LUCY'S LEGACY

Tia Day

ISBN: 0692930981
ISBN 13: 9780692930984
Library of Congress Control Number: 2017912907
Lucy's Legacy, Saratoga Springs, Utah

PROLOGUE

I am curled up under a bed with my arms wrapped tightly around my knees. My vision is blurred, but I can still make out the dirty ruffle of pink fabric in front of me.

I am praying quietly for comfort, but it fails to block out the shouting that is playing around me like a song on repeat.

That's when the panic finally sets in.

I insert my fingers into my ears and start humming to myself. I am humming a familiar tune, a lullaby.

The fear is unbearable.

Terror is resonating throughout my entire body, leaving all senses awakened and on high alert. I start to hum louder, in an effort to block out the chaos around me.

There are multiple footsteps dispersing in different directions throughout the house. I feel them make their way down the hall toward me. The floor shakes beneath my frail body with every step.

I wish to be invisible. I immediately stop humming and curl up tighter; sinking inward.

Please don't let them find me...

"Did you check the bedrooms?"

"All but one."

The door to my room cracks open.

I squeeze my eyes shut when I hear a pair of footsteps suddenly halt in front of me.

I force my eyes back open again to see a pair of black vinyl boots with black laces just below the pink ruffle.

The hair on the back of my neck stands up.

I cover my mouth with both hands to refuse the cries that are fighting for freedom.

Just then, a firm hand grabs my tiny arm and pulls me from my hiding place.

1

I am abruptly jolted awake by a loud *clap*! My eyes fly open, darting around the room. Sweat is pouring out of me, and for a moment, I am confused.

I attempt to catch my breath when I realize that my hands are still covering my mouth. I bring them down and wrap my arms around the pillow that is cradled against my chest.

"Caitlin? It's Dr. Thompson. You are in my office, and you are safe."

I pull myself up to sit on the black leather sofa belonging to Dr. Blythe Thompson, my shrink for the past five years. She is wearing a burgundy-buttoned blouse, black dress pants, and looking calm and collected as ever.

"How are you feeling, Caitlin?"

I fold my legs up onto the couch, and try to make sense of what I have just experienced, but like the many sessions before it, there was nothing more to gain in this one either.

"I'm not entirely sure how I feel," I say, quietly.

Dr. Thompson hands me a box of tissues to collect the tears that are streaming down my face.

After wiping my eyes, I am suddenly filled with anger and frustration. Leaping to my feet, I throw my hands up in the air.

"This isn't working! For weeks now this hypnotherapy has failed me! I'm not getting anywhere! *We* are not getting anywhere! And how do we know these nightmares are even *real?* I mean, the only thing they have *ever* given me is insomnia!"

I pace back and forth. "And what I wouldn't *give* for just one night of uninterrupted sleep. Just ONE! Is that *really* too much to ask?"

I finally drop back down on the couch and yank another tissue from the box. I blow my nose before grabbing another.

Dr. Thompson is sitting quietly, unfazed by my ranting as always. She gives me a moment to defuse, before standing up from her chair, and taking a seat next to me on the couch.

"Caitlin, your frustrations are valid, and you're right. We don't know what these flashbacks mean. Dissociative Amnesia is a complicated disorder. It's hard to decipher whether or not these flashbacks are lost memories or mere manifestations of your inner fears and anxiety. And, Caitlin, we may never know.

"But what we *do* know is that you need some sleep. I know you don't like taking medication, but I'm writing you a prescription for Ambien. Just five milligrams at bedtime, is all. You don't have to take it, but promise me that you will *at least* consider it."

I look onward, feeling numb. I have never really understood my aversion to taking medication, specifically pills, but anytime I try to swallow them, I immediately dry heave.

Dr. Thompson pulls out a green prescription pad from the drawer of her mahogany desk. She pulls her red-framed glasses from her salt-and-pepper hair, and scribbles something onto the pad. She then rips the script from the pad and hands it to me.

"Here you go."

I fold it up and scrunch it into the back pocket of my jeans. She watches my reaction, and I know that she is likely aware of my plan to discard it later, but rather than quiz me, she changes the subject.

"So, tomorrow is the big day, hmm? Tell me; how are you feeling about the move?"

I cringe thinking of all the boxes that are waiting for me back at home.

"Mackland is such a great school, Caitlin. I believe that you will feel right at home there, especially with how driven you are academically."

Dr. Thompson hands me a card with her contact information on it but I hand it back over to her with a smile.

"Dr. Thompson, I have your number programmed into my phone."

She smiles, and tucks it back in her desk.

"Yes, of course, I know. Just a reminder that you can always contact me if you need to. Otherwise, I will see you back here during the holidays." She walks over and gives me a big hug.

"Thank you, Dr. Thompson." I hug her back.

I then turn to leave her office, when I hear her shout from behind me: "Please tell Lucy, and the rest of the Capelli family, hello for me!"

Luciana Capelli, is my best friend, and soon to be college roommate. After two years of community college, and two associates degrees between us, we have finally been accepted into Mary Mackland University, near Washington D.C.

Lucy and I have talked about attending Mackland since we were Freshman in high school. Due in part to their stellar academics, but *also* in part to their campus housing option—which *just* so happens to sit a beautiful one hundred and twenty-seven miles away from our home here in, Allen, Maryland.

For Lucy and me, Mackland equals independence, and tomorrow, we will finally move in to our dorm, and begin a new chapter of our lives.

I only wish that I could remember the first few chapters of mine.

2

I open the front door to hear Lucy erupt into a giggle. I immediately roll my eyes, knowing all too well those giggles are being teased out of her by Cale Bradley, Lucy's high school sweetheart.

Cale comes complete with well-kept, and well-gelled, medium-brown hair. Complementing the brown, are the occasional blonde highlights dusted throughout the ends. He has compelling blue eyes, and I must admit, a delicious body to match. He's built, but not *too* built, and he carries himself with such confidence. Damn near every girl in high school wanted him.

That is, everyone except for me. I was too busy being happy for my friend's profound giddiness to think twice about him.

But the truth is, Lucy could not have found a more perfect match for her.

I head toward the kitchen to see that Cale is cradling Lucy in his lap, and whispering something in her ear. They are so lost in each other; they don't even notice that I've entered the room.

"Gag!" I say, startling them out of their dreamy state.

"Oh, stop it, Caitlin!" Lucy smirks at me.

"No, I mean it. I can actually feel the bile rising up my throat." I pretend to dry heave, then follow it up with a wink, and a smile.

I continue my walk around the marble island, and retrieve a pitcher of green tea from the fridge.

Lucy climbs out of Cale's lap—against his many failed attempts to pull her back in—and moves to the bar stool across from me.

"So? How was your therapy session? Any luck?" she whispers, trying not to let Cale hear—as if I care that he knows.

"Nope. Hypnotherapy has failed me again."

I open the cupboard below the kitchen sink and toss the Ambien prescription into the trash before grabbing a glass for my tea.

Cale moves in to sit on the bar stool next to Lucy. He then grabs her hand and kisses her knuckles.

"So, you're seein' a shrink, huh? That explains a lot," he says.

I pick up a grape from the bowl of fruit on the island and throw it at his head, just as Lucy withdraws her hand, and hits him in the chest.

"Cale! Don't be an ass!" she snaps.

"Owe, baby, you wound me," he says, rubbing his chest with a pouty look on his face.

Lucy's irritation immediately melts into a smile. She forgivingly nestles her face into Cale's neck, and he wraps his arm around her shoulders, in return.

Truth be told, Cale isn't being an ass. He's just being the unrelenting *smart* ass that I've actually grown quite fond of. We've become great friends, which is convenient, considering he will most likely marry Lucy one day, and I will be stuck with him, and lots of little 'Cale's and Lucy's' climbing all over me.

"Well, I better get home and pack," Cale says, standing from the bar stool.

Lucy walks him to the front door, and I can't help but listen from the kitchen.

"Have I told you lately that you're my prettiest girl?" Cale asks her.

"I better be your *only* girl."

He laughs. "One 'n only, for the rest of my life. I love you, baby."

"I love you, too."

Oh brother.

I grab my cup of tea, a bunch of grapes from the island, and make my way out of the kitchen—*just* in time to hear Cale raise his voice for my benefit: "I'll be here at eight am sharp, so the two of you better be ready when I honk!"

I reach the foyer and casually lean against the door jam. Cale sees me enter, and continues his lecture, "I would hate for you to have to walk to campus, Beck."

Beck is my last name, but for whatever reason, Cale insists on using it as my nickname.

"Now, I think we both know that lecture belongs to your girlfriend," I say, grinning at Lucy.

"Well, beauty takes time, Cait." She teases, "I mean, c'mon. Do you think I wake up like this?"

Cale locks his arms tighter around Lucy's lower back and draws her in close. "I happen to know for a *fact* that you do," he tells her. He then kisses her on the lips, her cheek, and finally, her neck.

"Jesus, get a room, will ya?" I pull another grape off the bunch I am holding and throw it at them.

Cale catches the grape mid-air, tosses it into his mouth, and winks at me.

I roll my eyes, and he chuckles in response. He then leans in to kiss Lucy's forehead and heads out the door.

Just then, Lucy spins around on her heels to face me and claps her hands together: "Alright, Miss Caity-Cait. We've got shit to do." She smiles and turns back around to head up the stairs that lead to our bedroom.

I fall in line behind her, not wanting to drag her down with my inner turmoil after such an intense therapy session. After all, Lucy has already dealt with her fair share of my inner demons over the years.

Hell, when it comes right down to it, Lucy saved my life.

3

Lucy and I met when I was around ten years old in Richmond, Virginia. I'd been in and out of foster homes by then, and my foster parents thought it might do me some good to spend time at the local Rec Club for Children after school.

Lucy was a bright and bubbly girl, with caramel-colored hair, dark olive skin, big brown eyes, and the longest eyelashes I had ever seen. The first time I laid eyes on her, I was sitting on a swing by myself, while the other kids laughed and played among themselves.

Looking down at my feet, I noticed a shiny pair of white saddle shoes suddenly walk into view.

Startled, I immediately looked up, and there was Lucy—folding her arms and tapping her foot. She was wearing a white cotton dress, white ribboned-pigtails, and a look of complete bewilderment on her face...

"Are you some kinda freak or somethin'?" she asked.

I shook my head and looked back down at her pretty shoes, which had suddenly made me self-conscious of my tattered and worn-out sneakers.

"Well if you aren't a freak, then why are you sittin' over here all alone? Don't you wanna play?"

I shrugged my shoulders, and continued to admire her feet, wishing I could trade her shoes.

"Well, I'm Luciana Capelli, but you can call me Lucy. Do you mind if I keep you company?"

I shrugged again. "Suit yourself."

"Good." She sat down on the swing next to me. "My mom is a volunteer at this place, but she won't be done for a whole hour. I used to play with Shirley Jenkins, but she moved away. You see those kids over there?"

I raised my eyes to see her pointing at the chain-link fence at the opposite end of the yard.

"Well, they really get on my nerves. That little Suzie over there is a real brat!" She pushed her nose up with her middle finger, and I couldn't help but laugh.

"Hey, what's your name anyway?" she asked.

"Cait," I said, without looking up. "Caitlin Beck."

"Well, you know what, Miss Caity-Cait? I think I could get used to you."

It was then that I forced myself to look over at her for the first time, and I will never forget the smile on her face in return.

Just then, a strange and unfamiliar feeling erupted within my chest. I felt my eyes start to water, as I realized the feeling—that was so foreign to me—was *hope.*

But the hope I felt that day would pale in comparison to the hope that was yet to come.

About a year after Lucy and I became friends, she broke the devastating news that her family was moving to Maryland. With tears in her eyes, she leaped forward to hug me and sobbed dramatically into my shoulder.

When I hugged her back, I could see that her father, Roberto Capelli, was witnessing our goodbye through the chain-link fence surrounding the Rec Club. His expression was sympathetic, and while I felt as though someone had punched me right in the gut, I did my very best not to let him see me cry; see me *weak*.

Then, after Lucy had demanded that I pinkie swear to write her every single day, she turned and ran toward her father's black sedan, that was waiting near the curb.

Out of fear that the other kids might see me cry, I ran around the brick building and found myself a corner to sag into.

Pulling my knees up to my chin, I cried to myself, and the sorrow completely overwhelmed me. I had never cared for anyone as much as I cared for Lucy, and I was certain that I never would again.

As time wore on, Lucy's move was hard on me and my nightmares worsened. I withdrew myself from others, and when I did choose to make myself heard, it was usually by throwing something against the wall. I felt so lost and spent most days sitting on the couch watching television.

But then, on July thirteenth, and exactly forty-four days, eight hours, and approximately fifty-five minutes since Lucy moved away, I was sitting on the couch watching television, when I heard a knock at the door.

Shortly after, Sylvia Lun, my foster mom at the time, entered the living room with an older gentleman following behind her.

Wearing a pinstripe suit, the man looked to Mrs. Lun for approval, before then, taking a seat next to me on the couch.

> *"Caitlin, my name is Derick Ryder, Mr. Capelli's attorney."*
>
> *I looked at him puzzled. "Lucy's father?"*
>
> *"Yes, dear." Ryder cleared his throat. "Caitlin, Mr. and Mrs. Capelli would like to adopt you into their family."*
>
> *My mouth gaped open in utter disbelief.*
>
> *"They have spoken with child protective services and completed most of the paperwork," Ryder continued.*

I maintained my blank stare; mouth still wide open in shock.

"Caitlin?" Mrs. Lun spoke up, "Do you understand what Mr. Ryder is saying?"

While I continued to struggle putting my thoughts into words, I knew exactly what he was saying...

I was going to be Lucy's sister.

"If you don't want to go, honey, you don't—"

"No! I mean, YES! Please take me with you, Mr. Ryder!"

I remember calling him my hero as I jumped to my feet to hug him. After all, I was gaining a family, and not just any family, but Lucy's family.

It was then that I finally reunited with that hope I thought I had lost on the day that she moved away.

It was then that Lucy changed my life forever.

4

I finish packing the last of my boxes in time to hear Cale's horn blaring outside.

"Cait, let's go!" Lucy calls out to me from the bottom of the stairs.

"I'm coming! Keep your panties on, will ya?"

I grab a few boxes and make my way down to greet them. After stepping outside, I see that Cynthia and Rob, my adoptive parents, are in a group embrace with Lucy.

Of course, Cynthia and Rob have asked me to call them "mom and dad" more than once, and it's not for lack of trust or love that I don't.

In fact, I love them both dearly.

That said, they did adopt me a bit late in the game, and calling them "mom and dad" just never came naturally to me.

Although, Dr. Thompson has a different take on this, *entirely*. It is her "professional opinion" that I resort to more "formal labels" for the people in my life, as a defense mechanism that stems from a deep-rooted "fear of rejection" resulting from my childhood trauma.

Dr. Thompson believes that I desire love, and want to show love, but *only* within my control, and without making myself too vulnerable to others. She also refers to the inner workings of my mind as "complicated."

Tell me about it.

Just then, Cale runs up and grabs the boxes from my grip. "Hey Cait, you ready to party?" He winks at me before carting my boxes off to the trunk of his red, not to mention, gorgeous, Ford Mustang.

Cynthia and Rob notice me walking across the lawn and open up their hug-circle to invite me in.

"Caitlin," Cynthia says somberly, "come here, honey."

I join them, and we all hug each other. I really am going to miss Rob and Cynthia. They are the only parents I have ever known, and I will always be grateful to them for taking me in.

Although, if you ask Lucy, they never had a choice in the matter. She will then tell you the story of how she would sit in front of her parents and shout: *"I'm going to hold my breath until you get me my best friend!"*

She would then make good on that threat, ballooned cheeks and all, and as stubborn as she was, continue holding her breath until she turned blue.

In reality, Cynthia and Rob had already begun looking into my adoption long before that.

Nonetheless, it hasn't stopped Lucy from taking all of the credit for their decision, after one of her tantrums had finally caused her to pass out one day.

"That lit a fire under their ass," she told me, during one of our many late-night conversations. *"I got your back, Miss Caity-Cait."*

And while Lucy may not have been the direct reason behind my adoption, I know that she *does* have my back, and I will always have hers—even *now*, as I rewind my arm back in preparation for a pillow attack onto her and Cale.

The drive from Allen, Maryland, to MMU, has been a rather *painful* two-and-a-half-hour trip, thanks to the nauseating PDA that is displayed out in front of me—and I have bitten my tongue, long enough.

"You know, I *am* still in the car assholes, and it's not a pretty sight from back here."

We all laugh, as I toss the pillow at the back of Lucy's head. She sticks her tongue out at me before picking up the pillow and tossing it back.

Cale looks at me in his rearview mirror. "I hear there are plenty of eligible bachelors at MMU, Beck. I bet we could find a man with your sarcasm and witty charm to sweep you off your feet."

"I doubt I'll have the time. I'm taking twenty-four credits this semester."

"Holy Shit! Overachiever."

"Well, frat parties and pep rallies will only get you so far, Cale."

"Oh, and the gloves come off! Well *maybe* if you would have come to a pep rally once in a while, you wouldn't have spent most weekends *only* dating the men in those books you love."

Cale looks in his rearview mirror, expecting a comeback, but I cannot argue with this, or take offense because it is true.

The men in my books are predictable and charming. They never disappoint me, and our relationships are completely one-sided. I don't have to share my inner fears, let my guard down, or extend any trust to them.

In truth, the idea of an intimate relationship with *anyone* scares the shit out of me.

"I got nothin', Cale. You win."

"Set-and-match, Beck! Until next time."

I roll my eyes and peer out the window to see our new home coming into view.

Cale pulls into the campus parking lot and finds a stall near the dorms. He shuts off his engine and the three of us jump out of his Mustang to start hauling bags from the car. From somewhere behind us, a familiar voice shouts in our direction: "Hey!"

I turn around to see that Lucas is heading our way with his arm wrapped around Angelina Dublin.

"When did *that* start up again?" Lucy whispers.

I shrug my shoulders. "Hm. Yeah, I don't know. Interesting."

Lucas Trout, *or* Luke, as we call him, moved into Lucy's neighborhood shortly before our eighth-grade year. He knocked on the door one day looking to mow our lawn for some extra cash, and our duo became a trio.

Lucas has always been intelligent, with stylish black-rimmed glasses to match, and while the glasses are the first thing you notice about him, underneath them, he is quite attractive, with that whole 'Superman behind Clark Kent' thing going on. Especially with his short and wavy black hair.

The three of us were always together.

Then, sometime during our ninth-grade year, Lucy and Luke became more than just friends. At first, it was a little awkward—that is to say, it was awkward for me, but after a while, I was forced to acknowledge how adorable they were.

Luke was overly-attentive toward Lucy, and he never left her side. As we reached the end of our sophomore year, however, their relationship fizzled out, and Luke was beyond devastated. After flowers and love letters had failed to get her back, he shut us *both* out for months. His sadness only worsened by the very public romance that blossomed between Cale and Lucy, in the fall of our junior year.

Then, *finally*, after six months of the silent treatment, Luke met Angie. She brought him out of the darkness, and back into our lives.

Surprisingly, Luke and Cale became friends shortly after that, and things have been great ever since. I only wish I could say the same for our relationship with Angie. Unfortunately, neither Cale, Lucy, nor I, like her much. She is majoring in Physics, which has made her usual condescension *worse*.

But anyone that Lucas chooses to love, we will love, because we love Lucas.

"What the hell? I thought they broke up!" Cale blurts out, upon seeing Luke and Angie wandering our way.

Okay, so maybe I should have said that we will *at least* choose to love Angie *in front* of Lucas.

"Luke! What's up my man?" Cale slaps his hand and turns toward Angie. "Hey Angie. Welcome back."

"Thanks, Cale," she says.

"Hey, Luke! Hello, Angie," Lucy and I say, in unison, our tones changing to a forced cheer by the end.

Angie offers us a pathetic version of a smile in response. She then whispers something in Luke's ear before giving him a quick kiss and heading off to the registration building.

Luke walks over to hug Lucy and I, with a huge grin on his face.

"Well you look disgustingly happy," I say, as he kisses my cheek hello.

"Yeah, man, what the hell happened?" Cale nudges his shoulder. "I thought you broke up with her."

"I did, but I just really missed her. So, I called her up, and after a very, and I mean *very*, intimate reunion"— *Gross*— "I decided that she would accompany me to MMU for school."

"*You* made the decision that she would accompany you? Why, that doesn't sound domineering at all." Lucy mocks, "And anyway, what happened to her acceptance into CIT?"

"Look, it was a mutual decision. We both realized how much we need each other, and Angie's grandmother lives close by, so she has a place to stay. We *both* feel really good about it Lucy, so please, back off, will ya?"

Lucy wraps her arms around Luke and ruffles his hair. "I'm sorry, Luke. You know I adore you." She then winks at him before reaching down to grab a box labeled 'Glamour supplies.'

"Oh, and by the way," Luke adds, "her dad got us both an apprenticeship at Brunick Solutions." He raises an eyebrow above the rim of his glasses, and we all look at him surprised.

Brunick is a rather prestigious software firm that specializes in programming for a variety of high-profile agencies, and being that Luke is a Computer Science Major, it is practically his dream job.

"Congratulations, Luke!" I say, wrapping my arms around his neck.

"My turn!" Lucy drops her box and falls in line for a hug. "I am so happy for you, Luke! You've been talking about working there since we were freshmen!"

"Well, once you girls get settled in, I'd say this news calls for a celebration!" Cale slaps Luke's hand.

"I'm there," Lucy says before kissing Luke's cheek and heading off to the dorm.

I pick up my boxes and follow behind her. After stepping through the entrance, we sign a security log and make our way up to the second floor.

Lucy and I locate our assigned room and throw our boxes on the floor. We look over at each other, both grinning from ear-to-ear.

"I can't believe we're finally here!" Lucy plops down on one of the twin beds. "Although, this room is lacking some serious charm." She reaches over to wipe some dust off the drab wall behind her.

"Ikea?" I suggest, being that it is our favorite store to wander in. It also happens to be the best place to buy furniture for small spaces.

Lucy nods. "Oh, hell yeah."

But after unpacking less-than-half of our boxes, Cale and Luke show up, interrupting our plans to go furniture shopping.

"It's time to stop unpacking, and start celebrating Luke's news," Cale says and removes a fifth of Tequila from the inside of his jacket.

Luke walks over and collapses onto my bed, before landing his legs on my lap.

"Maybe one drink," I say, and push Luke's legs back off of me.

Cale suddenly grins. "Why only one, Beck? Afraid you might end up in another game of strip poker?"

And cue in the mass hysteria.

Luke immediately sits up and joins Lucy in gasping: "*What?!*" Then, the two of them burst into laughter upon their unified reaction.

Lovely.

"Now, hold on a minute," Lucy continues, "where in the hell was I when this happened?"

Cale reaches out and pulls Lucy into his arms by her wrist. "You were upstairs with me," he says, touching his nose to hers, before slapping her on the butt.

Luke then pipes in, "But Cale, if you weren't there, then how do you know about it?"

"Why don't you ask Cait," Cale says, handing me a drink.

I snatch the cocktail from his hand. "Well, my guess would be, that Cale heard it from Marcus Gillman."

Lucy's laughter comes to an immediate halt—"Oh. Well let's move on then," she says, knowing all too well that "Marcus" is a topic I'd like to avoid.

"Thank you," I respond to her, and look back at Cale. "And besides, why in the hell would I be afraid to play a game that I won, Cale? I still had all of my clothes on after it was over."

Cale immediately laughs out loud, and I realize the trap I just fell into: while I *did* manage to hold onto my clothing *during* the poker game, I did *not* hold onto them later that night.

Ugh.

I feel my cheeks get red-hot and instantly slap my face down in my hands. I then have no choice, but to join Cale's laughter.

Lucy and Luke follow suit, and before I know it, it's several hours, and too many drinks later.

In fact, Cale and Luke's goodbyes are barely audible, as I finally pass out, and drift off to sleep.

5

I feel a thick pair of arms snatch me from behind.

The volatile nature of the grab causes confusion and fear to rip through the happiness I felt just moments before.

I immediately start to kick and thrash, when a hand covers my mouth.

I then feel a sharp rush of panic when I am suddenly tossed into a van. I fumble for the door handle—my only key to freedom—and frantically yank on the lever.

I expect to feel a cool breeze greet my exit from the vehicle, but my attempts are futile. The door will not open, and I realize...I am trapped.

My mouth gapes open with screams for help when a finger seizes the opportunity to push something toward the back of my throat. Its forced administration, combined with a smell of sickly-sweet perfume, causes me to gag.

But it's too late.

Within minutes, the pill's purpose takes hold. My legs begin to feel like dead-weight when at last, I can no longer lift them. A mix of fog and dread overwhelm my senses, and I collapse to my side...

I awaken to find that Lucy has taken up post beside me. She immediately moves into her standard routine of dabbing the sweat from my forehead, while handing me a cold glass of water.

"You were having another nightmare. Anything new?" she asks.

I grasp my forehead and sit up, trying to recall the fragmented details.

"I'm not sure," I say, gripping the glass of water with both hands.

I then take a drink, and I've only just begun to swallow when the instant recall of an object being forced down my throat triggers immediate repulsion.

I hurl the water back into the glass, causing it to explode in a spray around me.

"Shit, Cait! Are you okay?!"

Lucy takes the glass from my hand and sets it down on the nightstand. She then begins to wipe the water from my face.

I do my best to nod, as I desperately fight for enough air to cough.

"Can I get you something?" she asks.

I shake my head and close my eyes when finally, the sweet sensation of oxygen begins to flow back into my lungs.

"I remember...something was forced down my throat"—I cough a couple more times—"and I'm certain I passed out shortly after, so I think it might have been a pill of some kind."

"Well, that explains a lot," she says.

I nod my head and continue, "There was also a putrid smell of perfume coming from the hand that forced it down."

"*Really?* Do you remember seeing a woman? Had to be a woman there."

I just shrug my shoulders, and she sighs.

"I'm sorry, Cait. I wish there was something more I could do." She tilts her head into mine, and I pat her knee in reassurance.

"Thanks, Lucy, but you're here, and that's enough. Besides, this *is* something new and could explain why I avoid pills. Or it's all bullshit, and means nothing at all."

I look over my shoulder at the alarm clock to see that it's five-thirty in the morning, and regrettably, I am now wide awake.

"I'm going for a run," I say, throwing the covers back.

"Do you want me to go with you?"

"No, you go back to bed. I just need some air."

I open up one of the boxes on the floor and pull out my favorite lime-green jumpsuit that Lucy gave to me for my twenty-first birthday last week.

I throw on my running shoes and step in front of the mirror. I look like I have already run a marathon.

My rich blonde layers are draped around my neck in a pool of sweat, and my blue eyes could fool anyone into thinking they have already lived a hundred lifetimes by now.

I gather my hair up into an elastic band and repetitively pull the ponytail through it, until the last two loops, where I only pull it half-way through. I then grab some headphones and leave our room.

As I exit the dorm, I am greeted by a crisp autumn air, prompting me to flip my hood up over my head. I set my pace, and after round-ing the corner, I manage to trip over a garbage bag of leaves collected by the campus janitor.

"Oh shit! Sorry!"

I immediately try to pile the leaves back into the bag, when he shakes his head and shoos me off.

"Are you sure?" I ask.

He nods and bends down to clean up the mess himself.

"Okay, well, thank you, and again, so sorry."

He ignores me this time, so I put my headphones back in my ears, and resume my jog.

Once I have left campus grounds, a blanket of fog surrounds me as I reach the Potomac River. I connect with its accompanying path and steadily pick up the pace, doing my very best to squash the recent nightmare beneath my feet.

6

After a few weeks of grueling coursework, Lucy and I have decided to spend a Saturday organizing our room. I sit down next to the Ikea bookcase we put together last week and start arranging my books on the bottom shelf.

Midway through my task, Lucy hands me a colorful looking flyer that reeks of a frat party—not to mention a miserable time for me.

I immediately hand it back over to her.

"Oh, C'mon Caitlin! I know it's not really your scene, but I *also* know that you could use a distraction from all these damn nightmares you've been having."

I sigh, as the faint details of my latest nightmare flood back into view.

Lucy kneels down beside me. "Please, Cait? I would do it for you."

"Cheap shot."

"Yeah? Well, if it gets you to have some fun with me, it's a shot worth takin'."

"Well," I sigh. "I guess I can't really say no to a fun night out with you, now can I?"

"That's my girl, and you won't regret it. I promise."

Just then, we hear a short knock at the door, and only moments later, Lucas and Cale barge in.

I immediately look up at them annoyed. "Don't you think you should wait for an answer *before* you walk in? I could have been naked in here!"

Cale responds as he makes a beeline toward Lucy, "But Cait, how would we ever see your naked body beneath the cobwebs?"

My jaw drops to the floor, as I suddenly find myself speechless to yet another one of Cale's jabs. He is really gaining on me with the witty banter these days.

Dammit!

Then, as if he can read my thoughts, Cale looks down at me. "Off your game today, slugger? I mean, it's hard for me to revel in triumph if you won't even put up a fight." He is partially teasing, but looks slightly worried, as if something might actually be wrong with me.

Lucas bends down to pick up the flyer lying next to me on the floor and *thankfully* changes the subject.

"So, you ladies are in then?"

"Looks like it," I mutter.

Luke grins and sits down next to me. He *then* starts rearranging my already organized bookshelf.

"Excuse me, but I was doing just fine *before* you came along, thank you." I snatch a book from his hands, and he responds with a sly grin.

"So? Are you fine ladies ready to have some fun tonight?" Cale asks.

Lucy wraps her arms around his neck. "You bet your ass we are."

Cale takes her lower lip in between his teeth and pulls her in tighter, before then directing his voice at Luke and me: "Hey kiddies, mom and dad need some alone time." He then whips Lucy up into his arms and snuggles her neck, causing her to giggle.

Luke and I look at each other in disgust.

"Coffee?" he asks me.

"Coffee."

After a two-and-a-half-hour coffee break, Luke and I part ways to get ready for the party. I reach the dorm, hoping that my calculation of time has prevented me from walking in on Lucy and Cale.

After slowly peeking through the door to our room, I am relieved to see that Cale has already gone back to the frat house to "prepare for later."

With only three hours left to go until the party starts, Lucy and I decide to wrap up our day of decorating and do the same.

I grab a few toiletries and walk down the hall toward the community shower. Once there, I wrap my hair up in a clip and step inside an available stall. After lathering up some soap, I start to wash my body—and painfully recall Cale's comment from before.

Cobwebs. Ugh!

To Cale's credit, it *has* been a while for me, and I've only ever slept with two guys up 'til now anyway. Not to say there is anything wrong with that, but my limitations are stemming from a place of fear, as opposed to any real moral obligation—which isn't all that great either.

My first time was with Owen Phillips. We met at the library, just going into our Junior year of high school, so I was only seventeen at the time.

Owen was a rather good-looking and sweet guy. *Too sweet.* Every minute we spent together was filled by his zealous inclination to baby me.

How are you doing, Cait? Are you cold? Do you need my jacket? Can I call you?

We had fun together, so I tried not to mind it much. That is, until homecoming happened. We left the dance early that night and drove to one of the many after parties—*against* my better judgment.

After a few strawberry wine coolers, Owen led me into one of the bedrooms upstairs, and it was *over* before it *ever* began.

I remember laughing to myself, as I recalled a funny conversation that Cynthia had with Lucy and me, just a couple years prior...

> *"Girls, boys your age are more brawn than brain. I think it only safe to assume they are a walking penis, just looking to lure some poor unsuspecting girl into their beds. They will steal your virginity and spit you back out afterward!"*

I recalled that conversation, as I laid beneath a dinosaur themed blanket, belonging to our host's little brother. Owen was cuddled up next to me completely satisfied, while I was completely *not*, and suddenly, all the babying and gushing he ever bestowed upon me was making me ill.

So, I decided that Owen *"spitting me out afterward"* would serve as a huge relief. I mean, *surely*, he would dump me now that I had slept with him, right?

Wrong. Cynthia couldn't have been more wrong.

In fact, I cursed her name under my breath as I pulled out a white card from the long-stemmed, red roses that were waiting for me on the kitchen counter when I got home from running that next morning...

> *"My bounty is as boundless as the sea.*
> *My love as deep; the more I give to thee,*
> *the more I have, for both are infinite."*

> *"Oh shit, he's quoting Shakespeare?" Lucy asked, peering over my shoulder. "You must have given it to him good, Caitlin Beck."*
>
> *"Yeah, too bad it was entirely one-sided! I'm dumping him tonight!"*
>
> *Lucy left the kitchen laughing, as I dropped the entire vase of flowers into the trash. I then started to carry it out to the dumpster, when I suddenly heard Lucy exclaim from*

> *the living room, "Holy shit, Cait! Get your sweet lovin' ass in here!"*
>
> *I put down the trash and reluctantly walked down the hall to see that Lucy was peering through the living room curtains. She rapidly waved me over with a look of pure amusement on her face.*
>
> *I slowly took her place at the window and was beyond horrified by the nauseating masterpiece before me. Owen had written 'I Love You' in neatly arranged rose petals, each word easily approaching six feet in length.*
>
> *I stared at the embarrassing display, mouth wide open, as Lucy stood next to me shaking her head. "Poor bastard."*

I still dumped Owen that night. Though, I admit I was gentle about it after such an elaborate display. I was also relieved that we somehow managed to stay friends afterward.

The second guy I ever slept with was a drunken mistake after wrapping up my first semester of college. *Marcus Gillman.*

Marcus was one of Cale's jack-off football buddies, and participant in my *now* infamous game of strip poker. I had entirely too much to drink that night and decided that I was a powerful seductress. That one actually *did* spit me out afterward.

Dick.

I finish up in the shower and head back to our room to get dressed. I cross paths with Lucy, as she makes her way to the shower. She raises an eyebrow and displays a side-grin as she passes, which tells me she is up to no good.

A few steps later, I enter our room and immediately see the reason behind Lucy's grin. The outfit I had chosen to wear tonight, has become a pathetic pile on the floor, while in its place, lies a navy-blue cocktail dress that Cynthia bought for me a few weeks ago.

That little shit. No way am I wearing that dress tonight!

I return it to the back of my closet and pick up the outfit I had originally intended on wearing from its offended resting place on the floor: a pair of dark blue skinny jeans, a silky white camisole with delicate spaghetti straps, and a pair of gray Toms.

I've never been one to wear a lot of makeup, so I opt for a little mascara to accentuate my deep blue eyes, and a touch of soft-pink lip gloss. I toss my hair up into a loose bun, allowing pieces to fall where they may. I then put on a pair of diamond earrings, and after looking myself over in the mirror, decide to add a soft gray cardigan sweater as a finishing touch.

"Well, it almost worked—*until* you did *that*."

I turn to see that Lucy has entered our room. She closes the door behind her and sternly folds her arms.

"Where's the dress, Cait?"

"Where it belongs," I sneer, masking a grin.

Lucy releases her arms and sighs in defeat. She then opens the closet to retrieve her chosen outfit for the party and slips it on.

I turn back toward the mirror to add some final touches to my hair when I notice Lucy's reflection in the mirror. She is wearing a black cocktail dress with black stiletto heels, and it's times like this when I wonder how we ever became friends at all. She is so confident in that dress.

Whereas, I can't even manage to wear a camisole without wanting to cover it up with a sweater.

I sit down on my bed to play with my phone, while Lucy styles her hair into big shiny curls that fade from dark caramel at the scalp, to a lighter shade at the tips. Once the last curl is set, she walks over to the mirror and applies some red lipstick.

"All right, Miss Caity-Cait. Let's have some fun."

We head out into the cold air, and I find myself grateful that the frat house is conveniently located just a block from campus.

In no time at all, Lucy and I have reached an elegant brick Tudor with some alpha-omega symbols arranged on the eave just above the porch. As soon as we reach the front door, one of the pledges greets us wearing nothing but his underwear and a cape. He reaches into a cooler, and hands us both a beer.

"Welcome ladies. Mi casa y su casa," he says, beaming at Lucy.

We accept the pledges offer when he suddenly turns around and lifts his cape to reveal piles of cash tucked into his briefs.

Within seconds, Cale comes up from behind us and shoves the pledge out of our way.

"That's my girlfriend dumbass! No tips necessary."

Damn near every male in Cale's family are alumni from this fraternity, and due to his family's generous donations, he was able to forgo the "pledge" process, entirely.

Cale leads us through a crowd of coeds toward the kitchen, and I see that Luke is already there. He is fraternizing with the enemy by taking a shot from in between some bimbo's breasts.

"Traitor," I whisper in his ear.

"Hey, who am I to rob her of my company."

"I'd be willing to bet you're just one of many, Luke, and where is Angie, anyway?"

"One of her friends, who I can't stand, by the way, is also having a party tonight. Besides, it's not like we're married, Cait. Our relationship tends to be a bit more on the fluid side."

"And I assume that Angie shares your view?"

"If you must."

I gasp in disgust.

"Oh, relax, Cait. Of course, it's mutual."

Lucas removes a joint from the ashtray behind him and tries to pass it my way. "Here, I think you need some help removing that stick from your ass."

"No, thanks, and you shouldn't be taking hits off that either, Luke. I don't have the money to bail you out of jail if you get arrested."

"Hey, Marijuana is legal in the state of Maryland."

"It's legal for medical use *only*, Luke."

"Yeah, so? I use it for my anxiety." He laughs and takes another hit.

I roll my eyes, and lean against the counter, just as Cale hoists Lucy up onto the kitchen island.

Seated next to Jell-O shots, Cale reaches around Lucy's waist to grab one. He brings it up to her lips, and she parts them, allowing it to slide down her throat. She then lightly licks her lips with her tongue.

Cale's expression shows captivation, as he leans in to remove the remaining Jell-O from her lower lip. Anyone who knows anything would look at them and know just how much he loves her.

Typically, I would have turned away by now, but Cale's jab about my lack of romance has me feeling a bit out of sorts. I *now* find myself entertaining the idea of having what Lucy has—or maybe it's just her natural ability to trust someone with her whole-heart that has me yearning a bit.

My gaze into their sensual world becomes a blank stare, as I continue analyzing my thoughts. That is until I see Cale remove a quarter from his back pocket, and slam it down on the counter with a cunning and ambitious look on his face.

Cale has just invited me to a game of Quarters. The game is played by one-of-two people trying to bounce a quarter up and into the first of six shot glasses, arranged according to size.

You start with the smallest shot glass first. If you make the shot, your opponent drinks, and you move on to the next size up. If you miss, *you* take the shot, and remain with that size, until you eventually land the quarter in the glass. Only *then* can you move on to the next size up.

Typically, the game continues until someone has landed the quarter into the sixth and largest shot glass—*or* until someone passes out—whichever comes first.

Cale and I love this game, and we've yet to find any worthy opponent, outside the two of us.

"What do ya say, Beck?" Cale asks.

Lucy turns to face me from her stoop, smiling in anticipation of my reaction to Cale's proposition.

I slide the cardigan off my shoulders, tie it around my waist, and approach the island.

"You're on, frat boy."

I pick up the quarter and walk past him toward the large dining room table. Lucy erupts into cheers of excitement, prompting the rest of the coeds nearby to gather around us.

Cale then arranges six shot glasses on the table between us, while Lucy follows behind him with a bottle of Patron.

Several of Cale's fraternity brothers have gathered around us, and one of them starts rubbing his shoulders, like a boxing coach before the big fight.

"You got this, Cale. Don't be a chump and make us look bad."

Luke joins Cale's crowd of support, bimbo in tow. I catch his eye, and mouth the word *traitor* again. He just chuckles and says, "Kick her ass, Cale."

Lucy finishes pouring liquor into the last shot glass and takes a seat next to me. Cale looks at her and slaps his hand against his heart acting pained by her choice to side with me—*as if this is anything new.*

"Sorry, baby, but I gotta back up my girl."

Then, without breaking her eye lock with Cale, Lucy leans over to whisper in my ear, "Kick his ass, Cait."

Oh brother.

Sitting up in my chair, I take the quarter and slide it across the table toward Cale.

"Ladies first," I tell him.

Excitement erupts around the table, as Cale leans forward to pick up the quarter.

"Well, well, well. It's about damn time you showed up. I was start-ing to wonder if you'd lost your edge, slugger."

Cale takes the quarter in between his right thumb and forefinger and slams it down in front of the smallest shot glass. He projects the quarter up and into the silver liquid with ease. He then raises an eye-brow, as I grab the shot glass and take it down.

Lucy was right. I needed this.

I catch the quarter between my lips and set the glass back down. Once Lucy has filled it with more Tequila, I take the quarter out of my mouth, and send it right back into the shot glass it came from.

Cale takes the shot, and we now move on to the next size up. This cycle continues until we've come to the sixth and final shot.

Attempting to concentrate, Cale slams the quarter onto the table. We all watch, as it bounces up into the air, hits the rim of the glass, and finally lands on the table beside it.

"Dammit!" Cale hits his hand on the table, before leaning back in his chair.

I fail to hide my glee, as I reach across the table and slide the quarter back my way.

Taking aim, I slam dunk the quarter up and into the shot glass in one, flawless swoop.

The entire room of coeds explodes.

Lucy, who has been sneaking shots from the bottle this whole time, starts celebrating. "That's right bitches! No one fucks with my girl!"

I stand up and walk over to the other side of the table where Cale is sitting, and no doubt, seeing double by now. Whereas, I have always been able to hold my liquor better than he can.

Bending down toward him, I whisper, "Set-and-match, Bradley."

I grab the bottle of Patron off the table and remove Luke from the bimbo's arm. "Let's dance, traitor."

We all continue to dance and drink well into the night until I have finally had enough.

Luke is passed out, so Cale chooses to walk Lucy and me back to our dorm. After some hugs and kisses all around, Lucy and I drag our sorry asses through the front door, past security, and up to our room.

Lucy clumsily removes her heels, before patting my cheek with her right hand.

"I love you, my Caity-Cait-Cait."

"I love you more," I say back, and for me, those words between us are far more valuable than any others.

Lucy and I are sisters, but we are also each other's *person.* When she hurts, she comes to me. When she needs to share a gut-wrenching confession, she shares it with me. I know every single thing there is to know about her, and the same goes for her about me—of what I can remember, anyway.

It was this line of thinking that led to our decision to continue referring to each other as "best friends," as opposed to "sisters," even after my adoption was final. Lucy felt that relationships between sisters are "*obligatory*", whereas, best friends are "*chosen*".

Of course, we were just melodramatic children at the time, but no matter the label, our bond is unbreakable.

Relationships may come and go, but what Lucy and I have, will last a lifetime.

7

The next few weeks are a blur, as all of us are eyeball deep in textbooks, homework, and dreadful tests. Before I know it, we are sitting around a table enjoying Thanksgiving dinner.

Rob invited Cale to join us, after hearing that his parents had chosen to remain in France for the holidays. He also invited Luke, who opted to have Thanksgiving with Angie.

We all take our napkins and spread them across our laps when Rob rises to his feet, and holds up a champagne glass. We all raise our glasses in return, as he begins a toast.

"I would like us all to take a moment, and share what we are thankful for. I would like to start by saying how thankful I am for my wife, and two beautiful daughters, Lucy and Cait."

Rob motions toward Cynthia, who echoes Rob.

The order reaches me, and I stand from my chair, holding my champagne glass in the air.

I pause—realizing that I might actually cry if I speak. I take a deep breath, waiting for the emotion to pass, as Cynthia pulls a napkin from the table to dab her eyes.

"I am thankful for everyone in this room, and especially this family. Before I met you, Thanksgiving was the plot on a television show that never held any real meaning for me. I honestly don't know where I would be without you guys."

I sit down, and the order reaches Cale, who then stands with his glass held high in the air.

"I am thankful for so many things today. I'm thankful for my family, may they travel safely. I am also thankful for the Capelli family, for welcoming me into your home. I'm thankful for friends," he motions toward me, "and last, but never least..."

Cale exhales slowly, wiping beads of sweat from his forehead, as he turns his attention toward Lucy. "I am grateful for this beautiful angel by my side." He gets down on one knee and produces a small pearly gray box from inside his jacket.

I cannot believe my eyes. I mean, I knew this was coming eventually, but we all just turned twenty-one!

This is crazy, right?

I look over at Lucy, worried as to how she will even begin to process this, but immediately relax, when I see the adoring expression on her face.

It is then that I realize my worry was just me, projecting my inner fears onto her. That look on her face tells me this makes sense for *them*, and if they're happy, then I'm happy, too.

Lucy moves her right hand up to cover her mouth, as Cale then takes her left hand in his.

"Before you, I was living *a* life. It was a life with a predetermined and well-thought out future that I often struggled to identify with altogether. Until one October night, after a last-minute touchdown. I looked up in the stands to see this angel cheering in the crowd, and it was her smile, that set my future right."

Cale brings the box up and cracks open the lid. Inside the box, is a dazzling, canary-yellow, princess-cut-diamond, lined with tiny diamond baguettes, and a shiny platinum band.

"I'm not just asking you to marry me, Lucy. I'm asking you to complete my life, because as far as I'm concerned, a life without you, isn't a life worth living at all."

Cale removes the diamond from its box and places it onto Lucy's finger. "Luciana Maria Capelli, love of my life, will you marry me?"

"YES!" she gasps, and throws her arms around his neck with so much force, they fall onto the floor.

The entire room begins to clap and cheer, and I realize that Cale must have already sought the approval of Rob, who is now smiling down at them, with Cynthia close to his side.

Lucy stands, holding her hand out to admire the ring on her finger.

I look at Cale and nod approvingly of the ring, who certainly looks mighty proud of himself.

Lucy runs over and quickly hugs Rob and Cynthia, before then heading straight over to me.

"Cait! Can you believe it?! Did you know?"

And before I can even respond, Cale answers for me, "Are you kidding me? Hell no! The two of you aren't capable of keeping secrets from each other. She would've ratted me out for sure!"

I just smile.

That's right. No secrets between us.

Cale continues, "The only people who knew were my parents, your parents, and Luke. He came with me to pick out the ring."

Mental note: Must remember to kill Lucas later.

I give Lucy a big hug. "I am so happy for you guys," I tell her. "Although, this *does* mean that I'm officially stuck with Cale." I pull back, cross my eyes, and poke my tongue out to the side.

"Bite me, Beck," Cale responds and throws his napkin at me.

We all laugh, as Lucy takes Cale's hand and pulls him toward us. She then drapes her right arm around Cale's shoulders and her left arm around mine.

"We're all stuck with each other," she says. "I only wish that Luke were here, too." She removes her arm from my shoulders and holds her hand out in front of her. "I mean, I have GOT to thank him for helping you pick out this rock, Cale!"

"Well, actually, you can just thank me. Luke wanted me to give you a ring from his Cracker Jacks."

We all burst into laughter, and Lucy falls back into Cale's arms—where she remained—until we finally returned to campus late Saturday night.

We had originally hoped to stay through Sunday, but my English Professor was kind enough to assign a twenty-five-page paper before the holiday, and *then* make it due on Monday.

So much for Thanksgiving break.

And now, after a full night's rest, I am ready to commit my Sunday to writing this miserable paper.

I settle beneath the covers, laptop in tow, with a hot latte at my side. The weather is really starting to change. Dark gray clouds begin to swirl around a soon-to-be December sky, making it hard for me to fight the urge to collapse beneath my warm blanket and take a nap.

Lucy is lying on her bed, frantically typing the names and addresses of everyone she knows.

"The big day" has tentatively been set for next summer, just after finals. A summer wedding will allow for a timely return to school in the fall. Cynthia made it clear that the invitations must go out by mid-December during her crash course on "proper timelines for a wedding," and she would know.

Cynthia's career as an interior designer has landed her some rather extravagant weddings in the past, and she only reminded us of that, like, twenty times.

After the wedding, Cale's father has arranged for him to work as a part-time legal assistant at 'Bradley, Statton, and Myer'. This will allow Cale to continue school while providing necessary funding for an apartment.

Of course, this *also* means that Lucy will be moving out of the dorm, and I will be stuck with some stranger, but I'll cross that bridge when I come to it.

I look over at Lucy, and can't help, but feel incredibly happy *and* incredibly afraid for her.

Lucy is so clueless to the cruelties of life, and try hard as I might over the years to shield her from playground bullies, there are many things I cannot protect her from, and a blow to the heart is one of them.

If he breaks her, I'll kill him.

Lucy's phone suddenly rings, and I can tell by the look on her face that it's Cale.

"Hi baby! I'm making our guest list right now as we speak. Do you have yours ready?" She pauses for his response. "Well, maybe I should come over so we can figure this out together...Yep, I'll be over in fifteen."

Lucy hangs up with Cale and shuts her laptop.

"Cait, I've gotta run to the frat house so that Cale and I can sort through this list. Do you need anything before I go?"

I remain focused on my screen, as I respond, "Nope. Have fun, Mrs. Bradley."

"I plan to be back well before midnight, but would you mind shooting me a text reminder at eleven-thirty, in case I don't make it back by then? I can see myself getting too wrapped up in wedding talk to remember curfew." She puts on her denim jacket.

I look up from my screen. "You got it."

"I don't know what I would do without you, Miss Caity-Cait."

"And you'll never have to find out either," I say, with a smile.

Lucy smiles in return, and heads out the door, closing it behind her.

I spend the next few hours writing, as the day eventually turns into night. The brightness of my computer screen is causing my eyes to gloss over until at last, my eyelids become heavy. I finally give in to their weight and drift off to sleep.

8

I am startled awake by my laptop crashing to the floor. I immediately reach down to inspect the damage, when my vision adjusts, and I see that Lucy is not in her bed.

Shit!

All students residing on campus are required to sign back into their dorms by midnight, unless otherwise approved by the dorm mother, and I completely forgot to remind Lucy of this last night.

I check the clock and see that it's seven-fifteen.

Phew!

Lucy is an Art Major, and she has an early morning watercolor class on Mondays.

Now, any other night, it would be strange for me to sleep through her return last night and departure this morning, but I just happened to fall asleep with my earbuds in last night.

I chuckle to myself, as I stumble out of bed and head down the hall toward the bathroom to brush my teeth. After fixing my hair into a somewhat presentable coif, I decide to take a run around campus before class.

I return to my room and throw on a pair of sweats, with a long-sleeved t-shirt. I open up the closet to grab my favorite pair of running shoes when I notice that Lucy's art supplies are still tucked away inside.

Oh damn.

Lucy would never miss a class, nor would she ever show up to one unprepared. So, if she *had* slept here last night, she would have grabbed her supplies before she left for class. And even if she hadn't, she would have—*at the very least*—stopped by here to grab her things on her way to class.

This brings me to the following conclusion: Not only did Lucy, in fact, sleepover at Cale's, but she has *also* managed to sleep in.

She is going to kill me!

After snatching my phone from the end-table, I decide to give her a wake-up call. It immediately goes to voicemail, when I notice that she left her charger plugged into the wall.

So, rather than leave a voicemail, I hang up and call Cale instead.

"Hello?"

"Rise and shine to the happy couple. Would you put Lucy on for me?"

"She's not here." He pauses to yawn. "It's after seven, Cait. She's in class."

"Right, except that her art supplies are still here."

"So? Maybe she didn't need them today."

"Or *maybe* she was too caught up in chiffon and flowers last night to stop by and grab them this morning. And it's partially my fault because I completely forgot to call and remind her last night! I just hope this goes unnoticed, or you'll be gaining a new roommate *before* the wedding."

"Whoa, back up, Cait. What in the hell are you talking about?"

"Oh, C'mon, Cale. You know that we have a strict curfew. If the dorm-witch finds out, she'll be kicked out for sure!"

"Yeah, I know. Which is *why* I had her back by eleven forty-five, Cait."

"You mean she didn't spend the night with you?"

"What? No! I just told you I walked her back."

A nervous tinge, travels up my spine, as I leave my room and run downstairs to check the logbook.

"Wait a minute, why?" Cale asks.

"Hang on," I say, prompting an immediate sigh of agitation from him.

I reach the lobby and scan through the log book, when that tinge in my spine goes from high alert to downright panic.

She never logged back in.

"Cait, seriously. Why would you ask me that?"

"Cale, I just checked the logbook; she never signed back in."

"Well, that's impossible, Cait, because I dropped her off in front of the dorm, and I *watched* her go in!"

I can now hear Cale rustling through drawers in the background.

"I'm telling you, her signature isn't there."

I've already returned to my room, and thrown on a pair of shoes, before then bolting back down the stairs again.

"Cale, I'm gonna head over to the art building. I'll call you when I find her."

"*My ass you'll call me!* I've already left the house!"

"Fine. Let's meet at the art building. If she's not in class"—*Oh please be in class*— "we'll check the library. Maybe she went there to study instead. I'll try Luke, too." I hang up and dial Luke's number.

I'm halfway through a voicemail when I step outside and see a crowd of people gathered near the garden that serves as a scenic pathway between the various buildings on campus.

Unfortunately, the path *also* serves as the fastest route to the art building. So, I decide to walk around the mob when I notice that several police officers are attempting to clear the herd of people.

I move in for a closer look and run into some caution tape. Just then, a coed to my left tries to sneak a picture, provoking the officer blocking my view to abandon his post.

I scan the scene in front of me.

Just a few yards away is a nicely dressed man. He is crouched down, observing something on the ground. Resting firmly on his hip is a badge and gun.

A detective.

Lifting his head to survey the crowd, he eventually finds me.

Our eyes have briefly met when the officer standing next to him steps aside to reveal a glare.

Instantly catching my eye, I direct my gaze to the source to find that it's attached to a very pale and motionless hand.

Just then, I am hit with a brutal case of vertigo, as the image suddenly snaps into focus: A dazzling, canary-yellow, princess-cut-diamond.

Everything. Around me. Falls. Silent.

Time stops—and my surroundings fade. I cannot see anything, except for that hand.

Lucy's hand.

So, unnaturally fixed, without the slightest hint of life.

There is just...nothing.

Oh, God.

Somewhere deep—*very* deep, I can feel something...oppressive.

Heavy. Suffocating.

It's AGONY.

Pure gut-wrenching and unfathomable agony. It resonates throughout my entire body until I feel nothing but unbearable *pain.*

My eyes glaze over as I reconnect with a familiar sense of dread. A place of loss and despair.

Oh yes, I have been here before...but when?

I feel my mind wanting to shut me out, as the sounds around me start to fight their way back in. Faint at first… Getting louder… Sirens… Frantic chatter… Louder still…a man's voice. Somewhere nearby? My awareness sharpens: Yes, a man, and he is right in front of me.

"Ma'am? Ma'am, are you alright? Did you know the deceased?"

Oh, My God, no! Not Lucy. Please, don't take her. Take me!

Just then, I hear a familiar voice among the crowd. An *angry* voice.

"Get your damn hands off of me! That's my fiancée! Let me see her! I need to see her!"

Cale.

His voice pulls me away from the edge, and I can now make out the man, *um, detective,* that is kneeling down in front of me. I must have collapsed, as I, too, am on my knees.

"Cale," is all I can muster.

I reach out and use the detective's arms to steady myself onto my feet.

"Who is Cale, ma'am?" he asks.

I ignore the question and stumble my way past him until I see Cale. He is feverishly fighting against one of the police officers. I can barely get his name out, when his eyes suddenly lock onto mine. He stops fighting and his expression changes from anger to complete devastation. He is barely hanging on.

Cale's emotion instantly triggers my own grief to start fighting for center stage—*No! Cale needs you.*

I stuff the pain back down—*way* down.

I hurry over and wrap my arms around Cale's neck. He buries his face in my shoulder and the dam breaks. As he starts to cry, I do my best to comfort him, when I suddenly feel a tap on my shoulder.

I ignore it.

Tap. Tap.

Leave us alone.

Tap. Tap.

Go AWAY!

The tapping continues, followed by a "Ma'am?"

I finally whirl around, "LEAVE US ALONE GODDAMNIT!!"

I then realize my nuisance is that same detective that was kneeling down in front of me before.

I want to punch him in the face.

"Ma'am, I am so sorry for your loss, sincerely I am. I can see that the young woman meant a great deal to you both, but I'm afraid that I will need you to accompany me down to the station for an interview."

'Meant' a great deal to me?

His use of past-tense has prompted an entirely new level of pain in my chest. It's too much.

Keep fighting, Cait.

The detective then motions toward Cale, "You too, I'm afraid."

"Does this really have to happen right *now?*" I ask, trying to keep my anger under control.

"Yes, unfortunately, it does. A murder case is time sensitive, ma'am. The more time that lapses from this point on, the less likely we are to find the person responsible."

Murder?

I hadn't even begun to register that as a possibility yet! All of the air suddenly leaves my lungs, and I start to feel limp.

"Ma'am?"

"Fine," I say.

I feel numb. I turn my attention toward Cale. He is staring down at the white sheet, with tears flowing down his cheeks, and off his chin.

I then feel the detective's hand touch my upper back. "Right this way ma'am."

The detective leads Cale and me toward a mass of flashing lights in the parking lot, before then dividing us up into separate patrol cars.

I feel as though I have left my body.

Time loses all meaning. My mind checks in and out at random intervals until I now find myself sitting in a square room bathed in fluorescent light.

Every few minutes or so, reality slams into my consciousness, and I have to cringe it back out again.

It's not real.

I rest my head in my palm when the door opens, and I hear someone take the chair in front of me.

"Can I get you something to drink?" he asks.

I shake my head.

"Can I get your name?" His voice is soft. Almost soothing.

It takes all the energy I have, but I slowly lift my face from its resting place to scan the view from the table up...

A pen and a pad of paper, a platinum Cartier watch, and a black dress shirt rolled up just below the elbow. His jawline is strong, framed with light stubble that continues around the mouth. He has full lips, olive skin, kind-but-brooding, deep-brown eyes, defined brows, and very short, messy-like, dark-brown hair.

It's that detective.

"Miss? Name?"

"Sorry. It's Caitlin Beck."

"I'm Detective William James. We've identified the young woman as Luciana Capelli. I take it you knew her."

I nod my head, as I wrap my left arm around my waist and rest my forehead back into my right palm.

"I see." He continues, "And how did you know, Miss Capelli?"

"Lucy," I say.

"I'm sorry?"

"Lucy. Her name is...was, Lucy." I feel like a wet noodle.

"Lucy. Okay. How did you know her?"

"She's my best friend"—*Was*— "and my adoptive sister. We met when I was ten, and just three months shy of my twelfth birthday, her parents adopted—SHIT!" I slam my forehead against my palm. "I have to call them! Roberto and Cynthia—"

"Yes, the parents. They're on their way. American Airlines, I think." He scans some notes on his pad.

"Should be getting in at fifteen-hundred hours." He looks back up at me. "Please continue, Miss Beck."

"Cynthia and Rob adopted me when I was eleven years old, and I've lived with them ever since. That is until Lucy and I moved into the dorm."

The happy memory of settling into our new abode runs through my mind when it's abruptly met with a brutal crash of reality.

This is NOT happening!

I feel my mind wanting to go somewhere else...somewhere safe... somewhere *familiar*. A place where pain no longer exists...

"And how do you know"—he looks down at his notes again—"Cale Bradley?"

"Cale is Lucy's fiancée. They've been together for little over four years now. He proposed to her on Thanksgiving."

A canary-yellow diamond on a lifeless hand.

I shake my head to erase the un-welcomed image.

"Take me through the list of events, starting with the last time you saw Lucy, to the moment you arrived on the scene."

I replay the details of my night...when she left the night before, my attempt to call her, my call to Cale, and our plan to meet in the middle. My attempt to reach Lucas—

"Wait, who's Lucas?"

"Huh?"

"You just said that you tried to call Lucas. Who is he exactly?"

"Son-of-a-BITCH!" I wince, and once again, slam my forehead back in my palm. "I need to find a way to call my friend Luke before he finds out from someone else."

The door suddenly opens, and a police officer motions for Detective James to step outside.

"There is a Lucas Trout here. Says he knows the victim."

Too late. DAMMIT!

"Okay, just take him to room three. I'll be right there."

Detective James re-enters the room and reclaims his chair. "Well, speak of the devil. It would appear that your friend, Lucas, has found us. Now, how did you say you knew him?"

9

The incessant questioning carries on for what seems like hours. When we are finally released from our fluorescent prisons, it's almost four-thirty.

I step into the hallway to see that Cale is sitting down on a bench in the waiting room.

Across from Cale, are Lucas and Angie, who are locked in a tight embrace. I walk toward them when Angie spots me and whispers something to Luke. He immediately jumps to his feet and makes a beeline in my direction.

"Oh God, Cait." He pulls me in for a hug.

"I am so sorry you had to hear it from someone else, Luke."

Angie speaks for him, "My friend Steph called and told us what happened. She said that she saw you and Cale getting into a cop car, so we headed right over." She is looking at Lucas, worried.

I pull back and grip his face in my hands. I have to make him know, that I know, just how much he loved her, too.

Luke slowly nods his head in my hands. Then Angie tugs at his shirt, so he leaves me and clutches onto her.

I look over at Cale, who is staring down at the screen of his cell phone. I know without looking that he is gazing down at the picture I took of Lucy the day we graduated from high school. Cale loved it so much that he made it his screen saver, and hasn't changed it since.

Cale is stroking his thumb back and forth across the screen, as I sit down next to him. He opens his mouth to say something, but stops himself.

I look over at him with anticipation, inviting him to speak, when he finally does.

"I should have walked her inside. Not just in the building, but to your actual room. If I would have just done that—"

"Cale," I lean in and put my hand on his back. "This is not your fault, and Lucy would not want you doing this to yourself. There was nothing that you could have done. Nothing that any of us could have done. There is just no way to predict something like this. It's not your burden to bear, Cale." I try to sound stern, but the truth is, I'm exhausted.

"Caitlin?!"

I hear Cynthia's frantic voice behind me and I leap from my chair to meet her. We lock into a tight embrace, and within seconds, Rob has joined us.

Cynthia is crying so hard that it takes both, Rob and I, to keep her from collapsing onto the floor.

"Mr. and Mrs. Capelli?"

We turn around to see Cale. His expression projects shame, with an almost apologetic '*I failed to protect her*' look on his face.

"I am so sorry I wasn't there," he says and his bottom lip is quivering.

Rob breaks from our embrace and grasps Cale's right shoulder with his hand.

"Cale. You can't blame yourself for this, son. Now, you were the love of my daughter's life, and she still needs you to be strong."

Cale's head is down, but he nods, and Rob pulls him in for a "pat-the-back" hug.

Cynthia soon follows Rob.

I feel exhausted, and decide to walk down the hall in search of some caffeine. I find a vending machine just around the corner, but remember that I don't have any money, because I left my purse in the dorm.

Because I thought I would be right back.

Another dose of pain radiates throughout the inner core of my being. So much despair, and I know that if I allow it to surface, I won't be able to pull myself out of it.

I turn to walk back to the lobby when I overhear a conversation between Detective James and another detective around the corner.

"He was the first one at the scene. Says he could see that it was a young woman. He checked her pulse, and when he couldn't find one, called us. Says he didn't do anything to disturb the body."

The body.

Lucy, my vibrant and beautiful best friend of ten years, has just been reduced to nothing more than "*a body.*"

"Well, I don't like it"—I recognize this voice as Detective James— "Says here, he was charged with statutory rape ten years ago."

Rape?

"He's racked up a few assault charges since then, too." The officer adds, "I don't know how he landed such a job in the first place."

"Well, janitorial jobs are common for work release. Maybe MMU is running an outreach program for inmates. Get in touch with the Dean over there and let me know what you come up with."

My stomach churns, as I realize they must be referring to the campus janitor I practically ran over after my last nightmare.

It also occurs to me they have stopped talking, so I hurry my way back over to the waiting area. After a few short steps, I am startled by a voice behind me.

"Thank you all for coming down."

I turn around to see that it's Detective James. He looks past me, and toward Lucy's parents.

"Mr. and Mrs. Capelli?" He extends his hand. "Detective James. I've been assigned to your daughter's case."

"Have you found the person who did this to our daughter?" Rob asks, pulling Cynthia close to him.

"No, sir. I'm afraid we don't have anything of real significance yet, but I can assure you that once we do, you'll be the first to know."

His face turns softer as he then turns to address the rest of the room, "Unfortunately, I do need at least one of you to accompany me down to the morgue for an official identification."

Cynthia gasps and covers her mouth. She looks up at Rob and starts shaking her head, while Rob just looks green.

I don't know whether I want to protect them from the torture, or if I just want to see her one last time, but I suddenly find myself volunteering.

"I'll do it."

Rob pipes in behind me, "Oh, Cait, you don't have to—"

"I know, but it's okay. I can do it."

A wave of relief washes over Rob's face.

I turn back to face Detective James. "I don't have a car, if you re-member."—*Because you dragged us here.*

"Yes, of course. I'll take you to the morgue, and give you a ride back to campus afterward." He smiles sympathetically, and this time, I notice how beautiful his features are.

"Caitlin, we are having Lucy transported back to Allen for the funeral. Cynthia wants her buried in the Cemetery where your grand-parents are. We would like you to go back with us tonight, if possible," Rob says.

I open my mouth to respond, but Detective James cuts in before I get the chance to speak.

"Mr. Capelli, I'm not sure if anyone has passed this along to you yet, but we won't be able to release your daughter until the medical exam-iner has completed his examination and collected all the evidence."

"How long is that going to take?" Cynthia speaks out, voice cracking.

"Could be as early as Wednesday, but most likely Friday."

"*Friday!?* We can't have our baby until Friday?!"

Rob pulls Cynthia back into his arms. "Honey, if having to wait a couple more days to bury our little girl, means catching whoever did this to her, then so be it." His face shows an unchecked fury by the end.

Cynthia nods her head and turns into his chest.

"Caitlin, honey," Rob continues, "we've already purchased your plane ticket. Our flight leaves tonight at eleven. We'll pick you up from the dorm around eight-thirty."

"Of course," I say.

"Do you want me to go with you to the morgue?" Cale asks, but he is pale, and I worry he will pass out.

"No, Cale. Thanks, but I can do it."

He nods and hugs me.

Rob, Cynthia, Luke, and surprisingly Angie, all follow Cale, hugging me one-by-one. I have become a mere shell of my former self.

Hollow. Lost. Exhausted.

I turn around, and Detective James motions me toward the direction we are heading. We make our way out to the parking lot and he opens the door of an unmarked black car.

I take a seat and stare down at my hands.

Detective James joins me on the driver's side. "Seatbelt please," he says, and it's more of an order than a request.

I reach over my shoulder to pull the belt across my chest, as we leave the parking lot and head north.

"I'm sorry about your friend."

"Thank you." I continue looking down at my hands.

"We are going to do our best to catch whoever did this, Miss Beck. I promise you that."

"It's, Cait."

"Cait, it is."

"So, do you think it was the janitor?"

He looks over at me confused, as to how I would even come up with that.

"Unfortunately, Cait, I cannot discuss the details of this case with you." His tone has changed from comforting, to professional.

Yikes. Break the tension.

"So, Detective James—"

"Will."

"Will, it is. Aren't you a bit young to be a detective?"

"I'm twenty-five, and I can assure you that I'm qualified to handle this case. I've been in law enforcement since I was released from the Navy, special ops, three years ago. I'm a third-generation police officer, so it's all I know."

"Special ops? Wasn't the team who took out Osama Bin Laden five years ago, special ops?"

"Indeed." He smiles.

I somehow manage to return the gesture, which induces a wave of guilt for even *allowing* myself to smile. My face falls and I sink in my seat.

Neither of us speaks another word until we arrive at the county morgue.

We enter the front door, and after Will has signed the visitor's log, we are greeted by an older gentleman in dark blue scrubs.

"Detective James." He shakes Will's hand and turns to me. "I'm Doctor Hadfield, and you are?"

"This is Caitlin Beck. She was the young woman's sister. She's here to make the identification."

"Oh, of course." He shakes my hand and then encloses it in both of his. "I am so sorry for your loss, Miss Beck. Right this way, please."

Doctor Hadfield leads us down a hall with an outdated mint-green tile and white walls. He opens a door and motions for us to enter a small foyer with a large picture window that looks into a stark white room.

On the other side of the window is that same white sheet, draped over a sterile steel bed on wheels.

Doctor Hadfield walks through another door and appears through the window. He reaches the head of the stretcher and pulls down the sheet to reveal a face.

Lucy's face.

I walk up to the window and place both palms on the glass. The sight of her takes my breath away. Her hair still looks beautiful, but her rich olive skin has turned to stone. Her once richly-pink lips are pale.

I stare at her, and it takes every ounce of strength that I have not to break down. I finally nod to signal that it's her, my best friend—*my sister.*

Then, as the man is about to pull the sheet back over her face, I see ligature marks around her neck, and that's it. That is all I can take.

I run out of the room and lose what little I had in my stomach to a garbage can down the hall. I wipe my mouth with the back of my hand as Will gives me some damp paper towels.

I dab my mouth and plop down onto a metal chair near the garbage can. I can see that Will is unsure of what else he can do.

"Thank you for the paper towels," I say to him, and this seems to make him feel better; like he's done something.

"You're welcome." He smiles.

Will then offers his hand to help me up from the chair, but I bypass it and stand on my own.

So, instead, he just points toward the exit, and we head back to campus.

10

Today is the day that we bury Lucy. The shock that has overcome me since the day she died has been my saving grace, and I'm especially grateful for it now, as I nervously gather up the notes for my talk.

With every ounce of strength that I have left, I force myself to stand up and put one foot in front of the other. I reach the podium and do my best to dismiss the ball of nerves in my throat.

I will not cry. I will not cry.

"Lucy was my best friend. She—" I shake my head, trying to keep my composure.

"Actually, she was my sister, my family. See, I never knew what family meant before I met Lucy. Rob and Cynthia took me in to their home and adopted me shortly after we met. They saved my life."

I look at Rob and Cynthia, who are softly crying, and their emotion triggers my voice to wobble.

"I often referred to Lucy as 'my better half'. She was strong when I wasn't, caused me to laugh when I needed to, and to be honest, I'm not sure what I am going to do without her—" My voice finally cracks.

The emotion is just too much to bear, and I feel as though it will engulf me, with everyone watching.

When suddenly, and as if—*on cue*—I instinctively check out, and finish the rest of my speech on autopilot. It's a setting I find myself resorting to often since Lucy died and I've gotten to be quite good at it, too.

So much so, that I *now* find myself at the cemetery, and I have no idea how I even got here. I wish I could just stay checked out, to tell you the truth, but a light drizzle keeps releasing sporadic raindrops onto my face, disrupting me from my stupor.

In an effort to maintain my composure, I try to focus my attention on the mountain of white roses draped over Lucy's white coffin in front of me.

Somewhere nearby, a family friend sings a rendition of "To Where You Are" by Josh Grobin, which only intensifies my emotion.

Just then, I hear Lucas speak up behind me.

"What are *they* doing here?"

"I don't know, but now is not the time, Luke."

Cale is whispering, but his tone is furious, and not far from breaching the whisper barrier.

In spite of Cale's warning, however, Luke continues anyway, "And *why* is he staring at Cait?"

Someone is staring at me?

Cale then makes his opposition to Luke's disruption clear by moving up closer to me. I look over at him, but his attention is on Lucy's coffin.

He looks, how I *feel*.

I turn my head to face forward again when I suddenly lock eyes with Detective James.

He is standing off to the side, with another detective. He offers me a sympathetic nod, just before I break my gaze.

What is he doing here?

The music comes to a close, and Reverend Michaels calls for us to place our long-stemmed roses onto Lucy's coffin. One-by-one, family and friends make their way over, leaving endless roses until they have covered her coffin like a blanket.

I stand in place, unable to move, as the last remaining guests have dispersed to their vehicles.

Once Rob and Cynthia have left their roses, they turn toward me, but I can't even manage to look at them. All I can do is stand here, paralyzed by the realization that once I leave this rose on Lucy's coffin, she will be hoisted down, and covered up forever.

Rob and Cynthia must have come to the conclusion that I need more time because they leave for the limo without saying a word.

I finally gather up the courage to take my first step. I approach Lucy's coffin, clutching a white rose in one hand, and a pink, pocket-sized flashlight in the other. I grip the object tightly, as I recall the first time I had ever laid eyes on it.

We were just twelve years old at the time. After another terrifying nightmare of me hiding beneath a bed of unknown origin, Lucy had patiently waited for me to gulp down another glass of water. I was terrified and involuntarily shaking.

After handing Lucy the glass, she opened up the drawer of her nightstand and pulled out a pink, pocket-sized flashlight...

"We're gonna beat these nightmares, Cait." She turned on the flashlight. "But you have to get under the bed with me."

My eyes flew open, as I dramatically shook my head, warding off her cruel suggestion.

"Don't you trust me?"

I nodded.

"Okay, then get down here," she sternly whispered.

I was scared out of my wits, but I did as she asked, and lowered myself onto the floor.

"Now follow me." She scooted herself underneath the bed, and I reluctantly followed her lead.

Once we were shoulder to shoulder, she reached over and held my hand. "Are you scared?"

I rapidly nodded my head, as tears streamed down the sides of my face.

"It's all right, Caity-Cait. We're gonna make a happy memory to replace the bad one, okay?"

I nodded again, trying so hard to be brave.

She pulled out a tiny pocket knife and carved half a heart into one of the wooden slats before handing it over to me.

"Now, it's your turn. Finish the heart, okay?"

I nodded, as I took the knife and tried to do what she asked, but my hand was shaking too bad. So, she reached up and held the knife steady for me.

After completing my half together, Lucy took the knife back and carved the initials: 'L+C = BFF' in the center of the heart.

"There. Now, see? This doesn't have to be such a scary place for you anymore."

Tears still flowing, I nodded and attempted a partial smile to appease her efforts.

"Now, anytime you get scared by your nightmares, you can come down here and feel safe again because as long as we're together, nothing bad will ever happen…"

I am softly crying, as the painful memory fades away. After carefully lifting the lid to her coffin, I slip the flashlight into her right hand and wrap her fingers around it.

"In case you get scared," I whisper.

I hold her hand tightly in mine until I have finally found enough strength to let her go.

11

The guests from the funeral trickle into our home, where a caterer is serving up crab cakes and finger foods to a sea of black dresses and suits.

I am trying to keep myself busy by helping with the dishes when I hear Detective James offering some kind words to a family member somewhere behind me. Shortly after, he closes in on me and picks up a dishtowel off the counter.

"I'm sorry for catching you off guard at the cemetery." He takes a plate from my hand. "You wash, I'll dry."

What the hell?

Forget the cemetery, because it's the offer to share dishwasher duty with me, that stuns me senseless.

"You didn't catch me off guard. I mean, I guess I *was* surprised to see you there, but I just had a lot on my mind."

Will has a slight grin, as he opens a few cupboards to find a shelf for his dry plates.

After what I feel is an appropriate lapse of time, I withdraw my hands from the sink and turn toward him. "See, now this is where you would pipe in and actually *say* why you are here."

Will continues drying dishes as a rather coy smile appears on his face. "I'm sorry. I wasn't informed of the rules beforehand."

He then reaches into the soapy water on *my* side to retrieve one of the dishes I have been neglecting.

I grab it out of his hands and splash it back down into the water, slightly annoyed by the fact that he thinks he can just come in here and take over my dishes without telling me why he is here.

Will raises an eyebrow at me and begins to dry off his hands with the towel. He then turns around and leans his back against the sink.

"Well, a majority of murder cases are committed by someone the victim knew. Which means the person responsible for what happened to your friend could potentially be at the funeral. So, we decided to go and observe guests' behavior, to see if anything would set off alarms."

Someone she KNEW?

I am staring up at him in shock. "You think it was someone she knew?"

"Now, I didn't say that, just that it's a possibility we have to consider."

"Well, if that were true, I would know them too, and I don't know *anyone* who would want to hurt Lucy." I splash my hands back down into the soapy water to retrieve another dish. "Personally, I think you're on a witch hunt, and should probably just leave."

"Listen, I'm sorry I offended you. I'm just trying to do my job." He sighs. "But yeah, you're probably right. I apologize for the intrusion."

Will drapes the dish towel over my shoulder and walks out of the kitchen.

I feel terrible. After all, he is only trying to find the person who hurt Lucy.

I grab the dishtowel to dry off my hands, vaguely noting the remnants of his cologne on the cloth, and follow him outside.

"Detective James!"

He stops when he sees me approaching, and whispers something to his partner, who then continues toward the car without him.

"I'm sorry, you don't have to go. I know you are only trying to find the person responsible for this. Please do come back inside. I could make you two a drink or something."

Will takes the towel from my hands to wipe the suds off my cheek. "Thank you, Miss Beck—"

"Cait."

"Right." His lips form a subtle grin, as he drapes the towel back over my shoulder.

"Thank you, Cait, but we really do need to get back to the station, anyway."

"Did you find something?"

"Yes, but could also be nothing. I promise I will let you know once we have something worth talking about."

"Sure. Of course."

"You know, if it makes you feel any better, I don't necessarily think that anyone here is responsible. We just have to explore every option, you know?"

He almost appears to be looking for...*forgiveness?* But why? Why would he care what *I* think?

I look down and nod my head. "I know, and thank you for that."

"You're welcome."

Will smiles and heads down the sidewalk to meet his partner, before turning back around to give me a wave goodbye.

12

The clouds are creating a thick gray haze within my view through a window, and I suddenly feel a chill. It's the New Year, and I cannot figure out where the time went.

Dr. Thompson is patiently waiting while I struggle to find any words—until I finally manage to speak the only word that comes to mind: "Numb."

I continue staring out the window, as I try to figure out the best way to describe what this numbness actually feels like. How to put into words this...*vast emptiness.*

"Numb. Can you explain what you mean by that?"

"I'm trying to, Dr. Thompson."

I now realize that my inner suffering has me clenching my jaw—as if I could apply enough pressure to kill the pain.

So much pain.

"Time seems to move quickly," I continue, "and yet I feel as though I'm frozen. It's only been a few weeks since the funeral, and I can't remember much about it or anything since. Hell, I can't even remember Christmas. Days seem to skip, as though my life is playing out in short movie reels."

"Yes, well, the brain has a natural way of protecting us from the terrible things in life, and unfortunately, Caitlin, your testament to this phenomenon is greater than most.

"And while we may not have all the answers to your past yet, I don't believe this to be the first time that your subconscious has chosen self-preservation, over facing unbearable grief or trauma.

"This response may be your mind's default setting to prevent the effects from your past trauma from becoming *worse*. I mean, the human psyche can only take so much, and that limit is different for everyone."

I suddenly remember the nightmare I had that morning with Lucy. "Speaking of past trauma, I had something new appear in one of my nightmares a few weeks back."

"Oh?"

I shut my eyes, and try to recall every last detail.

"I was thrown into a car, actually, it was a van. I was trying to get away, but I couldn't. I also remembered smelling a woman's perfume, and then someone, perhaps the same woman, forced me to take some pills."

My jaw is starting to ache.

"Well, I think we may know why you don't like taking pills now."

"Possibly. *Or* it's just some fragmented version of the truth."

"Perhaps, but it's a new development." She looks up at the clock. "And I think it's worth exploring further, but I'm afraid we have run out of time for today, my dear."

"Right. Sorry about that," I say politely, but she has always allowed me to go over my time, and not once has she charged me for it, either.

"Thank you, Dr. Thompson. For everything."

She puts her hand on my shoulder. "You know Caitlin, I've been seeing you for a few years now, and I just want you to know that I am as eager as you are, to get to the bottom of this. By the way, how are Cale and Lucas holding up?"

"Fine, I guess. As fine as they can be, anyway. I worry that Cale is going to implode if he doesn't open up about how he is feeling inside."

Dr. Thompson looks at me with severe scrutiny, but before she can call me a "pot to the kettle" I quickly distract her—"But we're all heading back to school in a couple of days."

"Well, you guys drive safe and be sure to let me know when you are back in town. And of course, you can always use my number, if you recall anything new from these nightmares."

I wave her goodbye as it suddenly occurs to me that I may need to come up with another word for "nightmare." After all, its meaning suggests that it's a dark contrast to your daytime life, and for me, that distinction no longer exists.

13

After hearing the blare of Cale's horn, I carry my bags out to meet him.

Cynthia tried again to buy me a car during Christmas break, but the cost of my tuition and books equals to *less* than my student loans each semester, which leaves plenty leftover to pay for public transportation.

Besides, there are far better uses for that money. Reverend Michaels connected Cynthia and Rob with the COPE Foundation: *"A non-profit grief and healing organization dedicated to helping parents and families living with the loss of a child"*, and I would rather she donate that money to them instead.

I reach the curb and Cale takes my bags.

"You look like shit, Beck."

I look up at him, offended. "Yeah? Well, so do you."

"Feel like it, too," he says and opens the trunk.

"But seriously, Cait. You didn't say much at the funeral. How are you holding up?"

"I'm good, Cale. Don't worry about me."

"God forbid, right?" He nudges my shoulder.

I open my mouth to respond, when Cynthia calls out to me from the porch: "Cait! Honey, don't forget these!" She is holding three shopping bags full of winter clothing that she purchased for me over Christmas break.

Cynthia has taken up a shopping addiction to distract her from the pain of losing Lucy.

We lost Lucy.

I shake the reminder, and meet Cynthia halfway to accept the bags.

"Thank you. And not just for the clothes, but for everything you have ever given me."

I set the bags down and hug her. She hugs me tightly in return, and I can hear her sniffling over my shoulder. The numbness I feel, like a dam, threatens to give way to the overwhelming torment behind it.

"No *thanks* necessary, honey. You're my daughter, and parents dote on their daughters." She pulls back, and I can see the tears are barely holding onto her bottom eyelid.

"Now you promise to call me when you get there, missy." She then leans in and kisses my cheek.

"I promise. Tell Rob bye for me."

"I will, honey."

These past couple weeks, Rob hasn't been around much. He locks himself away in his den, no doubt with a bottle of Brandy. I always thought that men were supposed to be the "strong" ones, but whoever said that, wasn't considering the concept of "Daddy's little girl."

"All set over here," Cale says, slamming the trunk down.

Cynthia walks over to Cale and hugs him. "Now, you take care of yourself, Cale."

"I will, Mrs. Capelli."

"Oh, for crying out loud, Cale. Call me Cynthia."

"You got it," he says.

She then grabs his face and kisses his cheek.

We hop into Cale's Mustang, and within fifteen minutes, we have picked up Luke and Angie from her parents' house. By the time we have entered the highway, Luke has synced his cell phone with the car stereo and keeps anxiously fiddling back and forth between songs.

"Have you heard anything more from that detective?" Cale asks, and I assume he is directing this question at all of us, but no wait—he is looking directly at *me?*

"No. Is there a reason why you are only asking me that question, Cale?"

He looks in the rearview mirror toward Luke, and I turn around to see that Luke is now looking back at him, in return.

"Okay, what the hell you two?" I ask, but before either one can respond, Angie does it for them.

"They think that cop has the hots for you."

Appalled, I turn and direct my fury at Luke, who immediately throws his hands up.

"Now don't lose your shit, Cait. We just noticed that he seems to have an interest in you, is all."

"What in the hell are you talking about, Luke? He's not interested in *me*; he is interested in finding Lucy's killer!"

"Well, at the funeral, he—"

"He was just watching me"—I correct myself—"or rather *us*, for 'clues."

My air quotes carry a tinge of sarcasm and bitterness toward the idea that someone Lucy knew could actually be responsible for what happened to her.

Cale looks over at me. "What do you mean, *clues?*"

"He told me after we got back from the cemetery that in most cases like this, the victim knows who their killer is, or whatever."

"What?!" Lucas shouts, "They actually think that one of *us* did *that?!*"

"Trust me, Luke, I gave him an ear full about that, but they're just doing their job. He actually mentioned they had some new evidence to process when he left."

"Well, did he say what it was?"

Cale's hopeful tone makes me wish that I had an answer for him, but all I can do is shrug my shoulders.

"Well, if it's any consolation, Cait, I knew there was no way he was into you," Angie says.

"Jesus, Angie! Don't you think you've done enough?" Luke snaps.

"What? *She* said it. I just agreed with her."

Right.

"I'm sorry, Cait," Luke says.

"Do you *really* think I give a shit about what Angie thinks, Luke? It's you and Cale that I'm pissed at!"

Normally, I would be more mindful of Angie's feelings—*for Luke's sake*—but quite frankly, I just don't give a shit right now.

"Oh, my hell, Cait. We were just talkin'. Right, Cale?"

But Cale doesn't respond or even acknowledge what Luke is saying. His hands are clenched tightly around the steering wheel, wrenching in a backward and forward motion, one whose fury I immediately identify with, as I reach up to massage my jaw loose.

"Listen you two, Will, was just—"

"*WILL?*"

"Yes, *Will.* If you remember, Luke, he accompanied me to the morgue, which was plenty of time to learn his damn name."

"Just be careful, Cait."

"And what in the hell is that supposed to mean, Luke?"

"Oh, I don't know. Maybe it's just me, but I tend to think that getting involved with the Lead Detective investigating your friend's murder would be a somewhat, dumb-ass idea. I mean, it's a conflict of interest. He should be keeping his head in the game."

"It is NOT like that, Luke, and trust me, that is the very LAST thing on my mind these days."

Cale is still gripping the steering wheel, and I can see that he hasn't been paying much attention to us at all. I turn my attention forward when I spot a familiar photograph tucked inside the dashboard, behind the steering wheel. I know it well because Lucy kept it on her dresser—*Oh, Jesus, I completely forgot.*

Cale and his mother had offered to pack up Lucy's things from our dorm room and send them home after the funeral was over. Cale must have taken the picture then.

I instantly fill up with guilt. I can't imagine how difficult that must have been for Cale, and I was so numb with my own version of hell that I completely neglected to ask him about it.

I sigh as I lean back in my seat and continue to gaze at the photograph. I can't help but feel immense pain, as I close my eyes and remember the day that I took it...

"Hurry UP Cait!" Lucy shouted while standing at the top of what could easily be confused with Mt. Everest.

Or at least that is what my legs would have told you, had they stopped trembling long enough to get a word in.

"Get off my back, Yoga Queen. I'm right behind you."

Lucy was standing on the ledge, looking out into the vast horizon. She looked so much at peace.

Cale was standing behind her, with his arms wrapped around her waist, and his chin resting on her shoulder.

I remember thinking how beautiful they both looked together, in spite of a three-hour hike in the blazing sun.

I also remember seeing spots and thinking that I might actually die.

"Have I told you where you can locate my will?" I asked, reaching the top.

Lucy rolled her eyes, without taking them off the view in front of her.

"What the hell, Beck? You run like, a mile every morning. How in the hell are you tired?"

"Running and hiking are two very different forms of exercise, Cale, and I don't hike Everest every morning, smart ass."

Lucy suddenly spun around and found a tree branch to stabilize her phone onto so that she could capture the moment. I immediately noted the strands of hair that were stuck

*to my face, and the beads of sweat that were providing the
glue.*

    "No, Lucy. I look like hell in a handbasket right now."

    "C'MON, Cait! PLEASE?"

    *"No. No freaking way. Why don't I just take one of the
two of you?"*

    *Lucy continued pleading, as I continued exerting my
stubborn protest until finally, she gave up.*

    "Okay, FINE, Caitlin."

When she used my full name, I knew I was in trouble. She handed me
her phone without making eye contact with me, but I didn't care at
the time. I refused to capture that sweaty moment on her Instagram
feed. So, I just took the phone from her hand, and with a sense of
gratification for winning the argument, I snapped the picture.

    What I wouldn't give to be in that picture now.

    I squint my eyes tighter, as I feel disgust well up inside of me over
the memory of such a petty and vain argument. I'm about to fall
down the rabbit hole of *"what if's"* and *"should have's"* when Cale suddenly breaks his silence.

    "Hey, say they do find that piece of shit."

    We all remain silent.

    "You know, say they do find him, and there's a trial. What then?
Would he get the death penalty? Would they lock him up for life?
And what if—and I mean, I lose sleep over this shit, but what if he
gets caught, and they find him *innocent?*"

    None of us say a word and it occurs to me that I hadn't given this
much thought before now—when suddenly, a far worse idea comes to
mind, and it's one that Cale hasn't even thought of yet...

    What if they don't find him at all?

    I suddenly have a strong urge to contact Detective James for an
update.

    We pull into the campus parking lot, and after Cale has turned
off the engine, we begin to unload our bags in silence.

"Thanks for the ride, Cale," Angie says, before stomping off.

Luke rolls his eyes. "Great. Now I've got *two* women pissed off at me."

I chuckle, "Oh, it's okay, Luke. Let's just squash it, okay?"

Luke nods, and I walk over to give him a big hug. I then motion for Cale to join us, and I pull their heads into a circle with mine.

"I don't know what I would do without you guys right now," I tell them.

Cale lifts his head. "Wow, Beck. Sentiment?"

Luke laughs, as I hit Cale in the arm.

I then notice that Angie has stopped her tirade and is waiting for Luke near the dorm. I clear my throat and nod toward her.

Luke follows my nod, and upon seeing her, sighs, and scoops up his bag.

"Well, I guess that's my cue." He winks and then heads toward Angie, who is now walking toward him with a look of remorse.

I can only imagine their sappy reunion, as I break my gaze to look back at Cale, who is staring down at his keys.

"Cale?" I place my hand on the back of his arm. "Can we do lunch this week? We haven't had a chance to sit down and talk since—"

"Yeah, sure Beck, but I can't do it this week. I've got a paper to write."

Cale breaks his stare to smile at me, then bends down to grab his bags. Heading toward the curb, he turns back around to face me, while walking backward.

"I like the sentiment, Beck. Looks good on ya." He smiles, before turning around and heading toward campus.

14

The first couple weeks of classes are a hailstorm of homework, and I'm grateful for the distraction. Hyper-focusing on school is my forte, and I currently find myself spending yet another Friday night in the library, while the rest of my classmates seek comfort in their beer bongs and pot.

After obtaining my Associates in Science, I chose to enroll in the MMU undergraduate curriculum needed to fulfill my lifelong dream as a Child Psychologist.

You are a walking, talking, cliché, Beck.

I close my Bio-Chem book and look up toward some whispering that is taking place across the room.

What the hell?!

I immediately reach up and pull the elastic from my hair, and begin to smooth the whispies down, as the librarian motions Detective James my way.

As my hair makes its horror film debut, I suddenly realize that today is laundry day, and I am wearing a pair of sweats and an MMU hoodie.

Oh, screw it.

Detective James approaches the table and pulls out a chair, "Do you mind?"

"Of course not."

His posture is professional, until his eyes land on my book. He picks it up and inspects the cover.

"Bio-Chem," he says and starts to nod. "Makes sense."

"Meaning?" I ask, and take my book back.

"Oh, I don't know. You just have this whole, you know, scrutinizing eye-thing going on. Like you're looking for flaws—or proof that there aren't any, in everyone around you."

"Oh, I see. And what does that have to do with Bio-Chem, exactly?"

"I'm just saying that based on my observation, I can see why you would choose a topic that offers concrete answers. As opposed to Shakespeare, where you could find a hundred people, with a hundred different interpretations, as to what he was *actually* trying to say."

I should let this go and find out why he is here, but what I *really* want—is for him to eat his words.

"I happen to like Shakespeare. Symbolism and metaphors aren't lost on me, and I am actually working toward a field in Psychology."

So, bite me.

He leans forward with an irritating smirk on his face. "And exactly *how* is that different from what I've just said?"

"Behavioral Science isn't exactly '*concrete*.'"

"That may be, but it still puts you in a position to analyze others." He leans back in his chair. "Does it not?"

He is rather proud of himself.

I want to kick the chair out from underneath him.

"What can I help you with, Detective James?" I begin packing up my things.

"Will." He reminds me, but I ignore him and continue shuffling papers.

I then catch a glimpse of the campus librarian over his shoulder. "In case you aren't quite sure what that searing heat is on the back of your neck, the library is about to close, and Ms. Kent is going to miss her date with TiVo if we don't hustle our asses out of here."

I stand up and start to drape my bag over my shoulder when Will takes it and tosses it over his.

"Shall we?" he asks and motions for me to go first.

I am so bugged, but nod in assent anyway.

We make our way out of the library and into the chilly night air. The weather has been relatively warm during the day, with temperatures averaging near the low-fifties, but the nights are brutal. I zip up my jacket and fold my arms around my waist.

"So, you never answered my question, Detective."

"We found some skin cells underneath Lucy's fingernails. It's not a perfect sample, but we're hoping there is enough there to use for a DNA rule out."

"So, whoever that skin belongs to, might be the one who—"

"Yes."

I start to visibly shiver, prompting Will to remove his jacket and drape it around my shoulders.

"Anyway," he continues, "at the risk of pissing you off again, I'm here to let you know that I will need you to come down to the station for a DNA sample. Not because I suspect you, or anyone that you know, but because I am *required* to—per standard protocol." He masks a grin.

I look up at him and raise an eyebrow. "So *that's* why you didn't want me carrying any heavy books."

He laughs and leans toward me. "Hey, I'm just relieved you weren't holding any dishes this time."

"Touché." I can't help but grin.

"So, can you do that for me?" he asks, as we reach my dorm.

"Of course. Anything I can do to help you catch the asshole who did this."

I retrieve my bag from his shoulder, and suddenly remember what Cale said to us on our ride back from the holidays last month.

"Hey, there actually *is* something I've been thinking a lot about these past couple weeks."

"Anything I can help with?"

"I'm hoping you can."

He tilts his head in interest.

"If you do find whoever did this, what *exactly* would happen to him. I mean, assuming that Lucy's killer is a man."

"According to our profile, that is most likely the case, and are you asking me what his charges would be?"

"Well, yeah, *that*, and what his actual sentence might be."

"Well, we would seek the maximum sentence allowed by law."

"Which is?"

"Which *is*, life in prison without the possibility of parole."

"You mean, you wouldn't seek the death penalty?!"

"Trust me, Caitlin, if that were a possibility, you bet your ass I would, but unfortunately, Maryland doesn't offer the death penalty, nor does D.C. for that matter."

I am suddenly sick to my stomach. This *thing*, this horrific monster—who took Lucy away from me, away from Cale, away from her family, away from *our* family—could actually be allowed to live out the rest of *"its"* life in an environment that offers "rehabilitation."

Well, what about *our* rehabilitation? Where is the justice for Lucy that would, *at the very least*, help to heal some of the pain and suffering this evil bastard has caused us?

And what happened to "an eye for an eye?"

The anger is far too much to bear.

"So, let me get this straight. Prison—where the punishment is three square meals a day, a bed to sleep on, and the opportunity to earn a free education—would be this guy's *max* sentence?"

"Listen, Caitlin—"

"Cait."

"Cait, listen. I can assure you that when I do find this prick, and I will do my best to find him, he will never get the satisfaction of breathing free-air again. Not if I have anything to do with it."

"But you *don't* have *everything* to do with it. What if his defense attorney is better at arguing the case?"

"I can assure you that Bill Trainor is the best District Attorney this side of the East Coast. He won't go free."

"But what if he does? You can't *guarantee* that he won't walk away from this, Will. You can't, and you know it."

Will sighs and looks down at me with this serious look on his face. "If he does go free, that would be on me, not the prosecutor. It's on me to gather enough evidence to keep this asshole behind bars for the remainder of his miserable life, so it would be *my* burden to bear if he walked."

"Along with the rest of the general public. Sociopaths who kill, don't stop killing, Will. They just get *better at it.*"

I stop walking and look up at him.

"And do you really think that I would blame you, or anyone else for what happened to Lucy? There is only one source of blame for this, and none of it belongs to you. I know you are doing everything you can, and no matter what happens, when all of this is said and done, I would never hold you responsible for the outcome of it."

Will looks into my eyes. "Well, while I do appreciate that, you better believe that I *would* hold myself responsible." He starts walking backward, toward the parking lot. "I'll see you at the station tomorrow."

"Don't forget your jacket!" I pull it off my shoulders and hold it outward.

"Nah, you keep it. You're freezing, and I've got dozens." He smiles and winks at me, before turning around and heading toward the parking lot.

All I can do is stand here as my thoughts become polluted by the idea of this monster holding onto his freedom. He just can't go free.

I will not let it happen.

15

The sun has yet to break the horizon as I finally decide to give up all hope for sleep.

After my conversation with Will last night, I may never sleep again. The very thought of this bastard escaping the demise he deserves is far too much to stomach, and I know I will never rest again until he is found. Somehow, someway, justice *has* to prevail.

I lay there staring at a picture of Lucy sitting on my dresser when my phone rings. I pick it up, noting the time.

"Why are you up so early?"

"Well, good morning to you too, Beck."

"Sorry, it's just so early, you caught me off guard."

"I'm assuming you already know that we have to go down to the station today for a DNA sample?"

Cale's insinuating tone pisses me off. As if he and Lucas actually believe I'm in a relationship with Will.

"Yes, I am aware."

"Well, I have a class at nine this morning, so I've gotta go in early and get this over with. Thought I would see if you wanna drive up with me."

"Yeah, that would be great, actually. I can be ready in thirty."

"Great. I'll meet you in the south-east parking lot."

We hang up, and I start rummaging through my closet for something halfway decent to wear. I settle on a soft, pink-and-white-striped V-neck sweater, and some denim jeans. I throw my hair into a flirty ponytail, apply a light layer of makeup, and head out the door.

Cale is sitting on the hood of his car, staring at his phone. He looks like he has abandoned the notion of sleep entirely, and I think he may have even lost some weight.

"Wow, Beck. You look abnormally nice for a drive to the police station. Exactly how do you plan on giving your DNA to this detective anyway?"

I roll my eyes, as I get in the passenger seat and put on my seatbelt. "Just drive the car, frat boy."

We make our way toward the police station, and now that he is closer to me, I can see that he hasn't been taking care of himself at all.

"Cale? Have you been getting any sleep?"

"As much as I need. Why? Worried about me, Beck?"

"Is it really all that surprising that I love and care about you? I mean, really, Cale."

He laughs. "All right, all right. If we're completely honest, all sarcasm aside, no. It's not surprising at all. I mean, you're probably the most loyal person I know, not to mention the most protective. I always felt grateful that Lucy had you in her life because I knew if I couldn't be there, you would be, and she'd be covered, ya know?"

"Wow, Bradley. I like the sentiment. Looks good on ya." I dish back his comment from the other day.

Cale smiles. "Yeah? Well, you didn't really let me finish. I was grateful to have you in Lucy's life but in mine? Now, that's an entirely different story."

"Oh yeah, funny guy? Well if it weren't for me, the two of you may not have dated at all."

"What do you mean?"

"I distinctly remember Lucy telling me about this gorgeous guy, who was sweet and charming, but was *also* the first-string quarterback on the football team."

"Yeah? So?"

"So, you know what they say about jocks, Cale. They're all about cheerleaders, beer, and easy-ass."

"Wow, I am genuinely offended."

"Well, you have to admit that many guys on your team did very little to prove otherwise."

I should know.

"Anyway, stereotypes aside, I told Lucy that until proven otherwise, it wouldn't be right for her to apply labels without getting to know you first."

"Huh."

"Huh? Is that *really* all you have to say to me right now, Cale? I mean, you practically owed me your firstborn," I joke.

But the instant that Cale's smile begins to fade, the painful impact of my words becomes clear: There will never be a wedding. There will never be a baby.

"Jesus, Cale. I am so sorry."

He smiles and nods, but the pain in his eyes tells me the damage is done. I want to shove my foot a little further into my mouth until I choke on it.

I continue to curse myself, as we pull into the parking lot of the police station.

"Dang, Beck, door to door service?"

"What in the hell are you talking about?"

I look where Cale is motioning his hand, and see that Will is standing outside the door with another police officer.

"It's clearly a coincidence, Cale. It's not like he knew the exact time we were coming."

"Sure, Beck. Sure."

We step out of the car and cross the parking lot. Upon seeing us approach, Will cuts his conversation short and meets us halfway.

"Mr. Bradley." He shakes Cale's hand, then turns toward me. "Ms. Beck. Thank you, both for coming. I'll walk you inside."

"Thanks. That is mighty generous of you," Cale says with a snide look.

I give him a quiet elbow to the ribs as we step inside the station.

"Ms. Beck, we'll have you go first, and Mr. Bradley, if you wouldn't mind waiting here, I'll send another lab tech to grab you shortly."

Will motions for me to turn down a long corridor, where he leads me into a small, ten-by-ten room, with one of those one-sided mirrors inside.

"Well, this isn't intimidating at all," I joke while taking a seat on a green plastic chair.

"It's just a formality," he says. "Shirley will be here with her swab kit in just a few."

I look up at him and I think he might be avoiding eye contact with me.

"Can I get you a soda or something while you wait?" he asks. "You won't be able to drink it until you've given your sample, but I could get—"

"Maybe just some water, thanks."

He is acting so professional and so... *aloof.* It's almost as if we have never talked before. I can't help but think that I've done something wrong.

"Is everything ok?" I ask him.

"Sure. I'll be right back with that water. Hang tight."

Will leaves the room, and I start thinking back over our conversation from the night before... Did I offend him in some way? Maybe he took my anger about the inability to seek the death penalty personally?

Just then, I see an officer walk past the doorway and trip. I immediately run out of the room to assist him.

"Oh my gosh, are you okay?"

"Yeah, thanks. I feel like a fool more than anything."

I then notice the scattered mess of papers on the floor around him. "Here, let me help you with those."

I bend down and grab a few photos that are scattered near me. After flipping them upright, I begin to arrange them into a neat and orderly pile, when the sight of something familiar causes venom to start flooding up the back of my throat.

Lucy.

My vision tunnels until all I can see is her lifeless body. Her eyes are open, but there is no sparkle. No smile, just—*emptiness.*

Her shirt is ripped. There are deep scratch marks that start at the bottom of her cheeks and end just above a dark-purple ligature mark around her neck.

I imagine Lucy's fingers fighting to pry the object free from her neck. Desperate. Afraid. Fighting for her life with so much ferocity that she leaves deep gouges in her skin from her finger nails.

The brutal image tests my psyche until at last, the photographs begin to lose color.

The bile in my throat becomes a hard and bitter lump in my stomach.

Every muscle in my body begins to convulse, as the anger, *the hatred*, makes its way up through my body like an electrical current until I feel nothing but unbelievable *rage.* All around me is rage. I want to scream, hit, punch. I want the man who did this to suffer the way that Lucy suffered.

I want him to die.

I feel my jaw start to tighten again, trying to stop the pain, the anguish. The shock is so intense, I can hardly make out the voices behind me.

"Walker! You, dumb ass, that's her friend!"

"Oh shit! Sorry!"

I suddenly feel the pictures being removed from my hands, while I remain crouched-down, and staring at the wall.

"Cait?" I feel a hand on my shoulder. "Caitlin, it's Will. Are you ok? I am so sorry you had to see those. Goddamn, I am so sorry."

Pull yourself together, Cait. Can't lose it now.

I muster up as much normalcy as I can and turn toward him. "Yeah, yeah, I'm good. Okay."

Will helps me up and back into the room, where a lady with a swab kit now awaits my return.

I sit down, and I feel nothing.

"Open your mouth and say 'AH,' honey."

I do as she asks, and feel the swab meet the inside of both cheeks, while images of Lucy's lifeless body play themselves out in my mind, over and over again.

"Okay, you're all done!" The lab tech packs up her kit and leaves the room.

Will closes the door behind her and takes the seat in front of me. "Cait, are you sure you're alright?"

The anger inside of me has nowhere else to go, so it suddenly, and *irrationally*, settles on a target.

"Oh! So, it's '*Cait*' now? What happened to '*Ms. Beck?*'"

"What?" He leans back in his chair, astonished.

"Nothing, never mind. Can I go now?"

Will is looking at me completely stunned. He then leans forward, brow furrowed, clearly trying to figure out what just happened.

I start to stand from my chair, and he immediately stands with me, putting his hand up in protest.

"Wait, I'm sorry, can we talk about why—"

"I need to get back. Can I just go please?"

Will's body language relaxes in defeat. He takes a step back from me, giving me the space needed to walk out of the room, and I immediately regret my reaction.

When I return to the lobby, I see that Cale is waiting for me, but without stopping, I head straight for the parking lot.

Cale immediately falls in behind me.

"Cait? What's wrong?"

I brush off his question and continue my tirade through the exit doors. I can't manage to stop and look at him—as if he could actually *see* what I just saw, simply by looking into my eyes.

So, I keep walking, all the while fighting the urge to vomit all over the parking lot.

"Cait! What in the hell is going on?!"

I move to the passenger side and attempt to open the door, but Cale stands firm on the driver's side.

"Kiss my ass if you think I'm unlocking this door without you telling me what in the hell just happened in there! What did they say? Did they find him?"

Cale's voice has changed from badgering to desperation, and I immediately feel crappy for my erratic behavior leading to this hope for resolution.

"No, no." I intentionally relax my body language. "I'm sorry, Cale. It's not about Lucy's case. This has all just been one great big witch hunt. I mean, while they're collecting swabs from the people who loved her most, the real killer is out there roaming free!"

Cale's face and shoulders fall, and I am immediately sick, as I watch this man that loved Lucy more than life itself, suddenly sink back into hopelessness.

"Come on. Let's get out of here," he says.

He unlocks the doors, and I can't get in fast enough. I have got to get as far away from here, and those pictures, as possible.

We pull out of the parking lot and make our way back to campus while images of Lucy continue to be intrusive and repetitive still frames in my head.

"You know, Cait, they are just doing their job, and you're right. That murderer is out there somewhere, free to do whatever the hell he pleases. So, you know what? If taking an hour out of my day will get their focus off of me, and onto the real killer, I will gladly give them whatever the hell they want. The sooner they rule us out, the better."

He is white knuckling the steering wheel again.

"I know. You're right. I'm sorry, Cale."

"Don't apologize. Believe me, I understand the anger, Cait, but you're pointing it in the wrong direction."

Actually, I'm not.

Because it's not the cops, that I'm angry with at all. My fury is aimed directly at the vile monster who took Lucy away from us. I just can't better explain to Cale why this anger has so abruptly risen to the surface, without *also* mentioning those putrid photographs.

"I know, Cale. You're right. You're absolutely right."

"Can I get that in writing, Beck? Because I'll be stunned stupid if I ever hear you say those words to me again. In fact, where's my phone so I can capture this moment."

I reach over and pick up his phone to record a message. Of course, it won't be the one that he wanted to record, but what's he gonna do? I click on the video app and press record.

"My dearest Cale, this is only a dream, and I encourage you to enjoy this dream while you can because when you awaken, you will be wrong again. At least ninety-eight percent of the time. So, sweet dreams, frat boy."

"I hate you." He attempts to grab his phone from my hands, but I fight to hold onto it.

"Hey, I'm not finished! I haven't made fun of your hair yet!"

Cale stops reaching for his phone and looks in the rearview mirror.

"What in the hell is wrong with my hair?!"

"Well, Jesus, Cale. Have you looked in the mirror lately? I mean, when was the last time you brought some scissors to it?"

He continues to examine his hairline, and I immediately start to chuckle.

"Don't worry, Cale. You're still under there somewhere."

He then looks over at me with a cunning smile on his face. "You know what, Beck? I may just pull over and let you walk home."

"But Cale, if I leave the car, how *ever* will you find your way back home through all those locks of hair?"

"Alright, that's it!"

Cale attempts to pull over, as my zealous laughter causes him to start laughing, too. Just as he nears the curb, however, his phone rings.

"Ohhh, and she's saved by the bell," he says.

Cale then veers back into the lane and hits the answer button on the dashboard.

"What's up, Luke?"

"Hey, so were you and Cait asked by that detective to give a DNA sample, or do I just look homicidal to this guy?"

Cale immediately gets a smile on his face. It's just *too* good an opportunity to waste.

"Nah, man. I don't know what you're talkin' about. He must be after you for some reason."

"What?! Shit! Really?"

Cale is trying so hard not to burst out laughing, that I can't help but to giggle my ass off.

"Cait? Is that you?"

"Yes, Lucas, it's me."

"Is that true? Is he really *after* me?"

"No, Luke, of course not. We just left the station. I'm sure we're just a few-of-many they've asked for a sample."

"Cale, you DICK!"

Cale erupts into uncontrollable laughter. "Oh C'mon, Luke! You left yourself wide open for that one man, admit it!"

"Uh-uh, no way. When I see you, you're dead!"

"LUCAS!" I sternly snap at his words without thinking twice.

Cale has stopped laughing, and the car is silent. I try to regain my composure when Lucas speaks first.

"Shit, I'm sorry. I don't know why I said that. I shouldn't have said that."

"No, I'm sorry. I'm just a little tense is all. I think we all are. But listen, Luke, this DNA sample is a good thing. The sooner they steer their focus in another direction, the better." I look over at Cale. "Right?"

Cale smiles and squeezes my knee.

"Right," Lucas answers. "So, I guess I better get down there then. Thanks for the invite, by the way."

"Luke, I knew you were at Angie's, and I wasn't about to drive another forty-five minutes to pick up your post-coital ass."

My mouth drops open. "Oh my God, Cale, that is disgusting. And do you ever sleep in your own bed anymore, Luke? I mean, every time we talk to you, you're at Angie's house."

"Well, actually—"

"Oh, back off, Cait. They're happy."

"Yeah. *Disgustingly* happy—and often," Lucas adds with laughter, and naturally, Cale joins in.

I roll my eyes and decide to tune them out. I then close my eyes, and for the first time since she died, I speak to Lucy...

I cannot believe you left me alone with these two. You've gotta be laughing your ass off right now.

In fact, I know you are.

16

After arriving back on campus, I sluggishly make my way toward the dorm.

Before parting ways, Cale made another promise to do lunch with me this week, and while I trust his intentions were honest, the sorrow in his eyes told me he will break that promise again.

Hell, the very sight of Cale's rumpled appearance today has me worried he's already surrendered himself to complete desolation.

God knows I'm not far behind him.

I focus on putting one foot before the other, all the while contesting my body's inclination to collapse from exhaustion. A loud explosion of thunder suddenly announces a heavy rain shower around me.

Fitting.

I reach the front entrance to my dorm, but rather than go inside, I turn around to face the garden walkway where Lucy's body was found.

For reasons I cannot explain, I find myself walking toward it. Maybe because it was the last place she touched. Maybe because it feels wrong to turn my back on what she went through...or maybe because the pain I feel couldn't possibly get any worse.

I reach the garden perimeter, and without warning, photographs of Lucy's disfigured body become a merciless slideshow in my head.

I try to shelf them, but the horrific images, once rendered colorless from shock, have become brutally vibrant with color.

And now, as I stand near the place where she took her last breath, I am no longer able to evade the many questions that torment a loved one when something like this happens.

How crippling was her fear in those final moments? How long did she hold onto the hope that someone, *anyone*, would just walk by and see her, before finally giving up, and accepting her fate?

How long did she suffer?

The intrusive questionnaire continues to consume me, while my mind continues to offer the most horrific possibilities imaginable. The cycle induces a hurt and anger more burdening than any one-person should ever have to bear.

I think of everything we have lost. Every smile, every laugh, the memory of once was, and what will never be. All that potential joy. A lifetime of it—gone.

It is so unfair!

I close my eyes and grasp my forehead, attempting to re-ground myself, but the dizziness prevails. I drop to all fours and wretch into the nearest flower bed.

Once I am sure there is nothing left, I wipe my mouth with the back of my hand and kneel back onto my heels. Noting the nasty appearance of vomit in the bare garden, I begin to cover it up with handfuls of neighboring soil.

As I gather up one more scoopful of earth, I catch a glimpse of something buried beneath it. I lean in closer to brush the mud away and discover that it's a cell phone.

It's Lucy's cell phone!

But how did the police miss it?

Lucy was discovered near the center of the walkway, and I'm kneeling just twenty feet or so from where she was found.

Although, this does put me approximately two feet outside of where the caution tape was placed. So, I guess it *is* possible that police missed it somehow.

But regardless of how it was missed, it now rests before me, and I am faced with two options: I could notify police and trust that any evidence it might contain will help bring Lucy's killer to justice;

Or I could take matters into my own hands.

The grandiose sense of *relief* that I feel from the mere thought of avenging Lucy's death has me favoring the latter.

Offering additional relief is the idea of no longer having to trust anyone else to bring Lucy's killer to justice. And why should I extend such a faith to authorities in the first place?

I've spent most of my life searching for answers to a forgotten past that others, *including* the authorities, have continually failed to provide me.

So, why should I trust them now?

For the first time since Lucy died, my mind has become unbelievably clear. I was *meant* to find this phone. It gives me a new sense of purpose, and something *more*; something I was given on the day that Lucy and I met. It has given me *hope.*

17

It has been over a week since I found Lucy's phone and I still have no idea what to do with it. After retrieving a Ziploc bag from my room, I had done my very best to collect it, without leaving fingerprints, or disturbing any evidence that might have been on it, but what good is evidence without the proper means to collect it?

Somehow, I have got to find a way to examine Lucy's phone myself, without the police getting their hands on it. Without *Will* getting his hands on it.

I cringe recalling my temper tantrum at the police station last week. Why did I have to lash out at Will like that? It wasn't his fault I saw those pictures.

Then again, if I'm being honest, that wasn't the reason behind my meltdown. There was something about Will's formal greeting that day that got to me.

'Ms. Beck' just didn't land on my ears the same way that 'Cait' did, and particularly the night before. Something about his casual demeanor, the way he was teasing me, almost...flirting. While short-lived, he made me feel somewhat *normal* again.

But I threw normalcy out the window the second that I decided to obstruct justice by holding onto Lucy's phone. So, I guess if Will never talks to me again, it is probably for the best.

I shut the textbook I have been staring at for over an hour when there is a knock at the door. I look at my phone, surprised to see that it's past midnight.

I walk over and open the door to find Lucas standing there. He has a backpack on one shoulder, and a partly unzipped gym bag, with some sloppily packed clothing, hanging off the other.

"Are you moving in?" I ask him.

"Are you gonna let me in before the dorm-witch sees me?"

I move out of the doorway and let him enter.

"How did you get past her in the first place, Luke? It's after midnight."

"I have my ways." He bumps his brows up and down.

"All right, so what happened?"

I open my dresser drawer and pull out a bag of toffee peanuts. It's a love that both Luke and I share.

I walk over and pour some into his hand, as he plops down on the bed adjacent to mine.

Lucy's bed.

I have to fight the nightmarish still frames from re-entering my mind as I listen to Luke go into his drama.

"Well, Angie and I got into a big fight."

"Well, Luke, that's the nice thing about having a dorm with your very own bed in it."

I rewind my arm and toss one of the peanuts into his mouth. He grins in victory, as he aims with one from his pile.

"I haven't slept in the dorm since we got back from the funeral." He tosses the peanut, and it lands in my mouth with ease.

"Yeah, I kinda picked up on that Luke."

"Well, it hasn't *exactly* been by choice. On our way back from the funeral"—he pauses to accept another peanut—"Cale asked if he could use my room for a while. To get some space from those Frat-tards, and I was more than willing to oblige when I had a place to stay, but now, I'm out a happy home."

Luke tosses another peanut my way, but eager to talk, I snatch it with my hand, instead.

"Why didn't you tell me, Luke?"

"Because Cale asked me not to. Said you would worry, and he didn't want you randomly showing up for pep talks."

Oh man. I'll show him pep talks!

"Everyone grieves in their own way, Cait, and Cale's choosing to grieve by isolating himself in my dorm, and ditching classes."

"Wait—he's ditching classes?"

"According to Angie, yeah."

"And how the hell would she know?"

"Because they have a class together. Last week Angie missed some big review, so I suggested that she get the notes from Cale, and that's when she told me he hadn't been to class since we got back from the funeral."

"*The funeral?!* That was almost three months ago! Why the hell didn't she say anything to you before?!"

"I think she assumed that I already knew, but, how would I? I've been staying with her."

Luke opens his mouth for another peanut, which I intentionally drive straight into his forehead.

"Ouch! Shit, what did I do?"

"I cannot believe he's been ditching class this entire time. I am such a schmuck. We are both schmucks, Luke. Our friend has been drowning, and neither one of us had a damn clue."

"Yeah? Well, I'm sorry, Cait, but Cale isn't the only one grieving right now, so you'll have to excuse me for not coddling him."

"Shit, you're right. I'm sorry."

"And besides, I've been more worried about you."

"Me? I'm fine, Luke."

"That's bullshit, and you know it." He stands up and sits down next to me. "I know how much she meant to you; we've all been through a lot together." He takes my hand and squeezes it. "You need to stop worrying about Cale, and let someone else worry about you for a change."

The combination of an invitation to expose my Achilles heel of vulnerability, along with his show of affection, has me feeling rather uneasy.

"Luke, really. I'm doing okay." I hold his hands with both of mine. "But thank you for being there, and not just for this, but for everything. You mean a lot to me, and I just hope you know that." I lean in and kiss his cheek, as he kisses mine in return.

He then stands up and retrieves a Tee and boxer shorts from his bag.

"Now, I know it will be hard, but I need you to ignore the passionate desires that are sure to overcome you, once you have seen me in my boxer shorts."

"It's hard to get turned on by dinosaurs and race cars, Luke." I smile and pop another peanut into my mouth.

"Jesus, Cait, I was twelve!"

"Yeah, well, the classics never die."

18

I take a quick shower and throw on some clothes while mulling over the best way to approach Cale, and his choice to abandon his life.

My phone suddenly rings, and the caller ID reads: Detective James. I feel a series of nervous flutters in my stomach, which catches me completely off guard.

I had already concluded that Will and I could never be friends, based on my recent decision to withhold evidence—*Oh shit, the PHONE!*

What if that's why he's calling? What if he saw me take it? I mean, Mackland is a crime scene, so there could be undercover agents spying on this entire campus right now!

Yep, that's it.

Will knows I have Lucy's phone, and he is probably on his way to arrest me right now.

I start to imagine whether or not *orange* is my new color when I finally get my wits about me.

If Will, or anyone in law enforcement, had witnessed my obstruction of justice, they would have arrested me on the spot, and Will most-certainly would not have called to warn me first.

So, what does he want then?

I decide to squash my curiosity and let it go to voicemail. Right now, I have to go and drag Cale's ass back to reality.

It's Saturday, so I don't even bother calling Cale to announce my impending arrival. I reach the door to his room and give it a few knocks.

No answer.

I knock a bit more.

No answer.

I lose my patience and start pounding the door.

"SHIT! All right! Hang on a minute, damn!"

Cale's speech is slurred, which only adds to my pre-existing list of concerns. *And good-shit it's NOON!*

My patience runs out when he doesn't come to the door right away, and I resume my knocking—*louder.*

"Stop! Jesus, I'm coming!"

Cale finally cracks the door, and before he can open it wide enough to acknowledge me, I shove my way past him.

"Cait? What the *hell*?!"

I stop and face him, ready to deliver a lecture, when something about his demeanor stops me. I begin to scrutinize his facial cues, when—

"Dammit, Cait." Cale closes his eyes and grabs the back of his head in frustration. "You *really* should have called me first."

He almost looks ashamed when he says this, and I instinctively turn around to see the source of his shame sitting on the edge of the bed.

A tall, blonde, and busty *mistake.*

"Who the fuck, are you?!" I target the girl with a rather strong inclination to defend Lucy's honor, and she immediately starts putting her clothes back on.

"Cait, relax! Geez, you don't have to—"

I turn around and point my finger in his face.

"You were already on my shit-list, Cale Bradley, and now *this*?! I mean Jesus, Cale! What would Lucy say!"

"She would say nothing, because she is DEAD, Cait! She's fucking DEAD! She can't talk, or see, or hear, any of this conversation because she is DEAD!"

Cale runs his hands through his hair, tugging at it sharply, as he turns away from me.

Then, before I can even process what he has just said, he picks up one of the beer bottles on the dresser and chucks it against the wall.

The blonde girl jumps and screams in response to the glass shattering all over the room. I bend down and pick up her remaining articles of clothing, stomp over, and toss them out, and into the hallway.

"That's your cue." I hold the door open. "Now get the fuck out."

She rushes toward the exit, as a few more bottles of beer go hurtling past her. She screams again, as I slam the door behind her, and make my way back into the room.

"Have you lost your damn mind, Cale?"

"You know what Cait? *Who in the hell do you think you are?* Coming in here unannounced, attacking my guest—"

"Your *mistake!*"

"Well FUCK YOU and the pretentious horse you rode in on, Cait."

"*Pretentious?!* Do you really think I'm here on behalf of the *moral police,* Cale!? Because fuck you for not knowing any better, if you do."

Cale opens his mouth to protest but chooses to bite his tongue. He looks exhausted.

We both choose to remain silent, and I can see the anger is finally slipping away from his posture. He walks over and sits on the edge of the bed, and continues to slide down onto the floor while burying his face in his hands.

I stay stuck in my position, trying to figure out how he got *so* out of control, and *so fast* when he finally lifts his head up to look at me.

"What do you want from me, Cait? Do you expect me to be that well-kept and happy *frat boy* again? Because I can't. I can't because he's gone. He doesn't *exist* anymore. Not without her."

Cale's eyes fill with water, as he wipes his nose with the back of his hand. His grimace shows pain, as his bottom lip and chin start to quiver.

"I don't know who I am without her, Cait. I don't know who I wanna be, or how to even find the desire *to live* anymore. I take sleeping pills—JUST to get some relief from this *pain...*" He winces.

"But then I wake up, and the anguish reminds me that she's gone, and I swear to God, Cait, it's like losing her all over again."

Cale's words are becoming intermittent gasps of agony. He runs his hand through his hair and rests his head against the edge of the bed.

"I just wish I could relieve this pain, you know? I mean, it is just *so—fucking—unbearable!* I would give anything to relieve it." He grits his teeth. "And I would give my life to make that fucker pay for what he's done!"

That makes two of us.

I walk over to where Cale is sitting and kneel down next to him. He wraps his right arm around my waist and buries his face in my chest.

"Oh God, I just want her back." He silently weeps, "Please...I just want her back."

I cradle his head in my hands, wishing I could take his pain away; wishing I could take it away from all of us.

"Shhh...it's okay. It's okay, Cale. I got you."

I rest my face down in his hair and close my eyes. I continue to hold him while mulling over his words. He is begging for relief, and I hold the key.

Cale and I share an equal rage toward the monster who killed Lucy, and for *me*, that relief came the second I decided to take justice into my own hands.

And so, ultimately, it is my desire to relieve Cale's pain that has triggered a hostile takeover of rational thought.

"I think you need to get some rest, Cale. We have a lot to talk about, and I need you mentally sound for it."

He sits back up and wipes his face with his hands.

"Yeah, you're probably right. And Cait, I'm glad you're here. You are the one person in my life who truly understands the pain that I'm in."

And the one person who knows how to relieve it, too.

I smile. "I'm grateful for you, too, Cale. Now get some sleep."

"Are you leaving?"

"No, of course not. I'm going to stick around and clean up this shit-show you've been living in. I mean really Cale, Lucy would have your ass."

I smirk at him, but he is too tired to acknowledge what I'm saying. He just falls back onto his pillow, and within minutes he is passed out.

I roll up my sleeves and scan the room.

As I take note of the shambles that Cale's existence has become, I feel like a total failure.

Lucy would have both our asses.

19

I carry two cups of coffee toward Cale's room. Now that he is awake, I am going to pump him full of caffeine and deliver my newly desired...*goal.*

Though, I'm not entirely sure how to word it—or how he will take it, for that matter. He could flip out and turn me into the police.

Or maybe, he will just bring me to my senses; but either way, there is only one way to find out.

"Ah, the nectar of the gods. Thank you." Cale takes the cup. "Listen, I'm sorry about before."

"Don't, Cale. It's time to face forward. I'm good. You're good. Or at least, we're gonna be."

He lets it drop and takes a sip of his coffee.

I nervously open my purse and remove the baggie with Lucy's phone, that I ran back to retrieve while Cale was asleep. He suddenly registers what I am holding and chokes on his coffee, mid-sip.

"Holy Shit! Where did you get that? And why do *you* have it, and not the police?"

I slide it back in my purse. "Now, don't freak out, but I found it in the mud after we got back from the police station last week."

Cale's eyes fly open. "Are you kidding me? How stupid could you be, Cait?!" He abruptly stands up and walks to the other side of the room.

Then, while lacing his fingers to support the back of his head, he finally turns around to face me.

"Okay, so explain."

"I just don't trust anyone else to handle it, Cale. What you don't know, is that when Detective James stopped by to tell me about the DNA sample, I asked him what the maximum sentence would be for the bastard who did this—"

"AND?"

"And neither Maryland nor D.C. offers the death penalty."

"So, what you're telling me is, this asshole could live out a cushy existence in prison?"

"Yep, and that's assuming they catch him *and* find him guilty."

Cale walks over and sits down on the bed in front of me. "All right...okay..." He is nodding his head. "So, what's the plan, here? Do you really think we could handle that evidence better than the cops can, Cait? Because we could just be fucking it up ourselves."

"I know, it's crazy. And I have no idea where we would even begin. I mean, we would want to check it for fingerprints, DNA, and anything else we could find. *How* we are going to do that—I haven't got a clue."

"Okay, so assume we magically figure out how to accomplish what you're suggesting; what do you plan on doing with it then?"

I sidestep this question for now.

"Cale, that's not the only thing I haven't told you. While we were at the station, an officer dropped some photographs in the hallway by accident, and when I tried to help gather them up—"

"Yeah?"

"They were pictures of Lucy, Cale. Detailed pictures. You know... *after* she was found."

His color turns a faint green, then abruptly changes to red. "I cannot believe you have carried that shit around with you for over a week, Cait."

Cale props his elbows up onto his knees and presses his forehead against balled-up fists. I hear him take a deep breath and I *know* what's coming next...

"Was it bad? I mean, umm…did she—" He exhales and squints his eyes in pain. "Ah FUCK!"

Cale tightens his fists, as he stands up to pace the room again. I can see the defined muscle in his arms, as his body clenches with anger.

"The details don't really matter, Cale. All that matters, is that you and I—"

He is not listening to a word I say, as he continues pacing the room.

"Cale!"

He stops and walks back over to sit in front of me.

"All that matters, is that *we* find him, Cale. You and me."

"And then what, Cait?"

I lean forward and look intensely into his eyes. "And then we kill him, Cale. We have to kill him. It is the *only* option I deem acceptable."

Cale sits back, somewhat in shock, although not quite as shocked as I expected him to be.

"He cannot go free." I continue, "And even if the cops do manage to catch him, and he goes to prison, he will still *exist* in this world. Why should he be allowed to take Lucy's life, and still be permitted to hold onto his? It is not right."

Cale laces his hands behind his head again, absorbing what I've just proposed.

"Cale, say something."

After several minutes, he finally leans forward and looks at me with hatred in his eyes.

"I'm in."

"Okay."

"And, Cait?"

"Yeah?"

"I want him to suffer."

20

That next morning, the sun has brought some late winter warmth, and I decide to take a long and much-needed run around campus.

Cale and I agreed to meet up at the library tomorrow to see what we can come up with, in the way of amateurs attempting to retrieve evidence from a cell phone.

As I run back to campus, I imagine us finding enough evidence to catch the guy who did this. I even allow myself to plot his death, which causes me to pick up speed as if running toward an imaginary finish line.

When I finally do make it back to the dorm, I see that Will is waiting for me by the entrance and I'm hit with a wave of shock and anxiety.

"Hi there. I tried calling first, but when you didn't answer, I thought I'd take a chance anyway. I'm hoping you haven't eaten breakfast yet."

My fear settles, once I look down to see that he is carrying a black nylon cooler and *not* an arrest warrant.

"Um, no. I've just been running."

"I can see that."

BAH!

"Painfully obvious, is it?"

"I wouldn't say *painfully*." He grins, before raising the bag. "I've brought you some southern biscuits and gravy. My mother's recipe." He raises an eyebrow.

Out of breath, I nod and continue toward my dorm.

"Now, just so I'm clear. You bravely fought for our country with one of the most prestigious and honored military teams, spend your days and nights fighting crime, clearly respect your mother, and evidently know your way around the kitchen. Oh, and you just so happen to be incredibly good-looking. Anything else I should know?"

"I speak three different languages."

"Of course, you do."

Will laughs, as we finally reach the entrance to my dorm.

"I'm starting to wonder how you've managed to avoid becoming a contestant on *The Bachelor*," I add.

Will flashes a flirtatious smile across his face, as I pull the key card from my pocket.

"So, you think I'm good-looking?"

"As if you didn't already know." I roll my eyes, as I open the door and lead us up to my room.

Will walks over to my desk and starts removing Tupperware from the cooler, lined with a thick heat retention material.

I sheepishly think that my stink is probably ruining his appetite.

"Would it be incredibly rude of me to excuse myself for a quick shower first?"

"Actually, I'd prefer it."

"You know, I would really hate to disrespect your mother's cooking by dumping it all over your head."

Will smiles, as he continues to remove various food items from the cooler.

I grab some underwear, a bra, jeans, a white tank, and my favorite loose white sweater that slightly hangs from the tops of my shoulders.

After the shortest shower in history, I brush out my wet locks, before applying a thin layer of lotion to my skin. I quickly dress and head back to my room, and the most amazing aroma surrounds me as soon as I've entered it.

Will hands me a red, square-shaped, ceramic plate, with some biscuits and gravy, accompanied by a thin slice of pinkish-looking bread.

"It's strawberry. Big where I come from."

I sit down on the bed, as he then hands me a champagne glass filled with orange juice and a heavy dose of surrealism.

"Jesus, who *are* you?"

He laughs, "Just a good old fashioned southern boy, who loves to cook *and* eat in style."

"Shocking." I grin, as I sit Indian-style on my bed, and take a bite of food that was clearly made in heaven.

Will sits down on Lucy's bed across from me.

"Well?" he asks.

"Are you kidding me? It's unreal!"

He displays a rather proud looking smile and then digs in himself.

"Ok, William. So, tell me more about these recipes and where they come from."

"Well, I was born in Savannah, Georgia, but my dad was in the military, so we traveled all over. I think I was around eight years old when he made Admiral, and we were finally allowed to remain in one place." He takes another bite.

"And where might that be?"

"Charleston, South Carolina."

I imagine him sitting on a porch swing, surrounded by various smells of homemade bread, and living the perfect life. A life so painfully different than my own.

"So, your parents are still married then?"

Will nods, as he continues eating.

"Any siblings?"

"I'm the oldest of five. Three sisters, and one brother. Mallory is twenty-three, Jonathan twenty, Lizbeth's nineteen, and Maggie is sixteen. She's the baby."

"Wow. That must have been chaotic."

"Yeah, but we're all really close."

"And of course, you're the oldest," I say.

"Profiling me, are you?"

"Not at all." I coyly grin, as I take another bite.

"Okay, so tell me something about you," he says.

"Not much to tell, that you don't already know from our initial interview. I was adopted by Rob and Cynthia when I was almost twelve, and my family has consisted of them, Lucy, Lucas, and eventually Cale, ever since."

"So, when did Lucas and Cale enter the picture?"

"Well, we met Luke during the summer before eighth grade; though, he was home-schooled until we all applied to Mackland. He describes his parents as 'hippies,' and he always seemed embarrassed by them. In fact, I've only ever met them once. He mostly preferred to hang out at our house.

"Cale, on the other hand, showed up the start of our junior year. The All-American quarterback, with a 'bright future at Law.'"

"Care to explain the air quotes?"

"Well, Cale didn't exactly choose his own path. It was clearly laid out for him since birth. Although, he would only allude to that when he was drunk. Most of the time, he would talk about it as if he'd always wanted it that way, but Lucy knew otherwise. I think he was ashamed to admit that his parents had that much control over him."

"And *before* they all came along?"

"Couldn't tell ya."

"Meaning..."

"Meaning *exactly that*. I can't remember anything before the age of five."

Will eyes me inquisitively, and I change the subject.

"So, tell me more about your family."

I see him wanting to chase his curiosity, but thankfully, he chooses to let it drop.

"Well, we are traditionalists. So much so that I am required to fly home at least twice a month for Sunday dinner."

"*Seriously?*"

"I know. It's a little crazy, but can you blame me?" He motions toward my empty plate.

"No, definitely not. Thank you, by the way. Breakfast was amazing, and so undeserved, after the last time that I saw you."

"Listen, don't worry about that. I'm sorry you had to see those photos."

"Yeah, well, that wasn't your fault. And not exactly the reason behind my irrational behavior, either."

"Oh?" He masks a grin.

"Judging by that look on your face, you've clearly formed your own conclusion."

"Actually, I'm more curious than anything."

"Curious?"

"Yes, curious. As to why my hesitation to call you by your first name was such a source of contention for you."

"Hesitation? I considered your greeting to be more aloof by design."

"Maybe with Cale." He looks directly into my eyes. "But not with you."

I suddenly find myself paralyzed by a clutter of butterflies in my stomach.

Overwhelmingly uncomfortable, I break his gaze and stand up to rinse off my plate in the sink of our small kitchenette before returning it to his bag. I feel him looking at me from the corner of my eye as I tidy up the remaining breakfast items.

"Something I said?" he asks.

I instantly feel a tingling sensation run down my spine, as I realize he has moved in behind me. He reaches his arm around me to set his plate down, and I force myself to turn around.

We are now face-to-face, and my attraction to him becomes evident. It wasn't his friendly-flirty banter that distracted me from my loss before.

No, it was something far more magnetic, and it now demands my entire attention.

Will is searching my face for answers, but I fail to find any words. His tantalizing brown eyes show no wear, which I find rather odd, considering his time spent in combat and dealing with criminals.

"How is it possible that you don't carry a single ounce of skepticism in those eyes of yours? After all that you've seen?"

"I guess I just don't see the point in dwelling on it. Trust me, life is too short."

Will takes a step toward me, latching onto my shirt with his thumb and forefinger, just adjacent to my belly button, and gazes into my eyes.

I am completely mesmerized by his smell and the sweet tickle of his breath on my face.

"You know, you're rather good at changing the subject." He whispers, "But if you don't mind, I'd like to explain why I was hesitant to say your name the other day."

I am suddenly aware of the light swirling circles his fingers are making around my belly button through my shirt, and I feel as though my legs might actually give out.

Will continues, "I was afraid that if I allowed myself to say your name, my tone would give way to what I have been wanting to say to you since the day that you first snatched that dish out of my hands." He coyly smiles, sending a ripple of anticipation throughout my entire body.

"And what is that, exactly?" I ask.

"That you have the most amazing blue eyes I have ever seen; and when you aim that cynical grin my way, that dimple that follows makes me wanna tug on your bottom lip." He studies my mouth before making his way back up to my eyes.

I attempt to swallow, noting how unbelievably dry my throat is. "Well, as long as we're making confessions—"

"Be careful what you confess to me, Caitlin." He whispers, "I'm a cop."

"Well, I guess I should keep that whole bank robbery thing to myself then."

"Unless you wanna find yourself in handcuffs."

I suddenly remember my current obstruction of justice, taking the shape of a cell phone in the top drawer of my dresser.

This is such a bad idea.

I cannot allow myself to get involved with the Lead Detective in Lucy's case. Considering that Cale and I have *now* chosen such a homicidal path in life.

"You were saying?" he urges, but his close presence is making me too nervous to form a single thought.

He then reaches his thumb and forefinger up to grip my bottom lip, before trailing them off my chin. He continues to study my face intently, but after failing to complete my confession, he suddenly forms a grin.

"Are you choosing to remain silent?" he asks.

"I think that might be best."

"God forbid you should say something vulnerable."

All right, he knows far too much about me!

I part my lips to argue, when he suddenly moves his left-hand to my lower back, causing all words to evade me. He then embraces the side of my face with his right-hand and extends his thumb out to trace my lips. Moving in closer, he captivates me with his eyes, and lightly touches his lips to mine.

After taking in my bottom lip, he then closes his eyes, and parts my lips open with his, to passionately taste me.

I realize, as his kiss ignites goosebumps all over my body that I have never been kissed in this way before. Never felt such a desire to let a man in—*really* in.

Will brings his left-hand up to the other side of my face, before sliding his fingers through my wet hair to cradle the back of my head in his hands. His passion calls for my usual tension to unwind, completely.

I can feel every desirous move and sensation that follows. It calls for a deep yearning from within me.

Will slowly brings our kiss to a close by taking in my lower lip again, only this time, he takes his sweet time releasing it. He then begins to softly brush his lips back-and-forth against mine.

The instant that I open my eyes, his alluring gaze holds me hostage. I am so lost, so open, so *afraid*.

So, I feel an incredible sense of relief when my phone rings, jolting me back from la-la land.

"I should probably get that. It might be Cale. He's been struggling lately."

Will releases his grip around my waist and steps back, granting me freedom.

Right then, I become aware that his embrace was helping to stabilize my legs. I focus on putting one foot, before the other, and reach for my phone as it goes to voicemail.

"It's Cynthia. I should probably call her back."

"Right." He smiles, and I walk over to help him pack up the rest of his things.

"Thank you again, for breakfast. It was delicious."

"Among other things."

Will grips my waist again with his right hand and pulls me in for one last kiss. I want so much to shove him out the door, but that smile...

"What would you say to dinner at my place Wednesday night?" he asks.

"Um, can I get back to you on that? I've got a busy week. Midterms."

"Sure." He smiles but is clearly suspect to my response.

"Bye, beautiful." He kisses my nose and then winks, before making his way out of my room.

I plop down on my bed, trying to make sense of what just happened between us when he sends me a text:

> 508 Arlington Way
> Wednesday @ 8 pm
> In case you get hungry.

I decide to keep my response short with a smiling emoji when I suddenly remember his willingness to call me out on my insecurities—*which then* causes me to bypass the smile and go for the emoji poking out its tongue, instead. He really *can* be quite aggravating.

But that dormant desire for love, the one I've deprived of attention for so many years, is pleading to be nurtured—*No, Cait.*

I send it back to imprisonment, after reminding myself of the inevitable fate that's followed every close relationship I have ever had.

Will has no idea what he's up against with me. I'm just a mere fragment of my former self, whoever that 'self' may have been.

And once more, I hate the idea of replacing that sweet optimism in his eyes, with the brutal pessimism I carry in mine.

So, the best thing for me, and for him, is to move on and forget that kiss ever happened.

21

It's Monday morning, and I wake up late for an early class. I throw my hair up and run out the door toward the other side of campus. My phone alerts me to a text, and my knees instantly go weak when I see that it's Will. I can't believe that our unexpected rendez-vous only happened yesterday—and my resolution to forget about it has lasted a whopping twenty-four hours.

You're pathetic.

I drag my finger across the screen to reveal Will's text:

> **Good Morning, Beautiful. I have
> a busy day ahead of me, but I just
> wanted to let you know that I can't
> stop thinking about you.**

Good morning.

> **Hi ☺ What are you up to today?**

Headed to class. Late, actually.

> **Well, I better not keep you then.**

**You're sexy and all, but I just can't
date a girl that's failed out of college.**

You're hilarious.

Smitten, actually.

That may have gotten
you a smile.

**And I'd love to see it. Send me a
picture of that beautiful face.**

No way. I woke up late,
remember? I'm a mess.

Oh right. On second thought...

Why, Detective James, you really
know how to sweep a girl off her
feet.

**Oh, I haven't even begun to sweep
you off your feet, Caitlin. But
you may have swept me off mine.**

I'm flattered. <3

**Not exactly the response I was
looking for, but I'm so happy for
you.**

You're a smart ass.

And you're one to talk.

I got nothin'.

I find that hard to believe.

Sorry to disappoint.

**Actually, you're adorable, and it
drives me MAD. I'd be halfway
to your doorstep right now if I didn't
have an endless stack of DNA
reports to sift through.**

Sounds like a roaring good time.

**There are many things I would
rather be doing.**

That makes two of us. ;)

**Don't flirt with me.
There's no telling what I might do.**

Sorry about that…

You're such a tease.

And you're a distraction.

Not yet, but I plan to be.

You're rather sure of yourself.

**Don't worry, Caitlin. I'm not
expecting this chase to be easy,
but I have a feeling it's gonna
be worth it.**

You know, you really can
be quite adorable at times.
Pisses me off.

**I'll take it ☺ Have you
given any more thought to
having dinner with me?**

Jury's still out.

**You know, I could help you
study. I'm rather brilliant.**

Not to mention arrogant.

**No, just confident.
And incapable of taking no
for an answer.**

Ok fine, dinner.

**Great. See you Wednesday.
And I apologize in advance.**

For?

**For you letting your guard down
and falling madly in love with me. ;)**

Goodbye, Will.

Bye, beautiful.

I sigh to myself, as I tuck my phone in my bag. I honestly have no idea what in the hell I'm doing. I have no business flirting with Will, and yet, for whatever reason, I just can't seem to let him go.

Although, that may change the further that Cale and I get into this vigilante scheme of ours. I mean, nothing kills romance like conjugal visits.

After my class has finally ended, Cale is waiting for me in the hallway as planned. We have got to find something that will help us search Lucy's phone, and I am hoping the library will help us to find it.

As I approach Cale, I notice that he is holding a stack of books in his arms.

"Did you hit the library without me?"

"No, I just got back from the counseling office. They're working with me to get back on track."

"That's great, Cale. Really."

"Yeah, well. I figured I should at least finish my undergrad. At that point, I can always re-evaluate things, right?"

"Right. Well, let me put some of those books in my bag for you."

I take what I can from his arms when I suddenly notice the janitor is watching us from the other end of the hall. Cale turns around to see what I am looking at, causing the janitor to redirect his attention elsewhere.

"Cale, did I ever tell you the janitor was the one who found Lucy that day?"

"No."

"Well, he was." I make eye contact with Cale. "And he's got a criminal record, too."

"How do you know that?"

"I overheard Detective James talking to his partner about it that day, and get this—his past charges were statutory rape and assault."

"No, shit?"

"Yep, and I swear he's been watching me, too."

"All right, well? Let's go pay him a little visit then."

We make our way down the hall toward the Janitor, as he picks up the trash and scurries through the exit. The rush of coeds then delays our efforts, allowing the janitor to slip out of sight.

"Where did he go?" I ask.

This prompts Cale to start pushing people out of our way until we finally reach the exit.

We step outside and span our view across campus when I spot the back-end of a garbage cart heading down another pathway to the right of us.

"There!" I point toward him, and the two of us make a beeline in his direction.

We turn the corner to see him tossing the garbage bags into a larger dumpster near the back of the building.

"Act casual. We don't want to scare him off," I suggest, slowing my pace.

After heaving the last of the garbage bags into the dumpster, the janitor sees us approaching, and instantly displays a look of fear and anxiety on his face.

"Whoa—did you see that?" I whisper.

"Yeah. He definitely knows something."

The janitor nervously grips the side of the barrel to pull it behind him when Cale runs up and grabs the other side of it, causing the janitor to halt and face us.

"Hey d-d-don't touch that!" The man gives the barrel a firm tug back toward him.

Cale puts his hands up, "All right, all right. Calm down. We just wanna talk."

"I have t-t-to work." He tries to continue onward.

"No, wait! Please?" I speak out, and thankfully, he stops.

I carefully walk around to face him, and he lowers his head beneath the bill of his hat, as I enter his view.

"Do you know who I am?"

He nods.

"And how do you know me?"

"You kn-new that girl."

"That's right, and you found her."

He nods.

I soften my voice, "That must have been difficult."

He nods again.

"Have you met Cale?" I motion toward him, and the janitor shakes his head.

"Well, Cale and I, were very close to Lucy."

I intentionally humanize us, hoping to stir up an impromptu look of guilt, but he just continues to stare at the ground.

"What's your name?" I ask.

"D-D-Daniel."

"Nice to meet you, Daniel. My name is Cait."

"Nice to meet you."

"Daniel, we are very eager to find the person responsible for this, and I'm sure you can understand why."

He nods and lifts his eyes slightly to peek up from beneath his hat.

"Well... we were just wondering if you happened to see anything—"

He rapidly shakes his head and lowers his eyes again.

"You sure about that?" Cale asks, and his accusatory tone causes Daniel to flinch.

I give Cale a curt-look and try a new approach.

"Listen, I'm sure that finding her in that way came as a horrific shock, and sometimes our memories can fail us during times of stress. So, maybe we could start with the least consequential and work our way up. Can you tell me what you were doing when you found her?"

"I already t-t-told the police. I was salting the sidewalks."

"In the middle of the night?" Cale blurts out.

Daniel lifts his head and looks sternly at Cale. "I always do! So, it won't be slick in the morning!"

"And what time did you find her?" I ask.

"Around six that morning."

This timeline knocks the wind out of me. The police report stated that Lucy had died sometime around one am. If Daniel didn't discover her until six am, that would mean that Lucy's bruised and battered body, was left exposed and undiscovered for five hours—and while I slept just yards away, too.

Ohhh, Jesus. It's too much.

"Did you notice anything strange? Any footprints, or objects of any kind?" I ask, and he shakes his head again.

"Bullshit!" Cale's patience has dissolved.

"Cale, calm down."

"I have to get b-b-back to work now."

Daniel tries to leave, but I put my hand on his shoulder to stop him.

"Wait, please. Excuse my friend; he just wants to find the person responsible. He loved her very much."

I then feel an instant shiver, as Daniel raises his eyes to connect with mine. "Love can make you do crazy things," he says.

"Care to elaborate, asshole?" Cale takes a step toward him, and I immediately bring my hand up to stop him.

"Hey, this is harassment!" Daniel shouts, "I'm calling the police!"

Oh shit! Not the police. Not Will!

"Listen, that won't be necessary. Really. We're sorry we bothered you."

With my hand still on Cale's chest, I force us both to take a step back and allow Daniel some room to leave.

"Are you kidding me? This is such bullshit! He obviously knows something!" Cale shouts.

"Let him go, Cale." My tone is firm, as I watch the janitor scurry off.

Cale throws his arms up in the air and storms back toward campus. I follow behind him, trying to sort through Daniel's words, body language, and overall demeanor in my head.

Cale suddenly stops and turns back toward me, the frustration and anger boiling over the surface.

"How could you just let him go, Cait? I mean, you saw his reaction! That freak knows something, and I want to know what it is!"

"Cale, please lower your voice. Do you want him to call the police? Do you want them to know that we're going around interrogating people? How do you think that will look?"

"Screw the police and SCREW HIM!"

"Cale, stop! You have GOT to calm down!"

Cale turns away from me, and I'm starting to wonder if bringing him into this was a mistake. If he lashes out at every person we interview, it will inevitably catch up to us.

"Listen, if you can't keep your emotions in check then maybe you shouldn't be involved."

"Okay. Fine." He turns to face me. "I'll back off for now, but he *does* know something, Cait, and you better believe I'm gonna find out what it is." He storms off again.

Cale is right. Daniel definitely knows something, and my gut tells me that I am not going to like it.

22

I search the aisles, skimming through vast amounts of literature on the art of forensics.

Taking a couple of books from their shelves, I head back to the table where Cale and I have been camped out for the past three hours.

Cale is casually leaning back in his chair reading, *Forensics for Dummies.*

"Subtle, Cale."

"Well, what exactly would you have chosen?"

"Something less obvious."

"Yeah? Well, obvious or not, I can't find ANYTHING that would help us examine that damn phone."

"Shhhh…" I lean forward and dart my eyes around the room to see who might be listening.

Taking my lead, Cale lowers his voice to a whisper, "There is no way for us to examine that phone the way we need to, Cait. It would require all sorts of computers and stuff to run fingerprints through that National Database."

"CODIS."

"Yeah, that one."

Cale closes the book and tosses it onto the table in frustration, before leaning back in his chair again.

"So? What do you suggest we do?" I ask.

"Well, we could abandon this idea and corner the janitor again."

"I think we need to take a break from the janitor for now, Cale. You've pretty much guaranteed he'll be carrying a shotgun from now on."

He sighs and rubs his eyes with his forefinger and thumb. He then stops and leans forward.

"Hey, have you tried looking *through* her phone? We could look through it without removing it from the bag."

"Yeah, I thought of that, but the battery's dead."

"Right. Damn."

"Well, you guys look rather intense. What's up?"

Startled, we both turn around and see that Lucas is standing behind us.

I subtly nudge the books toward Cale, sending a cue to disguise them, as I stand up to hug Lucas.

"Hey, Luke! So, good to see you. How've you been?"

"Since I just saw you two days ago? Fine." His expression is analytical.

"Oh, right. I know I just saw you, but you left so early in the morning—and without saying goodbye. I just wanted to make sure you're good."

"I left you a note."

"You did? I'm sorry, I must have missed it."

Cale stands and positions himself next to me, further blocking Luke's view.

"What's up my man?" Cale slaps his hand.

Luke returns his greeting before turning his eyes toward me again. Angie suddenly appears, distracting Luke from his visual assessment, and for the first time *ever*, I find myself grateful for her presence.

"Hey, Angie!" I say with some real enthusiasm, which only increases Luke's suspicions further.

While we all pretend to like Angie, Luke isn't stupid. He knows that she is not our favorite person.

"So, what are you two up to?" Cale tries to redirect.

"Luke is helping me study for an exam," Angie responds. "I was offered a rather prestigious position at Brunick, and it calls for me to be licensed in certain areas."

Angie's arrogance removes my previous enthusiasm, entirely.

"How about you two?" Luke asks.

"Well, I've gotten behind in my school work, so Cait's been trying to help me get back on track. It's been a bit stressful, to say the least."

"Huh." Luke still looks suspicious.

He knows us all too well.

"Well, good luck with that. We have to be going now. My grand-mother is expecting us for dinner. Let's go, Luke."

"Yeah, I'll be right there."

Annoyed, Angie rolls her eyes and walks toward the library exit.

"Listen, I'm glad I ran into you guys. I was hoping we might be able to get together soon. It's been awhile since we hung out, and it's been hard, ya know?"

"I know, Luke, and you're right. It has been far too long, and I think we could all use some lax time. I'm sorry," I say and hug him, relieved to see that he has let his suspicions go.

"I'm helping Angie study for this damn test right now, but soon, okay?"

"You got it, buddy. First rounds on me." Cale slaps his hand before moving into what I like to call the 'Bro-hug".

"All right. I'll see you guys later then."

I wave to Luke as he makes his way out of the library.

"Well, I'd say we officially suck as friends, Cale."

"Yep. Did Luke spend the night at your dorm or somethin'?"

"Yeah. He showed up the other night after a fight with Angie. They must have made up."

"Why didn't he just come back to his own dorm?"

"Well, I asked him that very same question, and *that's* when he told me he hadn't slept there since the funeral because *you* had taken it over."

"And that's when you came pounding on my door like a mad woman."

"You had it comin'."

"Ahh, well this is all making a lotta sense now, Beck. Remind me to punch Lucas in the face later."

I chuckle, as I begin to gather up the books from our study session.

"So, what are we gonna do about that phone?" he asks.

"I have no idea, but we'll have to sit on it for now. It's late, and we've got a long day ahead of us tomorrow."

"Shit. I forgot about that."

"Yeah. I'm not looking forward to it either."

23

Cale and I pull into the driveway of the only home I have ever known, and we are instantly greeted by Cynthia and Rob as we exit the car.

"There you are!" Cynthia shouts and moves in for hugs with glossy eyes.

Rob then hugs me and kisses my forehead, before shaking Cale's hand.

"Hey there, son. You feel like helping me take down some Christmas lights out back? I've let it slip this year and Cynthia's ready to have my hide."

"Well, for crying out loud, Rob. It's almost March!" Cynthia says with a subtle laugh, "And anyway, Cale just got here."

"That's all right; I don't mind," Cale says.

"And I've only got one string left, anyway, Cyndi. It won't take but a minute," Rob says and pats Cale's back. "Sound good?"

"Yes, sir. Happy to help."

Cale follows Rob toward the backyard, as Cynthia leads me into the house.

"The boxes are upstairs. I've labeled them with your names, according to who I thought might want what's inside of them," she says.

I follow behind her, as memories begin to flood my brain. We step into Lucy's bedroom, which is now completely boxed up.

I observe the sight, stunned by how quickly they seemed to have *erased* her.

I remind myself that everyone grieves differently, and for some people, personal items can intensify their grief.

But the sight of her life compacted into nothing more than cubes of cardboard has me failing to hold onto logic.

"Caitlin? What is it, honey?"

"It's like she was never here! I mean, I know you wanted to give me a few things, but I was not expecting *this*."

Cynthia sighs. "Come here, honey." She takes my hand and walks me over to sit on a depressingly bare mattress.

"I know this might be hard for you to understand, but it was just too hard walking past a room that looked like she was still living in it. Each time that I did, I would catch an item in the corner of my eye; her vanity, the pictures on her wall, her endless collection of hats and scarves that covered shelves and hooks. I just couldn't do it anymore." Her tone reveals so much pain.

I lean in to hug her, and she starts to cry. The devastation I feel from the only mother I have ever known is causing a deep pain in my chest when she suddenly pulls away and tidies up her eyes with her fingers.

"Well, I'd better go and finish up that spaghetti. I'll give you some space." She smiles weakly and heads back downstairs.

I scan the room, recalling every moment we had ever shared within these four walls when suddenly, another memory is triggered by the very bed I am sitting on. I lower myself onto the floor and scoot beneath it.

Running my fingers across the wooden slats that support the mattress, I find our carved initials and recall her comforting words to me that night...

"...as long as we're together, nothing bad will ever happen..."

The hurt is insufferable because she was right. If I'd been with her, she would still be here.

I feel my stomach cave in, as gasps of sobs fight to reach the surface.

"Cait?"

Cale is clearly caught off guard by my position under the bed, but I can't find the will power to respond. He finally bends down and shoves himself underneath the bed next to me.

"What'cha doin' under here?" His tone is slightly humorous until he notes my expression. "Are you okay?"

I shake my head and reach up to show him why I'm here.

"Oh." He reaches up to touch the wood, and I no longer have the strength to fight it.

Bringing my hand down to cover my face, I finally start to cry.

"Hey, hey, shh…come here." Cale slides his arm underneath my neck and pulls me into the nook of his shoulder. He then brings his hand up to stroke my hair. "It's okay. I'm here."

I continue to weep softly for the loss of my friend, my sister. But the pain is too much, and I know that if I don't pull myself out of it, I will sink inward, never to return.

I sniffle and bring my hand up to wipe my tears away. "Well, I guess we should do what we came here to do."

I slide out from underneath the bed on the left-side and rise to my feet, as Cale follows my lead on the right.

"So, where should we start?" he asks.

I shrug.

We look at the boxes, unsure of what to do next, when Cynthia suddenly calls to us from downstairs, "Lunch is ready!"

"THANK GOD!"

Cale's response offers an unexpected comic relief, forcing me to laugh, and he smiles in return.

"Shall we?" He motions toward the door.

Still giggling a bit, I nod and take his lead.

As we begin our descent down the stairs, I spot Rob and Cynthia in the living room below. Cynthia is clearly worried about something, and Rob is attempting to console her.

"Is everything okay?" I ask.

They instantly break up their intense conversation.

"Oh, yes, dear. Everything is fine," Cynthia responds while slipping something into the living room hutch. "I hope you two are hungry."

Cale follows them into the kitchen, but my concern for whatever is in that hutch takes over. I slip into the living room and slide open the drawer to find a long-stemmed rose made from paper.

I remove the hand-crafted flower from the drawer when without warning, a stream of rapid flashbacks hit me like a ton of bricks...

> *I am sitting against the wall of that room...an image of something getting tossed through a cracked door...the sensation of old, scratchy carpet beneath my knees, as I crawled to investigate the object...the feel of paper in my hands...adjusting my eyes in the dark to reveal a long-stemmed rose made from newspaper...*

"Oh my God..."

The rose falls from my hand to the floor.

"Cait, what's the hold-up?" Cale calls from down the hall, but as soon as he enters the room, he immediately notes my expression. "Cait, what's wrong?"

"Food's getting cold!" Cynthia shouts from the kitchen, pulling me from my trance.

"Um, nothing. We can talk about it later."

I open the drawer and shove the rose back inside.

Cale scrutinizes me, as I walk out of the room and into the kitchen. "Don't think you're getting off that easy," he says.

"Later."

I can't make sense of what I've just seen, and without a logical explanation, I don't know how to relay this to him yet, anyway.

What I *do* know is that somehow that rose is connected to my past. A past shrouded in confusion and fear. But *how?* And why is it here?

Is it possible that Rob and Cynthia had possession of something from my past this entire time and never told me about it?

I become lost in thought of all the possibilities, even as we spend the afternoon immersed in superficial conversation.

Once we have finished lunch, Cynthia starts to pick up our dishes, when my curiosity becomes too great to keep quiet.

"Where did that rose in the hutch come from?"

Cynthia stops dead in her tracks.

Rob instantly stops shooting the breeze with Cale and looks over at Cynthia.

"Who gave it to you?" I ask.

"We don't know," Cynthia replies and resumes her task of hauling our dishes away.

"We started getting them a few weeks after the funeral," Rob adds.

"*Them?*" I ask.

He nods and scoots his chair back to leave the kitchen.

"Rob—" Cynthia immediately tries to protest his intentions, but he ignores her.

A minute or so later, Rob returns with a stack of wrinkled journal pages that resemble the paper used for the rose. He then hands me the rose I had recognized and sits down at the table.

"We've gotten one every week, and they all come in the form of a rose. The one you're holding showed up today."

"Where was it?"

"I found it sitting on top of the fence while I was putting the ladder away."

I feel a terrifying shiver, as I realize that whoever is leaving these roses was just here, *and* might be related to my past somehow.

I look over at Cale, and I can see that he is recalling my response to the rose from before.

"Each one is filled with abstract phrases," Rob continues. "In the beginning, we thought it was just an admirer paying his respects—"

"Wait, an admirer of Lucy?" Cale asks.

"Yes," Rob responds to Cale's question and hands him one of the pages. "But they've gotten more...concerning with each one," he adds.

Cale looks over the page and starts to read it aloud, "I feel your loss. Your pain is my pain, too. It's immeasurable, I know. Without relief. Nothing can ease it. Nothing can take it away. Nothing."

Cale is suddenly interrupted by Cynthia exiting the kitchen. Rob watches her leave before turning back to us.

"It's been difficult for her. Well, for both of us."

"Why didn't you tell me about these?" I ask.

"We didn't want to worry you. Hell, I wish we didn't have to know about them." He hands me one of the pages.

"Out loud," Cale demands.

"I think of her often. Her eyes. Her soft skin. She was a deceitful angel."

"*Deceitful?!*"

I hold my hand up to calm Cale, as I continue to read, "I could never tell her how I felt. I tried for years to muster up enough courage to tell her how much I loved her, but all I could do was watch. Watch and wait." I set the page down. "Somebody was watching her?"

"It would appear so." Rob takes the page from me.

Cale, who has a look of murderous rage on his face, picks up another page. His tone is flat, as he starts to read it aloud, "I miss her. Miss her laugh. Even from afar, it was one of majestic beauty." He clears his throat, "I miss observing her mannerisms. Her little habits. The way she would twirl her hair around her—" He stops reading, and I think he might implode.

Rob reaches over and takes the page. "As I said, they've become harder to stomach."

Cale's fists are balled-up tight, containing his anger within them.

"I'm taking those with me." I reach my hand out, but Rob shakes his head.

"I'm worried they might be related to what happened to Lucy somehow," he says. "Cynthia's convinced they're from the person who—" He runs his hand through his hair. "I think it's time we turned them in to the authorities."

Cale looks up at me with wide eyes, as I try to think fast. If those letters are connected to Lucy's killer, we need to get our hands on them.

"I think that's a good idea," I say, "but at least let me take a picture of them first. I mean, if this person was watching Lucy, it might be someone we all know. If I can analyze those letters, there might be something in them that stands out."

Rob hesitates, as I pull out my phone and reach for the stack in front of him.

"I could help the authorities," I add.

He finally leans back in his chair, allowing me to take them into my possession.

I move through each page, taking snapshots, as alarming words enter my view with each photograph. I try to ignore them and get through my task, but bits and pieces still filter through...

She blinded 'Mi Fiore' and blinded me too. I thought we could be happy and in love, but that love just wasn't meant to be...
She surrounded herself with such feeble-minded people...
I loved her more than he ever could. If only I had dared to reveal myself from the shadows where I hide...

I reach the end of the pile and pick up the newest rose; its contents still a secret. I gently unfold the paper flower to unveil another letter. Its dark words, so strategically hidden beneath something so beautiful, carry a nauseating punch-to-the-gut.

I force myself to keep the nausea at bay, so that I can take a picture, but my attempt is rejected by a low battery.

"Um, do you have a charger by chance?" I ask.

"Sure." Rob takes my phone and sets it down on a black platform.

"Hey Rob, is that one of those new cordless chargers?" Cale asks.

"Yeah. Cynthia picked it up for me the other day."

Still holding the unwrapped rose, I look back down to read the rest of its cruel narration, when Cynthia re-enters the room. Her presence causes Rob to start collecting the pages back into a stack, and I immediately ball-up the one I am holding and tuck it into my back pocket.

Noting the condition of her face, Cynthia had clearly excused herself to cry. I feel the anger course through my veins, as I think of this monster, who drained the life from her daughter, tormenting her with his deranged obsessions.

"You know, if you two wanna get back on the road before it gets dark, you'd better get on top of those boxes," Cynthia says, as she walks over to the sink to resume her previous task of washing dishes as if nothing ever happened.

Cale and I comply with her wish and silently make our way up the stairs.

"What did the last one say?" Cale asks.

"Later."

"You know, you are really starting to piss me off with that."

"We have enough to get through right now without you losing your shit, and upsetting Cynthia more than she already is."

"I wouldn't—"

"Oh, but you would. Trust me."

Cale and I sit in the middle of the room and silently sort through each box, one-by-one. My mind is far too scattered to be present, as we complete our task in silence.

I finally adhere the last piece of tape across one of my boxes, as Cynthia enters the room.

"Have you decided what you would like to keep?"

"Yep." I wave my hand over the boxes. "All of it. And whatever Cale doesn't want, too."

Cynthia looks over at me stunned until she finally smiles in a show of understanding.

"Well, okay then. Cale, honey? Can you fit them all in your car?"

Cale smiles at me. "We'll make it work."

"Well then. Let me help you haul them out."

Cynthia reaches down to grab one of the boxes, while Cale picks up the rest. I follow behind them, as we make our way down the hall.

Careful not to let them see, I reach into my pocket and remove the crinkled page I had stowed away. I read the note more thoroughly this time, and the blood slowly drains from my face with each word...

> *Do you dream of her? I dream of her often, but how contrary to your dreams, mine must be. Yours, filled with soft cocoa skin. Mine, void of color. You see sparkling brown eyes. I see vast emptiness. You had her life, and I have her death, and for that, she belongs to me.*

24

After stopping to buy a cordless charger from the nearest electronic store, we finally get back to my dorm after one in the morning.

Thankfully, Cale had been present enough to gain inspiration by the mention of Rob's cordless charger. Whereas, I was too distracted by the words in that last note to hear what he was saying.

Within a few minutes of placing Lucy's phone on the platform, the battery happily charges through the bag and turns itself on. I let out a sigh of relief, grateful for the waterproof cover that Rob insisted we use to protect our phones last year.

As soon as the charge hits fifteen percent, I can no longer contain my anxiety and remove it from the platform. I drag my finger across the screen through the plastic, and it prompts me to enter Lucy's password.

Cale takes note of the screen. "Shit."

I grin to myself and quickly type in her code.

"You know her code?"

"You mean, *you don't??*" I respond with a sense of pride and playfulness.

Yep. I knew all her secrets.

I begin looking through her texts, emails, and anything else that comes to mind. I pass through each app, one by one, finally reaching the *<rainbow photo app>* then *<all photos>* then scroll down to the bottom, searching for the last photograph taken.

At first sight of the image, an instant lump of fear fills my throat, followed by a whirlwind of confusion. I shut my eyes, and my subconsciousness reveals another snapshot of memory...

> *I'm sitting in the back seat of a van, faced forward, and stiff with fear...The blurry shape of a man in the passenger seat turns to reveal a gun in his right hand...The steel object is pointed right between my eyes...Just on the inside of the man's forearm is a tattoo...A black and gray design resembling a star...*

I strain under the shock of such a vivid flashback. The picture on Lucy's phone might be as blurry as my memory is, but the shape is unmistakably clear.

I can't get anything close to a word out of my mouth, as Cale leans over my shoulder to get a closer look at the picture.

"What is that?" he asks, before then looking over at me. "Cait, you are white as a ghost."

"I've seen this before."

This can't be real.

"Seen what? What is it?" His tone reeks of impatience.

"A tattoo. It's a tattoo, Cale."

He takes the phone from my hands and brings it in for a closer look.

"That's a tattoo?" he asks.

But I can't speak. I just close my eyes and fight to regain the feeling in my body.

"Cait?" Cale's voice has softened.

I feel his thumb brush away some tears from my cheek. Tears that have been unknowingly creating a puddle in my lap.

I hang my head in shame, as I absorb the confirmation that I've been dreading. Somehow, my past, or a man from my past, is connected to Lucy's death.

"That man... I mean, it could be nothing—"

"What man?!"

"Cale, did Lucy ever tell you about my nightmares?"

"Well, yeah, sort of. She told me that you had a hard time sleeping at night because of some nightmares, but she never really gave me any details." His eyes open wide. "Wait a minute, what does *that* have to do with this, Cait?"

"You know that I was adopted by Rob and Cynthia—"

"Yeah? So?"

"So, I haven't been able to remember much before the time I was like, five years old. *Except* for those nightmares. I would wake up in a cold sweat, terrified, sometimes screaming. Lucy was always right by my side, holding a glass of water, ready to hear about the latest detail, so she could help me attempt to piece them together. Only they would play out in the same scenarios, over and over again, and would never get anywhere."

I squint my eyes in anguish from the memory of having Lucy there to help ease my fears during times like this.

If only you were here with me now.

"Go on," Cale urges.

"Rob and Cynthia set me up with Dr. Thompson—"

"The shrink?"

"Yeah, the shrink. Do you want me to finish the story, Cale?"

"Yes, sorry."

"They made me an appointment with her because she specializes in hypnotherapy. We had hoped that she could help me remember more than just those repeated tidbits, but I never could—*until* now. I'm almost certain that I've seen that very same tattoo on the man in my nightmares."

"Shit, Cait. I had no idea." He pulls me into a hug, which does help some.

"Yeah, well, neither did I until now. To be honest, I still don't know if what I'm recalling is a hundred percent real, Cale. All I know is that tattoo is familiar, and I've seen that rose before, too."

"Yeah, I already figured that one out. Not that it was related to your past, but that you had clearly seen it before."

"Well, I kept that last one. I couldn't let Rob and Cynthia read it."

"Why?"

"I agree with Cynthia. I think whoever is sending those letters might have killed Lucy. At least, that is what it eludes to."

"Let me read it."

"Not yet. It will only send you into a rage, and we need to try and stay focused."

"Let me see it, Cait."

"Cale, just trust me. It's not the right time. Please?"

He looks frustrated, but rather than push any further, he moves on, "So, assuming these paper roses, and that tattoo, are related, they could lead us to the asshole responsible."

"Sure, but how?"

"Well, for starters, we might be able to track down the origin of that tattoo somehow."

"And how would we do that?" I ask, still struggling to reconnect with the here and now.

"I think tattoo parlors keep records of their tattoos."

"What makes you think that?"

"Hey, I watch CSI."

Note to self: Must buy the complete series of CSI.

"You know, you're proving to be quite an asset."

"Oh, C'mon, Cait. Haven't you figured it out by now? I'm the shit," he teases.

But I can't pick up the humor with him. I've sunk into a great depth of agony.

"Cale...do you realize what this means? I could have—I mean, what happened to Lucy...this whole thing could be my fault."

"Stop, Cait. This wasn't your fault. Yeah, maybe, it's connected to you in some way, but that doesn't mean it's *your* fault. All this connection means is that now we have a clue, and a damn good one, I think. Agreed?"

I nod.

"Okay, good. We should probably start by jotting down the names of tattoo parlors in Allen."

"Richmond, Virginia, actually. Lucy and I lived there before moving to Allen."

"Okay, so we'll make a list of Richmond tattoo shops and head down there this Friday. In the meantime, I think we should turn her phone over to police."

"Are you crazy?!"

"Hey, we have enough to get a head start on them. I mean, the police don't know that you've seen that tattoo before, and without the right forensics, the phone is no good to us now anyway.

"Besides, the longer we hold onto that thing, the higher the risk of us getting caught before we have a chance to do what we've actually set out to do."

I sigh with exhaustion. "Yeah, okay. I'll call Detective James and hand it over to him in the morning."

"Just let me take a picture of that tattoo, so we have a reference," Cale says, pulling out his phone.

I stretch the plastic flat against the screen so that he can get a clear view.

Once he has taken several shots, I walk him to the door, and he turns to hug me.

"I'm sorry again...about whatever happened to you."

"I know. Thank you."

He pulls back and kisses my forehead before then leaving my room.

I walk over and carefully put the plastic bag containing the phone back in my dresser drawer. I leave the phone turned on to run out the battery, which shouldn't take long, considering we'd pulled it off the charger so quickly.

Now, I just have to figure out how I am going to explain this to Will. I guess *technically*, I could tell him the truth: that I found it in the flower bed outside, and put it in a baggy to preserve the evidence.

That's not exactly a lie, *per se*. Sure, the authorities might get mad at me for handling it myself, but hey, I'm just a clueless layman.

And besides, there is no way for Will to know the exact date and time that I found the phone.

Right?

25

I wake up Wednesday morning to my phone ringing. As planned, I had called and left Will a voicemail last night, explaining how I'd found Lucy's phone and 'preserved evidence' by putting it into a plastic baggie. I cringe at the thought of having to sell myself as *that* stupid.

"Good morning, Detective James."

"Hey, I got your voicemail. I haven't left my office since yesterday, and I'm still swamped, so I've sent another Officer to pick up the phone."

He is all business today. I hate that.

"He'll want you to show him where you found it, and go over the steps you took to retrieve it, and for the record, I really wish you would have called me first."

"I know, I'm sorry. I just didn't want it to get disturbed. I panicked." The lie comes easy. *Too* easy.

"Just promise me that next time, you'll call me—"

"Okay."

"Good." Will sighs. "And now that we've gotten that out of the way, how was your day yesterday?"

"Painful, actually."

"Missed me that much, did ya?"

"I think you're projecting."

"Ouch!" he responds with laughter, and I can't help but laugh, too.

"I wish I could see the smile behind that laugh," he says.

"Maybe during dinner."

"Actually, that's the other reason for my call; I have to ask for a raincheck. I'm up to my ass right now in reports and interviews, but I promise to make it up to you, beautiful."

"It's okay, really. I've got a busy week ahead of me, too."

"You could at least pretend to be disappointed."

"It's only a minor delay, and I can be very patient, Will. In fact, I prefer to let the anticipation build. It's like foreplay."

"This conversation just turned into foreplay."

"Mm-Hmm."

"You know, on second thought, maybe I should be the one to come and get the phone."

"Say, when is that officer of yours coming, anyway?" I ask.

"Should be there any minute. I hate him."

"Aww, it's okay. You can always ask him to describe the nightie I'm wearing when he gets back."

"I swear to God, if he comes back with a description of you wearing anything but a moo-moo, he's fired."

I giggle, as I hear a knock on the door. "Oh, I believe he's arrived. I better get that."

"You're a shit."

"It comes naturally."

I hang up the phone and toss it on the bed before throwing on some jeans.

Why can't I stop flirting with this man? Hello, Cait. BAD IDEA, remember?

After handing Lucy's phone over to the officer, I lead him outside to show him where I found it, praying that my lies won't be visible.

"I found it by the garden where she was found. I just happened to drop something, and when I bent down to pick it up, I saw the phone poking out of the mud. I knew it was Lucy's the second I saw the case and that's when I called Detective James."

The officer is writing down my statement as two men with toolkits start dusting and collecting things, while another man takes some photographs.

"Okay, ma'am. Thank you for your statement. If you come across anything more in the future, please try and keep your lunch baggies in the kitchen. We have kits for this sort of thing."

"I understand."—*You, condescending prick.*

"Here is my card, in case anything new surfaces."

The officer hands me a business card, as the lab techs make their way back to the parking lot.

I politely take the card, and then toss it into the nearest trash can after he leaves. I turn to walk back to my dorm when I nearly bump into Lucas.

"What was that all about?" he asks.

"Well, actually, I found Lucy's cell phone near the garden—"

"Her phone? Really? Did it have anything on it that might tell them something or help them find whoever did this?"

"I really don't know, Luke. I called Detective James once I found it and handed it directly over to police."

I really hate lying to Lucas. He doesn't deserve it, but it's for his own good. Cale is already an accessory to my crimes, and that's bad enough without involving Luke, too.

"Right, of course. This whole thing is just so crazy, Cait. I mean, sometimes it doesn't even seem real, you know?"

"I do."

"Anyway, sorry to bombard you with questions."

"Are you kidding me, Luke? It's fine. I understand the urgency of wanting answers. But hey, where are you headed right now?"

"Well, I was coming to check in on you."

"Well, good. Can I buy you a cup of coffee?"

"Shit, you can buy me two. I was up half the night helping Angie study for that damn test."

We buy a cup of coffee at the campus java truck and make our way over to a rod iron bench in the courtyard next to a fire pit, which comes in handy during the early spring season.

Lucas slides his backpack off and sets it down on the ground, before taking a seat next to me. He is wearing a white, short-sleeved tee, underneath a burgundy, black, and gray-striped sweater vest, jeans, and a pair of black vans—and wait, no glasses?

"Hey, did you get contacts, Luke?"

"Oh! Yeah, last week. Angie likes them better."

Right then, I realize that while Cale and I have been playing cloak and dagger, I've failed to check in on Luke. I clearly have no idea what's been going on with him—but I plan to rectify that now.

I attempt to bend my leg up onto the bench to face him, just as he comes back up from putting his phone in his backpack and we bump into each other, causing my coffee to spill into my lap.

"Oh shit! Sorry! I'll grab some napkins!" he shouts.

I grab his arm. "No, Luke, really, it's okay. I got it." I stand and make my way toward the java truck for some water and napkins.

Wiping myself down, I walk back to the bench and stop dead in my tracks when I realize that amidst the chaos, my phone must have fallen out of my back pocket, because it is now in Luke's hands. His facial expression shows fury.

I approach the bench, terrified of what he's just discovered. An incriminating text from Cale? Or worse still, another flirtatious text from Will?

"You got a text." Luke hands the phone over to me, and I see that it was option number two.

Fantastic.

He tosses his coffee into the trash, before standing to throw his backpack onto his shoulders.

"You know, I cannot believe this shit. That jackass is supposed to be looking for the person who killed our friend, but *instead*, he's trying to get into her best friend's pants."

"Luke, it is NOT like that."

He holds his hands up. "Hey, listen. It's none of my business, and at least now I know why you haven't been around." He starts to walk away but changes his mind.

"You know, I stopped by today because I wanted to make sure that you were okay, but *clearly*, you're more okay than I thought you were." He throws his arms out to the side. "But HEY! Never mind the rest of us. We'll be just fine."

Luke turns to walk away, and I want so much to stop him. To fix it and make it better, but there are no words. No rebuttals to speak of, because there isn't a single word to justify what I'm doing. Whatever spark that has developed between Will and me, will need to be extinguished. I just can't afford to lose Luke over this, and God knows, Cale would feel the same way that Luke does, if he were to find out, too.

I toss my spilled cup and napkins into the trash, as I immediately start to rehearse my let down speech to Will.

26

Friday morning arrives and I have thrown my overnight bags into Cale's trunk.

Still plagued over my conversation with Luke, I'm finding it difficult to be up for the adventure that awaits Cale and I today, but I can't exactly share the source of our argument with Cale either.

So instead, I do my best to put on a smile as I enter his Mustang.

"Hey, Beck. You ready for this?"

"Yep."—*Nope.*

"I bought a notebook and wrote down some tattoo shops in there."

I open up the glove compartment to retrieve it. Not only has Cale written down the location of every tattoo parlor within a twenty-five-mile radius, but he has also ordered them in a path of least resistance, with a hand-drawn map on the next page.

"Wow, Cale. This is great."

"Yeah, well. I probably went a bit overboard."

"Are you kidding? This is genius. We'll get so much done with it organized in this way. Although, I suddenly feel like a loser. This clearly took you hours."

"Yeah, well. I'm all for distractions these days."

I instantly remember the feel of Will's lips on mine, and how wonderfully distracting *that* was.

"Well, that's one thing we have in common."

"Oh, I think we have more in common than that," Cale says.

"You mean, in addition to the nine-by-nine cell we'll be sharing someday?"

"Nah, I'm pretty sure they keep the men and women separate."

"Just don't drop the soap," I tease.

"Not a problem. I'll just hide a shank up my ass."

I look at him in complete astonishment and disgust, and he immediately starts laughing.

"You're such an easy target, Cait."

I shake my head and try to get that disturbing image out of my brain.

"But hey," he continues, "if killing this guy lands me in prison, then so be it. I'll do the time, because it's the right thing to do. I mean, if you really think about it, we're just taking out the trash, so to speak. People like that? They're not even human and I've always been pro death penalty, anyway. So, whether it's us that takes out this scumbag, or the government, what's the difference?"

"One of them has permission."

"Yeah, well. I try not to get caught up on the little things."

"That's hardly a little thing, Cale. The government gives people a fair trial, where you need a unanimous vote from twelve people just to get a conviction. It's a collaborative and societal decision, and there are so many fail-safes in place to prevent people from being falsely accused."

"So?"

"So, we cannot afford to take this lightly. If it takes twelve people in a court of law to convict, we need to be twice as certain about every decision we make. I mean, what if we're wrong about the one that we decide to—"

"We won't be. Come on, Cait. You said it yourself; this guy could go *free*. That shit happens all the time, and I won't let it. This is for Lucy, and I'm sorry, but she is all that matters."

I look over at him and nod in agreement when I suddenly notice his hair.

"Hey! You got a haircut!"

"Took you long enough."

We arrive in Richmond around four thirty in the evening, and the first three tattoo shops we visit are a complete disappointment. Not one person recognizes the design or has any idea as to where it came from.

Exhausted and discouraged, we decide to hit one more tattoo shop before checking into our hotel for the night.

We pull into the parking lot, and as soon as we get out of the car, I notice two guys standing in the parking lot, covered in tattoos—and eyeballing us up and down.

I offer them a sheepish grin. "We're lost."

"No shit." The one with a dagger on his arm responds, as his friend chuckles.

We step inside the shop, and we are greeted by a spunky young woman I would guess to be in her twenty's, with spiky red hair.

"Hey, can I offer you two some directions?" she asks, examining Cale's haircut.

"No, actually. Do you think we could talk to one of your artists? We have a question about a tattoo."

"I got it, Mel," a scruffy voice yells from the back.

"Looks like Charlie's free. Have a seat." She points to the lobby and goes back to answering phones.

Cale motions toward one of the coffee tables in the lobby. "Let's look through some of those portfolios."

We walk over and pick up one of the albums. As Cale turns each page, he holds his phone up next to them, comparing the tattoo photo we have, against the ones in the book.

"What can I do for you, pretty lady?"

I turn around to see a larger man, who I would guess to be at least six feet tall. He has short black hair on top of his head, but a long braid down the back. His eyes are kind, but the skin around them looks like he has lived a hundred lifetimes.

"Yes, thank you. We have a picture of a tattoo that we would like to show you. We're trying to find out where it may have originated from."

Cale hands him the phone, just as the bell above the front door rings. I turn to see that it's *Mr. Dagger* from the parking lot.

He walks up behind Charlie and looks over his shoulder. "What'cha got there, Chuck?" He peeks at the phone and then looks back at me with a look of surprise.

"Oh, it's just a tattoo these kids are trying to track down, but I'm afraid"—Charlie hands the phone back to Cale—"I couldn't tell ya where it came from. Never seen it before, sorry. Wish I could be more help."

I gaze over Charlie's shoulder toward *Mr. Dagger.* He is tinkering with a tattoo gun, and avoiding eye contact with me.

"How about you?" I ask.

"Me? Nah. Couldn't tell ya. Never seen it before."

Bullshit.

Charlie pipes in, "If you would like to leave a copy of the picture, I will—"

"Thank you for your time," Cale cuts him off and takes my hand. "Come on, let's go."

I continue staring at that boldface liar as we leave the shop and take note of the shops hours of operation on the glass door.

"Somebody was lying," I say, as we enter the parking lot.

"Yeah, but like hell, am I leaving him, *or anyone,* a copy of that picture." Cale snorts as we get into the car, "The very last thing we need is the police stumbling onto it and getting led back to us in the process."

"Which reminds me, I officially handed the phone over to Detective James."

"Do you think he could tell you were lying?"

"Well, it was actually one of his officers. He was too busy to come and get it, but the officer seemed to believe me. I mean, he didn't arrest me."

"And when did you say that was?"

"Wednesday morning sometime."

"So, it's been a couple of days then. I would assume that no news, is probably good news, right?"

"I guess."

It suddenly occurs to me that I really haven't heard from Will at all since the text that Lucas saw on Wednesday. Not even for some flirty small talk, and considering the turn that our relationship had taken *before* turning in the phone, no news from Will, may very well *mean* bad news for me.

"I think we need to come back after closing and push that guy for some answers. He clearly knows something," I say.

"I agree."

"But I don't think he will talk to me with you around."

Cale looks at me with complete astonishment.

"Kiss my ass, if you think you're coming back here to question that guy without me, Cait."

"Calm down. We can hide you in the backseat underneath a blanket or something."

"With my willy tucked between my legs?"

"What's more important, Cale, your pride or getting some answers?"

He sighs.

We head back to the hotel and eat some dinner before heading back out to question Mr. Dagger.

On our way, we pull off to the side of the road so that Cale can slip in the back. He lays down across the seat, and I spread a blanket over him, before then piling a few duffle bags on top. I jump back in the car, and within a few short blocks, we pull into the parking lot, and I turn off the headlights.

It's five minutes to nine, so it doesn't take long for the man to enter the parking lot with a few other employees.

"Now hold still and keep it tucked," I whisper.

"I hate you."

I smile, as I turn off the car and get out.

Mr. Dagger sees me and slows his walk.

I stare in his direction, standing my ground and he finally pauses.

Another tattoo artist is sitting in a blue Ford pickup, with the engine running. "You comin' Joel?"

"He's already got a ride," I cut in, and motion toward the Mustang.

"Go ahead, Donny. I'll catch up with you later," *Mr. Dagger* tells him. He then walks toward me and stops a few feet away. "You know, either you're incredibly stupid, or incredibly suicidal. This is a dark parking lot lady. Shit, for all you know, I could be a serial killer."

"Well, unfortunately, I made a promise to someone, and I don't have time for profiling."

"Is this 'someone' worth dyin' for?"

"She's already dead."

Speaking those words *out loud,* almost causes that festering lump inside my stomach to release its stored grief, but I can't afford to lose focus.

"And I think you know why I'm here," I add.

He paces, shaking his head to himself as if debating something. "Listen, lady. You don't want any part'a that."

"You let me make that decision."

"All right, look. I can't tell you where it was done, or who did it. I can only tell you where I've seen it, and who it might be associated with."

I walk around the car and open the passenger door for him, hoping to block his view of the backseat.

"Get in. You can tell me while I drive you home."

We pull out of the parking lot, and he points me north. "So, I got'a cousin who lives down in Newport, close to the docks, or maybe it's his buddy who lives out there. Yeah, it's his buddy's place. Anyway, he mentioned doing some—" He stops talking and looks over at me. "Listen, you're not recording this, are ya?"

"Oh, trust me, it would not be in either of our best interest for me to document this conversation."

I imagine Will sorting through pictures and recordings of us on our ventures, investigating his case behind his back, and suddenly, that flirtatious conversation I had with him just a few days ago, seems worlds away.

"Please, continue," I say.

He directs me to take a left.

"Yeah, so it's like I was sayin' his buddy lives over there in Newport News, by the docks."

Pretty sure we covered this.

"So, one time, we was drinkin' on his buddy's porch, and my cousin told me he had some business with a dealer. Said this dealer was a crazy son' bitch. Said he was involved in trade." He chuckles, "*Trade.*"

"What kind of—?"

"Take a right at this light." He cuts me off and continues, "Yeah, so he's shootin' the shit about this deal he's got goin' down, and one of the dealers shows up and collects some cash from my cousin. Well, on his arm, was that same tattoo."

He directs me to pull over in front of an old, and worn-down house, near the train tracks. "This is me."

I bring the car to a stop near the curb. He reaches for the handle and then hesitates.

"Listen, lady, do you got a missing kid or somethin'? Because I can't help you with none of that. Told you all I know."

"No? Why in the hell would you ask me that?"

"Well, that dealer my cousin did business with—"

"Yeah?"

"He sells kids."

27

That next morning, we decide to head down to Newport News and hit up some shops there, but after making it through a few from our list, we've come no closer than we were before.

Meanwhile, I can't get *Mr. Dagger's* last words out of my head. If the man from my nightmares is involved in sex trafficking, could it then be possible that I've been recalling the memory of my own abduction? If so, how did I escape it?

And furthermore, why would that same man show up in my twenties and kill Lucy?

The confusion is starting to give me a headache.

We're studying Google maps in the parking lot of our last failed attempt when we're startled by a knock on the driver's side window.

We both turn to see a young woman bent down and peeking through the window. She has on trendy purple-framed glasses, a diamond stud in her nose, and a nervous look on her face.

Cale rolls down the window and she tosses something into his lap.

"Here." Her voice is shaky, "Meet me there in about an hour and a half."

The words trail off as she immediately rushes away from the car, hunching into the hood of her black velvet zip-up.

Cale picks up the paper and reads it before then handing it over to me.

Take US-17 N.
Make a left onto Rte 614 and another on 632
It'll change to 644, but stay with it
You'll see some old brick ruins on the right.

"What have we walked into, Cale?"

"I have no idea, but did you see the fear in her eyes? Like she was expecting a bullet to the back for talking to us?"

I nod my head, as Cale pulls out of the parking lot and heads north onto US-17.

We pass through some toll booths, as we take George Washington Highway over the York River.

Shortly after turning left onto route 614, we hit a stretch of road that is well-guarded by dense patches of forest on either side of the highway. Cale pulls off to the side of the road and stops the car.

I glance at the map on my phone, confused. According to the digital arrow, we've stopped just a few turns, too early.

"Are you sure we're in the right place?" I ask him.

Cale gets out of the car without responding and retrieves something from the trunk.

When he returns, he is guarding a folded-up brown paper sack inside his jacket. He carefully unfolds the bag, and while holding it open with his left hand, reaches inside, and pulls out a black handgun with his right.

"*Holy shit,* Cale! Where did you get that?!"

"It's a Ruger nine-millimeter pistol. I bought it off some arms dealer before we left. It's untraceable because the serial numbers are scratched off."

He turns the gun to its side, showing me a silver strip with deep grooves treading across it.

"I didn't wanna come out here empty handed."

"But how did you even know where to find an arms dealer, Cale?"

"Remember when I told you I'd been taking some pills to help me sleep?"

"Yes."

"Well, I got those from a dealer that frequents the frat house. So, I got in touch with that guy, and he referred me to this one."

Jesus, he was using street drugs to sleep?!

I'd just assumed that he had a prescription for those. Thank God, I got to him when I did.

Although, drugs would have just landed him in jail, or substance abuse treatment. Whereas, the plan that I've involved him in could get us both the chair.

Yep. Much better, Cait.

I should have never brought him into this.

"Cale, maybe we should just turn back—"

"Oh, don't let a little gun freak you out, Cait. I know what I'm doing."

Cale pushes a button on the side of the gun, causing a cartridge of bullets to appear from beneath the handle. He then checks to make sure that it's fully loaded, before sliding the clip back into place.

After gripping it with both hands, he then holds it out in front of him to aim.

My eyes nervously follow the pistol, completely stunned by its presence, as he lowers it below the dashboard to start a tutorial.

"All right, Cait. See these buttons on either side of the pistol next to the trigger?"

I nod my head, still in shock.

"Those release your magazine." He presses the button, repeating the procedure I had just watched him perform a few seconds ago.

After sliding the cartridge back in place, he continues with his lesson.

"This switch is the safety button; up is safe, down is not. You'll also know the safety is off by this red indicator that appears when the switch is down. See?"

He toggles the switch up and down, showing me the difference. Then gripping the handle with his right hand, he cups the top of the pistol with his left.

"To load a bullet into the chamber, you just grab the top of the barrel with your non-dominant hand, and cock it backward, like this." He performs a cocking motion toward the back of the gun.

"Then, remove your safety," he shows me this step again, "bring your sites up, and once you've got a clear aim at your target, you'll shoot by steadily pulling back on the trigger."

He goes through the motions, before bringing the pistol back down and switching on the safety.

"Now, this is important, Cait, so I need you to pay attention." He pushes the magazine release button and completely removes the magazine.

"You see how I've just removed the bullets?"

I nod my head.

"Well, that bullet we loaded into the chamber by cocking the barrel back is still in there so we'll need to remove it for the gun to be completely unloaded."

I nod again.

"To accomplish that, we've gotta remove the magazine, and cock it back one last time, like this."

He demonstrates, and the remaining bullet pops out of the chamber.

"See that? Now it's empty."

He picks up the bullet and pops it back into the magazine. "And now, it's your turn."

He tries to hand the pistol over to me, but I instantly push it away.

"What? No way. Uh-uh. I am not touching that thing, Cale."

"Cait, this plan we have is a dangerous one. It's not a game, and we have to protect ourselves. Besides, how do you plan on killing this guy if you won't even pick up a damn gun?"

I was thinking strangulation.

"Listen, Cale; I don't—"

"Goddamn, if you aren't the most stubborn pain in my ass sometimes, Beck, but let's try this again, shall we? This is for your own safety, ergo, *not* negotiable."

Cale is looking at me intensely with his deep-blue eyes, as he nudges the gun toward me again.

And though I am scared shitless, I slowly reach my hand out and take it anyway.

"Okay, good. Now go through the motions like I showed you."

I go through each step, one-by-one, finishing with the ejection of that last remaining bullet from the chamber.

"You're a quick study." He looks up at me, impressed. "Just always remember your safety, and the removal of that last bullet, okay?"

"Okay."

"Now these are hollow point bullets, Cait. They'll do some real damage if you need 'em to."

Cale takes the gun out of my hands, and after making sure the safety is back on, he reloads the magazine, cocks it back, and stashes it beneath his seat.

"Where did you learn all of that?" I ask.

"My dad used to take us boys out shooting a lot when I was a kid. It was never really my cup of tea, but I'm sure as shit grateful for it now. You'll need some practice, too. Once we get back, I'll take you to the range, and we'll shoot some targets."

I open my mouth to protest, but he cuts me off, "Not negotiable, Cait."

28

We pull off the road and drive back into some trees. In front of us sits a red brick building that is practically in shambles.

Cale leans forward to take a closer look out the windshield. "What is that?"

"I'm not sure. It looks like it could have been a castle or something."

Cale breaks his gaze to turn off the car. Reaching underneath the seat, he pulls the pistol out and carefully tucks it into the backside of his jeans.

We step out of the car and walk toward the ruins. The hair on my neck stands up as I wonder what, or *who* might be out here waiting for us.

We walk passed a grove of trees when I spot the woman to our left. She is leaning against an old white car, and smoking a cigarette.

She looks up to see us and throws it onto the ground before stomping it out.

"Are ya'll alone?" She asks and wraps her arms around herself.

"Yes, of course," I say.

She looks me up and down. "You lose a kid, too?"

"Um...no."

She grunts, leaning back against her car.

"Did you?" I ask.

She grunts again, looking down at the ground. "Yeah. A daughter. Eight years old."

She reaches into her back pocket and pulls out a plastic album with some wallet-sized photos inside.

I open the album to see a little freckle-faced and green-eyed girl. She is standing on a bungalow style porch and looking proud, as she holds onto the hot pink straps of her backpack.

The woman lights up another cigarette and inhales, as she points toward the picture.

"That was her first day of Kindergarten."

She blows the smoke back out to her right, with a faint hint of a smile in her eyes.

"She's beautiful," I tell her.

I then flip to the next image and see the little girl holding a soccer ball...then another to see her sitting in the woman's lap at the bottom of a red, plastic slide.

"And that was her seventh birthday." She laughs. "We invited some of her friends from school to the park for some cake, and she didn't hardly talk to one of 'em. Kept wanting me to go down that damn slide with her."

She takes another drag of her cigarette, as her hand starts to shake, and her smile begins to fade.

I reach a photo that appears to be cut in half, removing the man belonging to a burly arm that is draped around the little girl's shoulders.

I lean in to get a closer look when the album is suddenly snatched from my hands.

"I shouldn't be talking to you," she says and cuts a nervous look over at Cale.

He responds by taking a subtle step backward.

"Hey, Cait? I'm gonna head back to the car."

He turns to walk away, then touches the inside of my left elbow. "But I won't be far behind."

He darts his eyes back, reminding me of the pistol that is resting near his lower back, and I nod.

"He seems like a nice one. Not the kind to beat ya," the woman says, as she watches him walk away.

"No. Cale would never lay a hand on me, or any woman, for that matter."

"Must be nice."

She tosses her cigarette that has now become a long stack of ashes, onto the ground in front of her.

I soften my voice, "Do you have a name?"

"Paula."

"All right, Paula." I restate back to her, offering a smile. "Well, thank you for taking the time to talk to us. My name is Cait, by the way."

She nods and looks down at her feet.

"Now, may I ask how you lost your daughter, Paula?"

She leans back against the car, eyes starting to water as she looks off to the right. "They took her."

"I'm sorry, who took her?"

"Them fuckers with that tattoo you're looking for!" Her eyes briefly connect with mine, before turning her head back to the right.

My stomach becomes queasy, as I recall the various clips from my nightmares.

"And the kicker?" She adds, "Her own daddy's to blame."

She lights another cigarette, and after bringing it in for a long drag, continues, "That arm you seen in the photo? That was her lowdown, dirty excuse for a father. He was helpin' those sick bastards sell other people's kids! Got paid better than his construction job to do it, too. Only I didn't *know* he was doin' it. Would tell me he got bonuses for doin' such a *great* job, and like the dumb bitch that I am, I believed him." She shakes her head and chuckles, "Lyin' bastard. He ain't never done nothin' worth a damn. I should've known it was a lie."

She pauses to take another drag.

"So, one night, I got home early from workin' a grave and heard these strange voices comin' from my basement. I started to head

downstairs when I heard this man talkin' to my husband about a little girl he needed shipped off to some goddamn place I ain't never
heard of. Told 'em she was bein' held back at his place." She chuckles
again, "And *then* I actually hear my husband tell 'em that he's 'got it
covered.'"

"Did they ever mention a name or where they might have been
staying?" I ask.

"I wasn't there long enough to hear any-a-that. I immediately tried
to sneak my ass outta there, but once they heard that floor creak, it
was all over. I just sat in the kitchen chair, arms raised out in front
of my face, just waitin' for one of 'em to hit me. My husband finally
got 'em to leave the house, but they kept arguin' on the porch. I was
shakin' so bad, I couldn't hardly stand up."

She tosses her cigarette onto the ground, as she blows another
stream of smoke outward.

"Anyway," her voice cracks, "that next morning, after sending my
little girl off to school, they took her, and just like that, she was gone.
Got a note on my door warning us to stay quiet or they'd kill her. I
kicked that prick father of hers out of my house, and spent every day
since then, livin' one minute at a time. Never called no one. Never
spoke to the police. Just hopin' that one day, my silence would be
rewarded, and I'd come home to find my baby girl waitin' for me, but
that day has never come." She wipes some tears from her eyes.

"Do you mind if I ask you when that was?"

"Eight years ago. We'd be celebratin' her sixteenth birthday next
month."

My stomach sinks, as I look at this woman, who has spent every
day for the past eight years, just waiting for her daughter to be returned to her.

"So, now it's your turn. If you ain't lost a kid, then what the hell do
you want with that tattoo?"

"I think that maybe...I was taken by the same people."

"When were you taken?" She is suddenly frantic.

"I'm not exactly sure. I lost my memory, but I recall being thrown into a van—"

"Do you remember if there were any other kids around? Do you remember my daughter? Maybe if you look again, you'll remember somethin'."

Paula grabs the album from her back pocket and holds it up in front of my face, tapping it with her finger. "Did you see her? Do you know where I could find her?"

I feel the tears start to pour from my eyes as I shake my head. "No, I'm sorry. I don't remember her—or anyone. I am so sorry."

She brings the album back down and gazes at the picture of her daughter. Defeated. Broken.

"It's okay. Not your fault." She catches a tear from her cheek. "I bet your mom was sure happy to see ya though, huh?"

"Actually, I wouldn't know. I can't remember anything before the age of five, to tell you the truth. I spent my childhood in foster homes before I was adopted at the age of eleven."

She continues to look down at the picture of her daughter.

"Paula, do you happen to know where your husband is now? I'd love to speak with him."

"Honey, unless you're a medium, you ain't gettin' nothin' outta him."

Damn.

"That dumb bastard sent me a letter a few years back sayin' he wanted to do right by me. Said he was gonna turn that bastard in to police."

She reaches for another cigarette but realizing she is out, crunches the empty pack and tosses it to her side.

"Turns out, he'd only given it to 'em after being arrested for sex trafficking. He was offered a shorter sentence for some information. Pretty sure that's what got him killed, too. Stabbed to death in the shower."

"Did he ever tell you what he told the police?"

"Nah, he never told me nuthin', but I did have an uncle who was workin' as a prison guard at the time. He told me he never gave 'em nuthin' about the asshole that took my daughter. Just gave 'em information he had about a murder. My uncle said some poor bastard had been falsely-accused of the crime, and the information my husband gave 'em was enough to get 'em released from prison."

"Did he ever share any details about the actual murder itself?"

"Well, if memory serves me right, and it's shotty at best these days, I believe it was a woman. Her body was found in a field somewhere. He said she was strangled to death with a rope or a cord of some kind."

Her words invoke a flash of recognition.

"I'm sorry, can you say that again?"

"Yeah. She was strangled with a cord. A black one, I think."

A black cord.

I suddenly feel my knees begin to buckle inward.

I bring my right hand up to grasp my forehead when the dizziness starts to flood in. I feel my knees meet the cool, hard ground beneath my feet, as I lose all sense of awareness, and collapse to my side.

29

"It's okay, baby girl," my mother says.

Her voice rushes over me, warm and safe, comforting me the same way she always does when I get hurt.

"Shh...it's okay, baby. I'm here," she says again, as the van speeds away from the curb.

"SHUT UP, BITCH!"

A hand hits my mother, sending her flying back against the seat.

She says nothing afterward, but looks at me with so much love, ferocity, and terror in her eyes.

There is blood pouring out of a cut on her cheek.

I start to cry hysterically, my throat still raw from whatever that finger shoved down it.

I try to keep my eyes open and on my mother, but like my legs, my eye lids become heavy.

The next thing I know, I feel something being tied around my head, blocking my view.

Somewhere, just outside the van, I hear vicious shouting coming from the man who took us, followed by a torturous whaling from my mother.

"Mama!! I can't see!"

I reach my hands up to remove the blindfold that has taken my mother from view when someone instantly grabs my wrists.

"What did you do with my mama?!"

I begin to kick and thrash when my feet connect with whoever is feverishly binding my wrists in front of me.

Realizing I have successfully kicked someone, I gather up my inner strength and kick them again as hard as I can.

The person at the other end of my blows finally breaks their silence, and I am shocked to hear that it's a woman.

"Hey! Now you wait just a damn minute." Her voice lowers to a stern undertone. "Trust me, little girl, I am doing you a favor by covering your eyes. You do not want to see what's out there."

She readjusts the fabric, making sure it is snug over my eyes, and I decide to let her do it this time. Something tells me deep inside my tummy that she is right.

I begin to cry so hard that I choke on my snot and tears.

In the background, I can hear the screams beginning to fade a little further away. Screams from my mother calling out to me with such urgency.

"It's okay, baby girl! I'll always be with you! It's okay! Mommy loves you! I love you!"

My cries resurface into deep belly sobs, as I hear that man's voice interrupting her, but I can't make out what he is saying over my cries.

I try with all my might to stop so that I can hear; hear where he is taking her, and hear if they will be coming back.

But all I can hear is my mother pleading with them not to hurt me, and her words are becoming less audible, as they travel further and further away from me, too.

"PLEASE LET MY DAUGHTER GO! Please! Let my.... GO! .... can HAVE me, ... her go.... Please!"

I feel the sadness and fear well up in the back of my throat, as I choke on the sounds of my mother's desperation.

I begin to plead with the woman, "Please don't hurt my mama. Please let her come back. I won't fight anymore, pleeease..." I start to cry, and the lady remains silent.

So, I begin to pray. Pray for God to help us. Pray for him to save my mother.

A wave of exhaustion overwhelms me, as I continue to pray harder than I have ever prayed in my life.

When all at once, the screaming stops.

There is no more begging. There is no more noise.

And for a brief moment, I feel a rush of relief that they aren't hurting my mama anymore.

Maybe God listened. Maybe he saved her, and they are bringing her back to me.

I hear the door open, and my breath gasps inward with desperation, as I call out to her, "Mama?! Is that you?"

I feel my chest retract, as I become overwhelmed by the extreme longing to hear my mother's voice again. Feel her hug me and tell me that it's all going to be all right like she always does.

But there is nothing. No answer.

Instead, something is flung onto the backseat next to my leg. The door shuts again, and I hear some voices arguing outside.

Scared to death, I choose to take a risk and peek at whatever has been thrown at me.

Just below the cloth that is covering my eyes, I can see something resting on my thigh.

It's a black string or maybe a rope—no, it's a cord. Yeah, that's it. A black cord.

Just then, my body fills with fear and dread, as I hear that man with the tattoo finally speak.

"She's dead. The bitch is dead. Strangled. Now let's get back to the house and make some calls."

The words carry a punch that my body is too frail to bear, that my mind is too fragile to comprehend.

Each syllable rings loudly in my ears, pushing my mind closer and closer toward the edge.

I feel myself starting to sink inward, withdrawing from my surroundings, as my mind works hard to find any place for me to hide.

Until finally, a welcomed sense of relief.

All self-awareness, identity, and any remaining sense of who I was has unequivocally faded to black.

30

"Cait! Cait, what happened!" Cale shouts. "Do you need me to call an ambulance?"

"No…" I bring my hand up to my forehead and attempt to sit up. "No, I'm okay."

Feeling dizzy, and trembling with the realization that my mother was murdered only a few yards away from me, I look around Cale and notice that Paula is gone.

"Where did she go?" I stand to my feet, still a bit shaky.

"Cait, maybe you shouldn't stand—"

"I'm fine, Cale." I walk to where her car was, and turn full circle. "Where is she?"

Cale hangs his head. "When I saw you hit the ground, I thought she had done something to you, and I got freaked out. So, I pulled the gun from my pants—"

"Oh my God, did you…*shoot her?*" I whisper.

"Yes, Cait, I shot her. And then somehow managed to discard her body, *and* her car, in the last five minutes."

Five minutes? It felt like an eternity.

"No, I didn't shoot her! She saw the gun and took off."

"Okay, I know. That was a stupid question. I'm just so…I don't know. Confused."

I grasp my forehead and feel my stomach sink from the understanding that our best source of information has fled, and our next best source of information was killed in prison.

I bend down, resting my hands on my knees, feeling hopeless.

"I'm sorry, Cait, but seeing you laying there...I just panicked."

"Cale, she knew details about my past. I mean, she didn't *know* they were related to my past, but she knew things. I just wish I could have had more time with her."

"And I scared her off." He shakes his head, self-loathing as he raises his hands to the back of his head in frustration, and turns away from me.

"SHIT! I am such an idiot!"

"Cale, you are not an idiot." I walk up and place my hand on his back. "You didn't know, and let's be honest, if I were in your position, I would have done the same thing."

"I am so sorry, Cait."

"It's okay. Let's just get back to the car. I need to get the hell out of here."

We jump into Cale's Mustang and turn onto the highway, as a numbness envelops my body.

"So...is it okay for me to ask what she said to you back there?" Cale asks.

"Well, Paula said her husband got arrested a few years back for sex trafficking and negotiated a shorter sentence for some information he had on a murder. Apparently, the information he gave them helped to release some guy from prison that was falsely-accused of the crime."

"And why do you think that it's related to you?"

"Because she knew it was a woman who was murdered, and when she mentioned the murder weapon...it triggered another flashback."

Cale nods slowly, absorbing what I have said, and clearly afraid to pry any further.

So, I throw him a bone and continue to explain, "The weapon was a black nylon cord, and the woman was...my mother. I remembered seeing a black cord lying next to me on the backseat of the van—the same van that I keep recalling in my nightmares. I also remembered…" I clear my throat, "I remembered hearing that man with the tattoo telling someone that he strangled my mother."

"Are you telling me that you were there when this happened?"

"I mean, I can't be sure without additional information, but—" I sigh. "If I take everything into account that we've gathered up so far, then, yes. I think I was there when it happened. I also think the man who took us planned on selling me to some perverse sicko, and my mother was just collateral damage for them."

Cale runs his hand through his hair and huffs out a long breath of air.

"Jesus, Cait. I don't even know what to say. I mean, I'm just….man, I am so fucking sorry."

"I know. It's okay."

"Um, no, Cait. It's not okay. It's not even *remotely close* to being okay. None of this is okay."

Cale's right. It's not okay. But I have lost the energy to feel right now. All I can do is continue staring out the window, deflated.

"So, listen, I know you've already got a lot to digest right now, but I'm just trying to piece this together. Are you fairly certain the man who strangled your mother had the same tattoo on his arm that we found on Lucy's phone?"

I nod, and I immediately know where he is going with this. If that picture was a snapshot of Lucy's attacker, she could have been strangled by the same man that strangled my mother. I mean, even if he were in his thirties when he took my mother and me, he would still be capable of murder in his fifties.

But why now? Why would he suddenly show up after all these years? I mean, why even come out of hiding *at all?*

It then hits me like a ton of bricks.

"Oh, Jesus, Cale, of course! Paula's husband exonerated the man who was believed to kill my mother—"

Cale cuts in, "So, the case was reopened, and the *real* killer is back on the chopping block now."

"Right. So, he's—"

"Tying off loose ends."

"Exactly."

We sit in silence, absorbing this information, but something doesn't quite add up for me.

"But why kill Lucy, Cale? It doesn't make any sense. She had nothing to do with what happened to my mother. And how do we factor those roses into all of this?"

"Is it possible that the guy who killed your mother has been writing those, too?"

I consider this possibility, but something in my gut tells me that it's not the same person.

"No. I don't think it's him. I don't know *how* I know that. It's just a feeling that I have. I mean, obviously, they're related. I'm just not sure how."

"So, we're looking for *two* guys now?"

"Honestly, Cale, the only thing that I'm sure of right now, is that we need more information."

"Well, I say we go and talk to Paula's ex-husband—"

"He's dead. Killed in prison."

"Damn," he says.

"Yeah. Damn."

"But I guess that makes sense. He was just another loose end."

"Right."

I look forward, feeling lifeless when my phone suddenly rings. I look down to where it lies in the middle console and see that it's Will.

Shit.

I give the button on the side two clicks, sending it to voicemail.

Cale glances down at my phone and shoots a look of scrutiny my way.

"What?" I ask.

"I didn't say anything."

It rings again.

He looks down at my phone. "It's 'Will' again."

Without taking my eyes off Cale, I reach over and send it to voice-mail for a second time.

"Why aren't you answering his call, Cait? It could be about the case."

I set my right elbow down on the window, resting my forehead in my hand, and sigh.

The truth is, I'm deathly afraid that he is just calling to arrange our dinner plans, and I'm far from ready to share that with Cale just yet.

"Do you have something you'd like to tell me, Cait?"

My phone rings again.

Damnit!

"Just answer it already!" he shouts.

I pick it up, and it's already gone to voicemail. I attempt to check my messages when he calls back again.

"Hello?"

"Cait, where are you?"

"I'm…back home, remember? I told you I had—"

"Oh, that's right. I completely forgot."

I hear him cover the mouthpiece, as a conversation ensues in the background.

"Dispatch Twelve."

"Twelve, Shelby. Go ahead."

"Copy Shelby. I found Miss Beck, she's not at home. You're off the hook. Fifty out."

"Copy James. Shelby over and out."

"Will?"

"Yeah, I'm here. Listen, Cait, I need you to come back as soon as you can."

"Is everything okay?"

"I just need you to come back. Can you do that for me, please?"

I can hear the exasperation in his voice. I look over at Cale, skittish, and he mouths the words 'what' as Will becomes impatient with my delayed response.

"If you need me to, I can send a car—"

"No, no. That won't be necessary."

"So, you'll come?"

"Um, yeah. Of course."

"Great. When can I expect you?"

"I could probably be there within the next few hours."

"Great. Come straight to the station and text me when you're thirty minutes out. Okay?"

"Yeah. Okay."

"I'll see you in a bit."

Will hangs up and my stomach begins to turn.

"Cait? What's going on?"

"He wants me back ASAP."

"Yeah, I gathered that much on your end. Now I need his."

"He just said that he needs me to go straight to the police station."

"What do you think he wants?"

"I don't know, but…it sounded serious. What if he knows about the phone?"

Cale sets his elbow down on the edge of the driver's side window and starts to rub his forehead.

I can already picture myself behind bars, inmates laughing about how I thought I could fool a detective.

When suddenly, the thought of facing Will becomes too much to bear. Those eyes that once looked at me so adoringly, changing to pity and disgust. The idea has me ready to hurl out the window.

"Okay, well listen. We haven't done anything illegal, *per se*," Cale says, "I mean, yes, we held onto the phone—"

"And therefore, interfered with a murder investigation, and *then* preceded to lie about it."

"I know, but Cait, that wouldn't necessarily land you in jail. I mean, Lucy was your sister, and you'd just been told by the Lead Detective working her case that the killer could potentially go free. After a conversation like that, anyone with half a heart would understand why you did what you did."

"Well, actually, that is *exactly* why I chose to hold onto it."

"See, there you go. You could easily plea insanity for something like that."

"Well, if we're completely honest with ourselves, I don't think a plea of insanity is off the table for either one of us, Cale."

He chuckles. "Touché, Beck."

31

Cale and I enter the front door of the police station, and I walk over to a desk where a uniformed police woman has just gotten off the phone.

"Hi, I'm here to see—"

"Caitlin!"

I turn to see that Will is walking down the hall toward us. I toss my hand in his direction, letting the officer know that he is who I am looking for.

Will approaches us and his eyes connect with mine before looking over at Cale.

"Cale," he shakes his hand. "I do appreciate you giving Cait a ride, but if you don't mind, I just need to speak with her this time. Alone."

"Yeah, sure. Of course. I'll just wait around to make sure that she gets home—"

"Thanks, but I can take it from here."

Cale looks at him as if he is quite possibly the most pompous man on earth, which I wouldn't disagree with at the moment, but the look only prompts Will to pat his upper arm.

"Promise, I'll get her back in one piece."

Then in unison, they both turn toward me.

"Are you okay with that?"

Will pulls back, giving Cale an inquisitive smirk, as if Cale's show of protection over me is completely uncalled for.

Cale, however, completely ignores him, and looks to me for an answer. He needs some reassurance.

"Will, can you give us a minute?" I ask.

"Of course."

I take Cale's arm and lead him down the hall and out of the station.

"It's ok, Cale."

"Jackass."

"Yeah, jackass, but I'll be fine."

"And what if they arrest—"

"Just promise that you'll bake me a cake with that shank tucked inside."

Cale tries to hide the grin behind his aggravation and worry.

"But really, Cale. Now that I'm here, I'm not worried about that anymore. They would have arrested me the second I walked through the door. It's something else, and it may be something we can use."

"Yeah. You're probably right."

"I promise, I'll be ok." I reach up and wrap my arms around his neck and hug him.

"Fine. Call me when you get home."

"I will, promise."

I turn and walk back inside.

Will is standing in the middle of the hallway, with a look of confusion on his face. He is looking over my shoulder toward the parking lot.

"Did I interrupt something?"

I follow his gaze to see that Cale is still standing on the sidewalk and *still* hesitating to leave me here.

"Oh. No, he just worries." I look back at Will. "Like a brother would."

"Right. I can see that."

I can tell he is skeptical, as he carefully studies my face, which no doubt looks as though it's aged a couple more years since the last time we saw each other.

"So? Why am I here, Will?"

"Right." He takes me to an elevator at the end of the hall and pushes the up arrow. "Is everything all right, Cait?"

He is clearly not ready to let this go.

Must divert.

"You mean *other* than the fact that you called me here in a panic?" I look over at him, and see that my diversion has worked, as his expression changes from inquisitive to apologetic.

You are going straight to hell, Caitlin Beck.

The doors open to a long hallway lined with blue Berber carpet and offices on either side. We reach one toward the end of the hall on the left, and I can see that it belongs to Will by the brass nameplate on the door.

He leads me into his office, and I see a woman, who is wearing formal attire, seated on a chocolate leather sofa to my left.

Directly opposite of the woman are two matching chairs, with an end table in between them, and there is a man I do not recognize sitting in one of those chairs.

They both stand at first sight of me and extend their hands, as Will makes the introductions.

"Caitlin, this is Gretchen Baldwin, our Department Psychologist, and Patient Care Advocate."

Patient Care Advocate?

The woman smiles as she shakes my hand.

"Lovely to meet you, Caitlin."

Will then motions toward the man from the chair.

"And this is Police Chief Larry Sanderson."

The man nods and shakes my hand.

Will motions toward the leather sofa, "Have a seat, Caitlin." His tone has switched to a professional one again.

Will then takes one of the chairs and motions to Gretchen. She pulls a folder out of a leather bag that sits next to her feet on the floor and sets it down on her lap.

"Caitlin, we have some information, we would like to share with you. Would that be all right?"

Yep. Definitely a shrink.

"Yes," I respond.

"Now, it's my understanding that you were adopted by Roberto and Cynthia Capelli, after befriending their daughter Luciana. Would that be accurate?"

"Yes. We met at the local Rec Club when I was ten, and they adopted me just shy of my twelfth birthday."

"Right, and before that, you'd lived in a few different foster homes, is that also correct?"

"Yes."

The one word is all I can manage, as I am suddenly all too aware that Will is sitting four feet away from me, hearing the dark and depressing details of my tainted childhood.

"Caitlin—"

"Cait."

"Yes, of course, Cait. Do you remember much before you were placed in foster homes?"

Oh, God. What does she know? What does Will know?

"No. I mean, not much"—I hesitate, wishing that Will wasn't listening to this— "I remember being dropped off at my foster home, but anything that happened before that has remained elusive to me, except for some incomplete details that have surfaced in nightmares and occasional flashbacks. I've been trying hypnotherapy, but I still haven't had much luck."

Why does Will have to be here?

"And may I ask for your therapist's name?"

"Blythe Thompson."

She writes this down. "So, you've only been able to recall some minor details then?"

Not quite.

But the latest details, which offer the greatest amount of information, were prompted by a photo of a tattoo that came from Lucy's phone—a phone that I was never meant to have touched in the first place.

"I started having dreams that felt like they could be memories shortly after Rob and Cynthia adopted me, but they've never been of any real value."

"I'm not surprised to hear that at all. Dreams, or flashbacks, are common with repressed memory; especially when the suppression occurs as a result of trauma. Our brains have a survivalist ability to protect our psyche when it's called for."

Old news, Gretchen.

"Yes, I am familiar with the concept," I say, dryly.

"Yes, of course. I'm sure you are." She clasps her hands together. "Caitlin, has anyone ever spoken to you about your childhood? Like a Social Worker maybe, before your placement into foster homes?"

I shake my head.

"I see, and what about your parents? Has anyone ever spoken to you about them before?"

My stomach sinks as I remember my latest flashback. I continue to sit in silence. Afraid of saying the wrong thing, afraid of what Will might be thinking, and afraid to lift my eyes from their fixed position on my fidgeting hands.

"Caitlin?" I hear Will's voice to the right of me, but Gretchen raises her hand up toward him, suggesting that he hold off.

After a minute or two, she tries again.

"Caitlin? Has anyone ever spoken to you about—"

"No. Not directly. At least not that I remember."

"I see."

Gretchen reaches her hand out and Will hands her another folder. She opens it up to reveal a sheet with what appears to be a graph of some kind. Removing it from the folder, she then hands it over to me.

"Caitlin, do you know what that is?"

The title of the report tells me that it's a 'DNA Profile,' and there are two graphs arranged side by side on the page. In the top, left corner of the first graph is my name, date of birth, and all the usual demographic information. Whereas, the profile to the right is simply-identified as 'male.'

I carefully read through the details on the page, not exactly sure what I am reading, or what it all means. That is until I reach the bottom of the report:

Findings:
Sample from female specimen has matching numbers within each set of loci taken from a male specimen. These results suggest a >99% probability of a paternal match.

Interpretation:
Sample belonging to unidentified male is <u>NOT</u> excluded as the biological father of female sample.

I feel a wave of shock radiate throughout my entire body, as I carefully read the words, again and again. It occurs to me that I have yet to obtain any details about my father, through dreams, or otherwise. His existence has never lent itself to any formal idea, as to who he was, or where he might be.

I close my eyes, as I suddenly remember the unmeasured sense of fear that I felt within the walls of that van. The desperate attempts to flee, as I prayed for God's protection. Prayed for him to make me invisible. Prayed for him to save my mother, and prayed for him to— *help my daddy find us.*

I bring the fingertips of my right hand up to guard my lips, as droves of repressed memories flood back into my brain. I feel that retraction in my chest again, as I recall how much I had longed for my father to rescue me from the hell I was in.

That same father who had taught me to ride a bike and kissed my knee when I crashed; who would run all over the yard with me laughing on top of his shoulders. A father who would sing me to sleep with that all too familiar lullaby I had hummed to myself, as I lay underneath that bed in fear.

Memories of a happy childhood then become intermixed with the desperate screams of my mother, as her life was viciously taken away from us, and just feet away from me, too.

It's too much.

My breathing becomes rapid, fighting against the intense wave of pain that is now crashing against the surface of my mind. I start to shake my head in protest, struggling for air.

"Cait?" I can feel that Will is right next to me.

"Gentlemen, I am going to have to ask you both to leave now." Gretchen's voice interrupts Will's efforts to comfort me.

Chief Sanderson immediately rises to his feet.

"Yes, of course, Gretchen. Will?" He motions for Will to accompany him out into the hallway.

I can feel Will's hesitation, as my breathing begins to intensify.

"Please, Will." Gretchen's tone shows authority.

"Yeah, okay. I'll just be right outside if you need me." He says this to her, but I know that it's meant for me.

I close my eyes and start rocking back and forth, as the pain becomes unbearable.

Gretchen reaches into her bag, and the familiar rattle of pills from inside a bottle causes me to immediately withdraw my hands and start shaking my head in protest.

"No! No pills...please!" My sobs breach hyperventilation.

"Caitlin, it's just an anti-anxiety medication. It will help to calm your nerves, and allow you to breathe."

I suddenly remember that Will is right outside the door with ring-side seats, should a creepy man in a white coat suddenly appear and drag me off to a padded room somewhere.

The idea forces me to reach out and toss the tiny blue pill into my mouth.

Gretchen then hands me a bottle of water to wash it down. I lean back against the couch, overwhelmingly consumed with anguish, embarrassment, and shame.

My mind starts to walk through the barrage of details I have been given over these past couple days.

My mother and I were abducted, and she was murdered sometime after that, but who knows when. I clearly have a father, and at one time believed him to be a loving and protective man, but if that were true, where is he now?

It's all too much for someone to take, in such a short period of time.

I start to debate on whether or not I will survive any of this when the sweet and gentle mercy of that pill finally starts to take effect. I feel my body start to relax, as my breathing becomes more controlled. A warm and welcomed haze has filled me from within.

"How are you feeling, Caitlin?"

"Better."

"Good."

Gretchen stands up and fetches a pillow from the couch and lays it down behind me. She then helps to guide me onto my right side, resting my head on the pillow.

"You rest, for now, dear. We can talk again later if you'd like."

She takes off her sweater and drapes it over me, as the warm and comforting haze finally demands that I drift off to sleep.

32

I open my eyes from a nap of an unknown length of time to find that Will is sitting on the floor next to me with his right arm bent up and placed beneath his head on the couch.

He looks to be sleeping, as he lay nestled in between the nook of my chest and bent knees.

It feels as though I have not seen him in months, and with all that's happened to me these past couple days, it might as well have been months.

I study his face, as I reach out to run my fingers through his hair, prompting his eyes to open.

"Hey there," he says while lifting his head up and taking my hand inside both of his.

After kissing my knuckles, he leans forward so that he is face-to-face with me. "Are you okay?"

His show of sympathy brings more tears to the surface—tears I expected to be all tapped out by now.

He closes his eyes and brings his forehead down to rest on our united hands.

"Oh, Caitlin. I am so sorry." He sighs.

My chin quivers, as I try hard to fight the vulnerability when suddenly, a sick feeling washes over me.

"Will?"

"Hmm?"

"Is my father related to all of this somehow?"

"I don't think so, but considering the circumstances, we can't rule anything out just yet."

"So, he's alive?"

"Yes, he is."

"Where is he?"

"I can't tell you that yet."

"Well, how did you come across his DNA in the first place?"

He pauses, still looking down. "When we were comparing DNA samples to the one we collected from Lucy, his came up in the system as a familial match to yours."

"Why would his DNA be in a national database?"

"We're trying to figure that out, but I can't offer you anything more than that right now."

"You know, I think I've had enough for one day"—*or a lifetime*—"Could you take me home?"

Will finally lifts his head to look at me and softly grins. "Yes, of course, beautiful. Whatever you need."

He helps me to my feet, and suddenly, the idea of going back to an empty dorm after all that I've been through these past couple days becomes unbearable.

But where else could I go? I just can't bear to rehash all of this with anyone else right now.

"On second thought, do you think we could go back to your place instead?" I ask.

"Absolutely." He kisses my forehead before leading me out of the police station and back to his place.

After a relatively short drive, we turn onto a street lined with two-story, art-deco condominiums. Each one is a different color, with driveways that decline into a garage that sits beneath the home.

Will turns into one of the condos, and I can't help but feel like a juvenile, recalling his stylish breakfast in my childish dorm.

Will opens the door, and we enter a small mudroom that joins an immaculate kitchen.

Taking note of the steely-gray walls, stainless steel shelves, and dark blue cabinets with fogged glass, I am now able to see a connection between his modern chinaware and stylish meal behavior.

Will sets his keys down on a side table and takes my hand. He leads me down the hall and up a set of dark wooden slats, guarded by a railing made of silver wire.

We reach his bedroom, where a king-sized wooden platform houses a mattress covered in gray satin bedding. He then lets go of my hand to enter a large walk-in closet, lined with dark mahogany shelving and rows of pristine clothing.

I do NOT belong here.

Will reappears with a white undershirt and a pair of flannel pajama bottoms.

"This is the best I could come up with I'm afraid. You can change in the bathroom. There should be an extra toothbrush in the bottom left drawer, too."

"Thank you."

I walk in his bathroom and cringe at the red and splotchy face that is looking back at me in the mirror.

I immediately splash some cold water against my skin, before removing my clothing.

Pulling the undershirt over my head, I take note of Will's delicious smell laced throughout every fiber.

I then retrieve the unopened toothbrush from the drawer and brush my teeth.

Remembering my promise to Cale, I send him a quick text, letting him know that everything is fine and I will call him tomorrow.

I walk back into the room, feeling flushed and wiped out. I still can't reconcile myself with all the memories I have suddenly been given, and have no idea what to do with them, now that I have them.

Will reaches for my hand. "Come here, beautiful. Let's get you into bed."

I follow suit and slide beneath the satin sheets he has already pulled back for me. He then moves to the foot of the bed and lifts my legs out from underneath the covers. Then, after resting them on his lap, he starts to massage my feet.

I grin to myself and close my eyes.

"You know, if you keep this up, William, I may never leave."

"Promise?"

I open my eyes to see him looking back at me, and the implication of "forever" in his response suddenly makes me want to run—*far* and *fast*.

Noting my expression, he smiles with exasperation. "Would that be so terrible?"

Most definitely.

Nearly everyone I love is taken from me, and everyone else, I keep at arm's length.

"I don't have the best track record with relationships, Will."

He tilts his head at me, and I can tell that he is about to ask me a follow-up question.

But I'm not in the mood to discuss this right now, so I rush in to interrupt his thought before he has a chance to—"Thank you for being there today. Although, I do wish that Gretchen would have kicked you out just a bit sooner."

"Yeah, you're lucky that I don't have the psych ward on speed dial."

My jaw drops, as I cock my legs back to playfully kick him—and fail *miserably*.

In one swift motion, Will has fended off my kick by wrapping his right arm around my legs and pulling me toward him with one yank.

Then, while stabilizing both wrists above my head, he climbs on, locking me into place between his knees.

I have no words. I just lay there caught off guard and completely turned on.

"What's a matter, beautiful? You look a little stunned."

"Cheap shot, *Navy Seal*."

He laughs, "I think you enjoyed it."

"I think I would enjoy calling your previous employer with the Navy to inform them of your inappropriate use of military skills."

He laughs again, and I try hard to keep mine hidden beneath a stubborn smirk.

Still holding onto my wrists, Will bends down to nestle my neck. Then, after brushing his nose along my jawline, he reaches my lips and slowly coaxes them apart with his. I feel every ounce of tension wash away with his passionate embrace.

Will brings our kiss to a soft close and releases my wrists. He then falls onto his right-side and rolls me over to face him.

Cradling the side of my face in his hand, he softly kisses me again, before reaching up to pull a pillow down beneath our heads.

He then looks deeply into my eyes, as he trails his fingers up and down my arm, eventually finding my hand and bringing it into his chest.

"You know, Caitlin." He kisses my hand. "There is no other place I would have rather been, than with you in that office today, and there is still, no other place I would rather be, than with you in this room, right now." His expression has turned from playful, to serious.

Ugh. We are approaching dangerous territory here.

I'm not entirely certain that engaging in a sexual relationship with Will right now is the best idea, let alone a *romantic* one.

But I find myself torn between the 'Caity-Cait' that Lucy always believed I could be, and the fearful Cait the world has made me.

Will smiles at me, and I decide that having a distraction wouldn't be the *worst* thing in the world.

"Hmm…well, in that case, I'm sorry I almost ratted you out to the government," I tease.

We both start laughing, as he leans over and plants little kisses all over my face.

"You can stop with the kisses, William. I am not for sale."

"Ah, I see. Well, lucky for me, that is not a problem."

"Oh yeah? And why is that?"

"Because I don't buy, Caitlin. I take."

Every inch of my skin becomes hot with that statement, and I find myself wanting to bite him—but involuntarily yawn instead.

"I'm sorry, am I boring you?" he asks, amused.

"Of course not." I yawn again.

Will laughs and rolls off the bed.

After then scooting me up to the head of it, he pulls the bedspread over me and sits down on the edge. "I've got some work to finish up if that's alright?"

I nod sleepily.

He grins and bends down for one last kiss.

"Goodnight, beautiful."

I nuzzle my head into the cool silk, as he turns off the lights and leaves the room.

It's unfortunate that my life has to be so complicated because I really *could* get used to this.

33

The effects of another pink pill are starting to wear off.

I open my eyes and look around, but my vision is fuzzy.

My tummy starts to hurt and I realize I am hungry. I wrap my arms around my waist and start to whimper.

Just then, a blurry shape in my peripheral vision runs out of the room.

Shortly after, I see a plate with a sandwich slide across the floor and hit the foot of the bed.

I adjust my eyes, but all I can see is one eye and some hair, carefully peeking around the door jam.

I sit up and hurry over to get the sandwich, before hustling back into bed. Pulling my knees up to my chest, I devour the sandwich and realize that I haven't eaten in what feels like days.

Every so often, the eye peeks around the door jam, watching me.

"What's your name?" I ask with a mouthful of peanut butter when a voice from downstairs suddenly yells, almost causing me to choke.

"HEY! What are you doing out of your room? Get your ass back to bed!"

The man's voice causes my invisible friend to run down the hall and into the neighboring room.

I step off the bed and tip-toe across the floor to sit down next to the wall.

"Hey...are you in there?" I whisper through the air return separating us, but there is no response.

"Hey, I know! Let's do 'one' knock for no, and 'two' knocks for yes. Okay?"

I hear two soft knocks on the wall.

"Okay, yes. Have you been here a long time?"

Two.

"Yeah, me too, I think. Are there other kids here?"

One.

"So, we're the only ones?"

Two.

"Are you afraid?"

Two knocks.

"Me too. Sometimes I sing to myself. Do you ever sing to yourself?"

One.

"Hey! Maybe we could be friends. Do you wanna be my friend?"

Two.

I feel a small sense of relief spread throughout my body because at least, I am no longer alone.

34

My eyes fly open, and I sit up, leaving Will's embrace to sit on the edge of the bed.

"Cait? Is everything alright?"

I feel him sit up behind me. He starts tracing the back of my right shoulder, and then kisses my left.

"Yeah, sorry. Just a nightmare." I close my eyes, trying to recall the details, but they're a bit cloudy.

I feel Will slide off the bed behind me and head downstairs to the kitchen. I then hear some cupboards open and shut, the chime of some glasses, and finally his footsteps making their way back up the stairs. He re-enters the room and hands me a glass of water, before taking a seat next to me on the bed.

I look down at the water, and the very sight of it reminds me of Lucy and her post-nightmare ritual.

I want to hurdle the glass into the air and shatter its cruel mockery with a violent impact to the wall.

I have so much anger coursing through my veins for the man who took her life—for the man who took my mother's life—and I want so much to savagely take *his* life in return.

Managing to keep my wits about me, I set the glass down on the end table and turn to face Will.

I look into his eyes—his beautiful brown eyes, and suddenly, I don't want to be *this* girl. The one with a tragic backstory, who is so afraid to love.

No. Tonight, I just want to be...*normal.*

I gaze intensely into Will's eyes, sending him a clear message with mine. He reaches up and runs the back of his right hand down the side of my face. As he nears my chin, he pulls my bottom lip down with his thumb and forefinger. This is becoming a pattern of his, and it sends shivers down my spine every time he does it.

Will leans in and kisses me with so much passion, inviting me to leave my anger behind, and replace it with a ravenous desire.

I take up his offer and increase the tempo of our kiss, as I reach down to find the bottom edge of his shirt. I begin to slide the white cotton tee against his chest, allowing my fingertips to graze his skin while propelling it upward.

Will then takes over by gripping the back of his shirt with one hand and pulling it up and over his head.

I admire his chest, before leaning in to sample his skin. His smell is stirring up an insatiable hunger inside of me that is impossible to resist.

Will is firmly stroking my back when he suddenly makes his way up to grab my hair.

I continue to help myself to the taste of his skin until I reach his mouth and we fall into a kiss.

His lips are so soft, yet so firm.

Every so often, I feel his five o'clock shadow tickle my cheek, igniting a tingle in my lower back.

Our kiss comes to a close, and I bite on his lower lip as we lock eyes.

Just then, I feel his hands reach down and grab the bottom of my shirt. He slides it up and over my head.

I raise myself up to straddle him on the edge of the bed, before removing the clasp of my bra and coaxing it off.

While gripping my lower back with his right forearm, and gaining momentum with his left, Will scoots us both back toward the middle of the bed.

Sitting back up, he connects his mouth with my breasts, lightly teasing them with his tongue.

I firmly wrap my hands around his head, commanding his lips to do more, and he obeys by taking my nipple into his mouth.

Resting my face in his hair, I am taking in his delicious smell when intense emotion overwhelms me. I now realize just how much I have longed for this—longed for *him*.

Gripping my waist, Will pulls me off his lap and lowers me onto my back. He palms my face, as he gently kisses my lips, promoting an intense addiction to his taste.

Resting on his hip to the left of me, Will then slides my bottoms down and gently removes them from my legs. He makes his way back up my body by trailing his fingers along my left leg. I feel them pass over my knee, briefly dip toward my inner thigh, and finally settle on top of my lower pelvis.

I close my eyes and revel in the light sweeping motion he is making with his fingertips, as they graze back and forth between my hips. He then stops somewhere in the middle and bends down to land a soft kiss below my belly button.

I twirl his hair in my fingers, as he begins to circle the outer ridge of my belly button with his tongue. He gently tops it off with a kiss to the center and a light squeeze to my inner thigh with his left hand.

He then continues to leave a trail of soft kisses, as he makes his way up toward my chest, stopping at one of my nipples. I feel his wet tongue swirl around it before savoring it between his lips.

Gripping Will's biceps with my hands, I want so badly to sink into this heat we've created, and become lost in a world where pain and malice no longer exist.

Will climbs on top of me, as I reach down and unfasten his pants. Then, after helping them down to his lower thighs with my hands, I reach my right foot up and catch them with my toes to continue forcing them downward.

Will reaches for the nightstand, and I know that he is after a condom—but I've been on birth control for years, and I want nothing between us.

I grip his wrist. "We don't need that."

"Cait, you sure?"

"I am."

Without hesitation, Will rolls over on his back and hoists me up onto him.

I allow my knees to part and fall firmly against his sides, permitting him to gently enter me.

He slowly begins to alternate his grip between my bottom and thighs, steadily leveraging himself in, and out of me.

The world around us disappears, as it drowns beneath a delicious pool of sweat.

Will sits up and passionately kisses me before resting his face in between my breasts.

I then feel his palms stretch out across my bottom, as he gently drives my pelvis up, and down, and all around, commanding circular patterns with my hips.

When suddenly, I can no longer put off the inevitable rush of shivers that are welling up inside of me. My head falls back as I start to feel an immense wave of pleasure wash over me from within my lower abdomen.

Taking my lead, Will locks his forearms around my lower back and drives me into a smooth and steady rhythm by using his grip to coerce deep and continuous thrusts toward him.

My breathing becomes heavy, as he pulls me into him with such feverish intent that I finally commit to an explosive relief that sends shock waves throughout my entire system.

I whimper and moan, as I cling tighter around him, making every effort possible to force him deeper inside of me.

Will meets my demand, and maintains a burrowed rhythm, allowing my euphoric climax to reverberate outward, and ripple across my thighs.

I tip my face back down and lean my forehead against his for support—all the while absorbing generous aftershocks that allow my pleasure to multiply itself, over and over again.

Just then, I feel his body begin to tense up. Every muscle in his arms, chest, and abdomen, becomes rock hard, as Will finally permits himself to let go of all previous restraint.

While firmly holding my bottom in place, I feel him start to release, and the sensation of his climax causes an unexpected mass of pleasurable aftershocks to erupt within me *again*.

As we come together, I have no sense of where I end, and where he begins. The pleasure continues to seep between us until, at last, it fades; reduced to nothing more than a fond memory.

Compelling me to remain still in his lap with his left forearm, Will draws my bottom lip down with his right thumb and pulls me in for a slow and salty kiss.

He holds our kiss to the most affectionate pace until I feel him slowly relax his grip around my waist, allowing for movement. He then brings our kiss to a close with a bite to my lower lip.

I gaze into his eyes and he rewards me with the sexiest smile I have ever seen. He then falls back onto the pillow and pulls me down to rest on his chest.

We revel in gratification until at last, we succumb to a post-climactic crash.

35

I am awakened by the sun as it peers through the bedroom window. Glancing at Will's alarm clock, I am pleased to find that it's after ten. Somehow, I have managed to sleep in, and I have never slept so soundly in all of my life.

I can hear the shower running, and I imagine Will's naked body beneath a stream of hot water, causing my desire from the night before to return.

Oh, Jesus. Get a grip, Cait!

I slide out of bed and fight the urge to join him. After putting my clothes back on, I walk downstairs to make us some coffee.

I enter the kitchen and shuffle through some cupboards until I find what I need to brew the first pot. After pressing start, I head back upstairs to ask Will if he would like a cup.

I hear the shower turn off when I enter his room, and once again, I have to reign in my hunger for him.

I lightly tap on the door. "Will? I hope you don't mind, but I've started some coffee."

I turn away from the door when it suddenly opens, and I find myself whipped around to face him.

Flashing that intoxicating smile, Will wraps his arms around my waist and squeezes.

"Mmmm...good morning, beautiful."

His appearance excites me in too many ways to count. He is wearing a white towel wrapped around his waist, and his chest glistens from the beads of water that are dripping off his wet and disheveled hair.

After locking me in tight, Will buries his face in my neck and releases a groan of infatuation.

With that, I finally allow my body to anticipate another wild and passionate affair—yet he *only* maintains our embrace.

He feels so relaxed, and it seems as though he might actually be planning on doing this for *a while.*

Just standing here, and holding me, with no end in sight. Sending a very clear message that he doesn't want me to go—that he *needs* me.

It's a message that will most-certainly call for me to exhibit the same need in return, and it is *this*, I cannot take. Sex is one thing, but *this?*

It's too personal.

After what seems like an eternity, I can no longer take it, and abruptly pull away from his grip.

I've already begun my descent down the stairs when I offer him some coffee over my shoulder.

After retrieving two mugs from the cupboard, I turn back around to see that he has followed me into the kitchen.

"What just happened?" he asks.

"What do you mean?"

"You practically jumped out of my arms just now."

"I just thought you might like some coffee."

I suddenly feel like a cold-hearted bitch, as I casually reduce his assessment to nothing more than an overreaction.

"Sugar?" I ask while pouring a cup.

Just then, Will hangs his head and exhales, as if he has just failed a test for the one-hundredth time in a row.

"So even after last night, how incredible that was, I *still* don't have your permission to be intimate with you? To show you how much I enjoy you or tell you that I don't want you to go—"

"Stop. Please."

I set the pot down and brace my hands on the edge of the counter.

"Really, Cait? Is that all you've got for me?"

He is clearly hurt, and I hate that I've hurt him, but I just can't allow him to feel this way about me.

Hell, I can't allow myself to feel this way about him, either. I can't need him or wish he would never go because he *will* go—*or I will*—eventually.

"Will, listen. Everything you heard last night about my childhood? That's just a small fraction of how messed up it was. And yes, last night was incredible, but I just can't have someone needing me like that."

"You mean, you don't want to need them—need *me*."

"Why can't we just enjoy each other without complicating things? Why does it have to be all or nothing?"

"Because it just does. I can't have a casual relationship with you, Caitlin."

"Well, I don't want to ruin what we have."

"Well, I guess that's where you and I differ because I don't see intimacy ruining what we have. I want to be able to call you in the middle of the day and tell you that I can't stop thinking about you. I want to hold your hand as we walk through the mall. I want to laugh and talk for hours, and stay up late watching old movies. I want all of those things with you." He walks over and sets his fists down on the counter. "Don't you get it, Caitlin? I'm falling in love with you, and I don't want to be nothing to you."

"Will, I know this is my issue, and I know that it's fucked up. So..." *No pain, Cait. Make it quick.* "I completely understand if you need to end this now. I have no expectations after last night, and I promise, I'll be fine."

"Are you fucking kidding me with that?"

"I'm sorry, Will, but I just can't. I can't give you what you want. I'm too broken."

Will hangs his head and sighs. "Christ, Caitlin, you're not broken. In fact, you are very much intact. There is not one point of weakness displayed in that armor of yours."

Will starts to leave but then turns back around to face me. There is so much hurt in his eyes that I can barely stand to look at him.

"Broken is me, Cait. After hearing you permit me to walk out of your life, and then promising me that you'll be fine once I do.

"That, Caitlin, is what broken feels like, but you? You can't claim to be broken when you won't even allow yourself to be vulnerable."

Will walks out of the kitchen, and even though my heart is begging for me to chase him, I decide that it's best for me to call a cab instead—*until* I remember that I left my wallet in Cale's car yesterday.

Fuck.

Cringing with dreadful anticipation of the wrath I am about to face, I reach for my phone.

"It's about time, Beck."

"Cale," I sigh. "I need a favor."

"But I've given you so many already."

"I am *so* not in the mood right now, Cale."

"Wake up on the wrong side of the bed, did ya?"

"Jesus. You have no idea how true that is."

"Huh?"

"Forget it. I left my purse in your car last night, so I'm without cab fare and could use a ride home. I'm at 508 Arlington Way." I quickly hang up without giving Cale an opportunity to ask where I am.

I then nervously head upstairs to let Will know that I'm leaving, but he is in the bathroom getting dressed. I walk over to knock on the door, when the thought of looking into his pained brown eyes again, becomes too much to take.

So, I opt for a more "valiant" approach and leave a note on the nightstand instead.

You have truly sunk to an all-time low, Cait.

After propping it up against the lampshade, Cale's horn blares, prompting me to flee down the stairs and out the door, like the weasel that I am.

I reach the passenger side of Cale's car and look up to see that Will is watching me leave from his bedroom window. My heart sinks, as I shamefully break my gaze to enter the car.

As soon as I do, I see that Cale has also caught sight of Will through his windshield.

"Lovers spat?"

"Not now, Cale."

"You know, I probably don't need to tell you what I think about this, Cait."

"You're right. You don't. But it doesn't matter now anyway."

"And why is that?"

"Because it was over before it ever began."

"Wanna talk about it?"

"Nope."

Cale continues to drive, though he peeks over at me every so often, trying to read me.

I only hope he can't sense the utter disgust I feel for myself right now.

"My guess?" Cale finally speaks up, "He was getting too close, and you pushed him away."

"Wrong. He just wants more than I can give."

"You mean, he wants more than you are *willing* to give."

"No—"

"Yes. Don't bullshit me, Cait. I know you. It's what you do."

"That is not true! What about you and Lucas? I'd do anything for the two of you, and you don't see me pushing either of you away!"

"Ah, but that is very different."

"And why is that?"

"Because we're safe zones, Cait. Our friendship isn't contingent upon you having to open up to us. You can be cynically closed-off to your heart's content, and our relationship would still remain intact because we never demand anything deeper than a sarcastic limerick or two, over a shot of Tequila."

Cale's words knock the wind right out of me, as I realize just how lonely and shallow they make me out to be.

"We're a constant, and he's a variable, and let's face it, Cait, you hate variables."

Cale then looks over at me with the most arrogant expression on his face.

"Proud of yourself, are ya?"

He shrugs while flashing a subtle grin of victory.

"You know what, Cale? You should give Will a call sometime. I think the two of you might *actually* hit it off."

"Oh, yeah? And why is that?"

"Because you've been stealing your wisdom from the same fortune cookies."

Cale bursts out laughing. "All right, so maybe I'll give him a call."

"I hate you."

"I know."

36

After giving Cale a complete account of events from the night before—minus my intimate evening with Will—I had asked him to give me a few days to recuperate.

I have completely immersed myself in schoolwork. Though, the very nature of it fails to distract me from my pain, entirely.

Too many assignments centered on the inner psyche that painfully calls me out on my own maladaptive behaviors. Ones that somehow became obvious to everyone around me, if Will, and Cale, are any indication.

It's been days since I last spoke to Will, and while I continue to work hard in my classes, the effort I put in to forget about him is unmatched.

It's been absolute hell, too.

Yesterday, I thought I smelled his cologne in the hallway and spent the next sixty seconds feverishly spinning around in place, expecting to see him materialize in front of me.

Of course, he didn't, and as the cologne faded away, my hope faded along with it. I keep telling myself that it's for the best, but I know I'm a liar.

Leaning back in the library chair, I take note of the brisk, but sunny, early March day outside. The warmth coming through the window offers a hope of spring, and with spring, comes new possibilities.

I realize just how much I miss Cale and Luke when my phone suddenly vibrates.

It's a text from Cale:

> **I know you need your space right
> now but I could REALLY use your
> help at the frat-house.**

As it turns out, space is overrated.
When do you need me to be there?

> **An hour ago, would have been nice,
> But I'll settle for right NOW.** ☺

I clean up my things and head for the frat house. I ring the doorbell, and a pledge opens it up, inviting me in.

"Master Cale is upstairs," he says.

I run up the spiral staircase, taking in two steps at a time until I finally reach the top.

"Cale?"

"Master Bathroom!"

I follow Cale's voice to a larger bedroom at the end of the hall—just in time to hear someone violently vomit into the toilet.

When I turn the corner, I see that Lucas is the victim, and Cale is seated just behind him on the edge of the tub with a damp rag in his hands.

"Jesus, Cale! What the hell did you two drink?"

I take the rag from his hands and kneel down next to Lucas, who is now resting his face on the toilet seat.

"Oh no, not us. Just him."

I start to dab Luke's forehead with the rag when he clumsily takes it from my hands.

"Well, well, well. If it isn't my good friend, Missss Caity-Cait."

I immediately feel sick to my stomach at the mere mention of this nickname, but Luke only looks at me with a shit-eating grin on his face.

"Oops! Sorry 'bout that," he says, falling back against the wall.

I glance over at Cale, who looks as though he has already heard this tune before.

"Luke, what is the matter with you?" I ask.

"What's a matter with me? No, Cait. What's a matter with you? *Both* of you. You're off living your lives, and leaving me out of everything!"

Luke suddenly tries to stand up, and Cale immediately gets up to assist him.

"I don't need your help, *frat-boy*."

"Yeah, yeah. Just shut up, Luke." Cale helps him out of the bathroom and tosses him onto the bed.

I lean against the doorframe and realize just how rotten Cale and I have been. We'd noted it after running into Luke at the library, but we got caught up in our plans, and *again*, failed to catch up with Luke.

We've all been spinning in our own way, but Luke has been spinning alone.

Within minutes, Luke is snoring, and I see a look of relief wash over Cale's face. He lays a blanket over the top of Luke and motions for me to follow him out of the room. As soon as we enter the hallway, Cale closes the door behind him.

"I am so glad you're here. Thank you for coming."

I laugh at the exhausted sight of him. "Why? What did he do?"

Clearly, on a mission, Cale grabs my hand and leads me downstairs, and into the dining room.

Several pledges, including the one who let me in, are cleaning up broken glass and endless fragments of decorative items that were previously arranged throughout the room.

My jaw drops.

"Exactly," Cale says, as he stands there shaking his head.

"Why would he do this, Cale?"

"Apparently, he came here looking for me, already liquored to high heaven, by the way, and just started breaking shit. The guys called me, and when I finally got here, he'd already puked a few times."

Cale turns and motions behind me, where another pledge is scrubbing the carpet beneath him.

"Wow. How did I miss all of this on my way upstairs?"

"You're one-track minded," he states, matter-of-factly. "Anyway, he's spent the last hour puking and cursing *both* our names."

I sigh and walk over to sit on the bottom step, and Cale takes a seat next to me.

"We are selfish people. I mean, we've practically abandoned him, Cale. He tried to tell me the other day, too. I should have listened."

"Yeah. I guess we have been a bit hyper-focused these days."

"I was gonna say bat-shit crazy, but we'll go with yours." I smile, as I sway into his shoulder.

"So? How was your mini hiatus?"

"It was only mini because you dragged me out of it," I tease.

"Well, somebody had to. Anyway, I'm glad your back. I was worried. And I may have even missed you a little bit."

"Me too." I lock my arm around his and rest my head on his shoulder.

"So, now what?" he asks.

"Now, we are going to sober him up, and fill him in on the horrific tale that has become my life."

"We're gonna do *what?*"

"Only the details surrounding my history, and the fact that we know who my parents are. Nothing about our plans."

"And nothing about the tattoo, or the guy wearing it, for that matter." Cale adds, "We need to keep him under wraps as long as possible. I mean, from what I gather, the police still think that 'Ramirez' chick acted alone, and that gives us an advantage."

"Right. Wait—what?" I lift my head and look at Cale confused. "What in the hell are you talking about? What Ramirez chick?"

"Cait, after I dropped you off at the police station last week, I stayed up and performed several Google searches by arranging what information we do have in a combination of different phrases."

"What did you come up with?"

"A lot, actually."

"Why didn't you tell me?!"

"Because you'd been through so much already, and let's be honest; with your baseline of sanity already teetering on edge, it's hard to know what will eventually push you over."

"Do you *want* me to stab you, Cale?"

He laughs and takes my hand. "All right, come on. My laptop is in the other room."

We walk passed the cleanup crew and head for the den. Cale pulls a leather desk chair out for me to sit on and logs into his laptop. He then maximizes a screen from the lower right-hand corner.

An image of a family portrait appears, inflicting an enormous blow of shock.

Wearing brown corduroy overalls, a ruffled collar shirt, and pigtails, I look to be around the age of three.

My father is wearing a tan, long sleeved sweater, and my mother has on a pink button-up blouse, a brown silk infinity scarf, and some ivory pearl earrings.

My mother's hair is styled into thick blonde curls, with faded caramel highlights. Her smile looks like mine, and her blue eyes, just the same.

Cale has taken a seat next to me. "Isn't she beautiful? Looks just like you."

All I can do is sit and stare at this family, wearing their perfect colors, and their perfect smiles.

But what I really want to do, is smash the screen with a brick because it is all a lie.

The people in that photograph are nothing more than a bunch of strangers.

Just then, I spot an article below:

Local Mother and Daughter Abducted;
November 10, 1999; Christina Jeffries and her five-year-old daughter, Marin Jeffries, were abducted early Wednesday morning, as the little girl walked toward another day of Kindergarten.

Bystanders at a nearby park reported a blue van speeding around the corner, with what appeared to be a little girl inside. One eye-witness told reporters the little girl was, "Clearly terrified."

Cale reaches over and hits the back button to click on another link below that one:

UPDATE: **Local Woman's Remains Found;** *February 8, 2000; The remains of Christina Jeffries, wife to Joseph Jeffries, and mother to Marin Jeffries, have been found. While investigators failed to comment, sources say there is speculation as to whether or not the young mother had been strangled to death; Five-year-old Marin Jeffries has yet to be found.*

Cale pushes the back arrow again, clicking on each "UPDATE" one by one.

UPDATE: **Marin Jeffries Found; Investigators Name a Suspect;**
April 6, 2000; Charlie Hunton, Lead Investigator of the Jeffries case, has named a suspect in the murder of Christina Jeffries after a convenience store owner turned over some film from one of the surveillance cameras located on the roof of his market.

Robert Johnson, the store owner, told reporters that after his store had been robbed two nights ago, he went back through the surveillance footage and discovered something that he knew was related to this case.

"I noticed a blue Chrysler minivan turn the corner like a bat outta hell, and even though the angle is high, it must have been God at work, because I immediately spotted that little girl's face in the back window, and I knew that face. I mean, hell, we all knew that face! It's been all over the news!"

Investigators were able to obtain a license plate number that led them to an old house in Newport News, settled near some train tracks.

Police rushed the house, and none of them were prepared for what they would find inside. Marin Jeffries had been locked up in a bedroom of the home since she was taken almost six months ago.

"She is terrified, hungry, and notably dehydrated, but otherwise, okay," Hunton confirmed. Though, he would not divulge anything further about the little girl, or any evidence that may have been found in the home.

However, Investigators have confirmed that Eileen Ramirez, the woman seen in the surveillance footage, has been arrested.

Sources say that Ramirez has also named Joseph Jeffries as an accomplice to the kidnapping of Marin Jeffries and the murder of his wife, Christina.

UPDATE: Joseph Jeffries Charged with Murder;

April 16, 2000; Investigators have now confirmed that an impression taken of the weapon used to strangle Christina Jeffries is a perfect match to a spool of black nylon cord belonging to Joseph Jeffries. The match led investigators to arrest the man late this morning.

A trial date has not been set, as charges are still processing.

I read through each line until my head starts to spin. I knew about my mother, but the father I remember praying to would *not* have done this to her.

"Are you alright?" Cale asks.

"Honestly, I don't know what the hell I am anymore."

Clicking some buttons, Cale tries to show me the next article, but I can't read anymore. I slide the laptop toward him, and he closes it.

"With the exception of Ramirez's statement and the similar, *albeit* generic, spool of cord, they never found any real evidence linking your dad to the murder. So, the prosecutor had to settle for a kidnapping and abetting charge. Your dad and Ramirez were found guilty and sentenced to fifteen years in prison without the possibility of parole. Until his release in two thousand seven, after Freddy Stanza, husband to *Paula* Stanza, gave officials enough information to exonerate him of the crime."

"Well, I guess now we know why his DNA was in the national database."

"Yep. It also goes on to say that due to your father's suspected involvement, and no other family members to speak of, you were placed in protective custody and given a new identity. It also says there wasn't anyone else in the home that would qualify as a 'credible witness' to the crimes committed. Oh, and they also mentioned that you had appeared to be suffering from a 'dissociative condition.'"

You don't say.

I lean forward, placing my face in my hands, desperately wishing that Lucy was here for the unveiling of this psychotic plot that has become my life. And actually, not Caitlin's life, but *Marin's* life.

I really am three shades of fucked-up.

"Cait?" I can hear the worry in Cale's voice.

I reach over and pat his knee. "I'm okay, and thank you for this, Cale. I just think I need to sit with it for a while."

"Yeah, okay."

Cale stands up to pack his laptop away, as I sit and mull over the ever-growing shambles of my life.

37

"Holy shit! Did I do that?"

The pledges stop what they are doing, as Luke stands in the dining room, assessing his damage.

Cale and I emerge from the den.

"Pledges—*out*," Cale says, and his tone sends several young men scurrying out the front door.

Luke reads the anger on Cale's face and moves to minimization. "Oh, come on, Cale! We've done much worse than this before!"

Cale offers no response, making it painfully clear that I will be doing most of the talking.

I walk over to the dining room table and sit down while they both follow suit.

"Lucas, we owe you an apology." I start, "We really should have reached out to you more. I just think the close nature of our relationships with Lucy has brought us closer than we'd expected."

Luke leans back in his chair with a snide grin on his face and is inquisitively darting his eyes back and forth between Cale and me.

"No! Not *that* kind of close!" I snap, "Jesus, Luke!"

I am shocked that he would even consider that a possibility—while Cale is just pissed.

"Okay, okay." Luke puts his hands up requesting mercy from Cale's visual daggers.

I continue, "We've just been using each other to vent a lot, and anyway, we are both really sorry for not being there for you."

I shoot a look over at Cale, who appears to be biting his tongue for now.

Lucas sighs and rests his forearms down on the table while clasping his hands together.

"You know what, Cait? You *really* need to stop taking on everybody else's problems. I mean, this rather annoying habit you have of claiming ownership over everyone else's misery or demons? Well, it's not yours to take."

"Lucas, I—"

"Listen, my misery, is my misery, okay? All mine. It doesn't belong to you, or Cale, or anyone else. And I don't need you to fix me. So please, drop the God complex, and let me keep it for myself, okay?"

I am speechless. A God Complex? I've never put myself on a pedestal above others.

Have I?

"Did you *really* just say that to her, Luke? After she came running over here to help clean up your mess!"

"Of course, she did, Cale! That's what she does! She's the 'enlightened one,' and we're just the flock of rejects she takes care of. I mean, hell, even Lucy got sick of it every once in a while."

I collapse back into my chair, flabbergasted, as this person, whom I adore, won't allow me to comfort him, and worse still, he is suggesting that Lucy never wanted that from me either.

And did he just refer to me as "enlightened"?

"Cait, that is *not* true," Cale says.

"Oh yes, it *is*. In fact, Lucy would often complain about you too, Cale."

Luke's words have me extremely nervous that Cale is going to leap across this table and rip his head off.

"Yep. That's right. I had the inside scoop on *both* of you. So, see? You weren't the *only* ones she loved and had a close relationship with."

Oh damn.

My stomach sinks as I now realize this assault had nothing to do with Cale or me, and everything to do with my previous statement.

"Luke, it was not my intention to suggest that our relationship with Lucy meant more than yours did. That was a poor choice of wording on my part, and I am so sorry for making you feel that way."

"You're always sorry, Cait, but that's just it. I don't *need* you feeling sorry for me!"

And with that, Cale stands up and kicks his chair out behind him.

"Are you fucking *kidding* me right now, Luke?! You're begging for it! You go and get all smashed up, and come running through here like a Goddamn bull in a china shop, but you don't want us feeling sorry for you? BULLSHIT! That is *exactly* what you want!"

Cale turns to walk away from the table, then decides that he isn't finished.

"And do you know what *really* pisses me off? While you've been having your little pity-party, Cait's been going through some seriously fucked-up shit, and I'm sorry Cait, but exactly how many missed calls have you gotten from Luke lately? I know I haven't gotten any. This isn't *all*, on us."

I lean forward and rest my face in my hands. We are unraveling at the seams.

"Okay...okay, yeah." Luke's tone has finally calmed a few notches.

Cale walks toward a hutch in the corner to pour himself a drink.

"Pour me one too, will ya?" I ask.

Luke chuckles. "I guess I shouldn't ask for one?"

Cale turns and glares at him, as he finishes pouring mine.

"I'm kidding! *Jeez*, Cale, what happened to you? We've made plenty of drunken mistakes in our day."

Cale hands me the glass of our favorite liquor, "Yeah, well, I haven't exactly been myself lately."

"None of us have." I take down the Tequila in one shot, as Luke runs his right hand through his hair.

"Look you guys; I'm sorry okay? I guess I just missed this. You know? Missed us."

"I know. I've missed us too. ALL of us." I slide my glass across the table toward Cale, as the pain of losing Lucy begins to surface.

Luke then reaches across the table for my hand.

"I'm sorry, Cait. I didn't know you were going through something, and actually, I still owe you an apology for the last time I saw you."

Cale raises a curious eyebrow at me, as I graciously accept another refill of Patron.

"No, you were right, Luke. It's not a good idea for me to get involved with the Lead Detective in Lucy's case."

Cale then forms a "yep" smirk on his face, and I fight the urge to hurdle my empty glass at him.

"So, what's been going on with you then?" Luke asks.

"Well? After more than ten years of not knowing exactly who I am, or who my parents are, it turns out that my mother was murdered, and my father is a convicted felon. Cheers."

I take my shot, as Cale spits his back into his glass, laughing. I glare at him, before realizing just how ridiculous it all really is, and immediately start laughing too.

"What in the hell are you talking about?!"

"Oh, Lucas, I really do have a lot to tell you."

After a few hours, and almost a fifth of Patron later, Cale and I manage to catch Lucas up on the tragic details of my life—which become more amusing, the further we get into the bottle.

Of course, the five or six puffs off the joint Lucas provided isn't helping matters either.

"Wow, Cait. That is some real heavy shit," Luke says while passing me the joint.

"Yeah, man. Heavy." Cale is pulling at his cheeks, as if suddenly aware that he can't feel his face, causing Luke and me, to burst out laughing.

"You know what I think?" Luke blows out a stream of smoke and hands the joint over to Cale.

"I think the guy who exonerated your dad helped that woman out. How else could he know all of that? I mean, no offense Cait, but I don't see how a woman could force two people into a van by herself. No, way."

"Maybe she used Chloroform," Cale says, handing me the joint.

"And you don't remember anything about what happened? Not even a hint of who else might have been there?" Luke asks.

I shake my head.

"Seriously? *Nothing?*"

"Nope." I have become quite the shameful-liar these days.

"Wow. That is unbelievable," he says.

"To say the least."

"Okay, so what did that detective have to say about it? He can't really believe she acted alone."

"All *he* did was show her the DNA results, Luke. He never gave up any details about what happened to her. I came up with that on my own after a Google search."

"Well trust me, he may not have shared it with her, but he knows a hell of a lot more about it than you do. I've been assisting the guy who does the coding for their software, and you better believe their access to information far outranks your Google search."

Oh my God, of course!

I cannot believe this hadn't occurred to me before. Will knew the entire time! He knew that I was abducted by men who ship children off to the highest bidder. Knew that my mother was viciously murdered, and how I completely detached from myself. He knew every last horrific detail—and *then* had the nerve to sleep with me while omitting *that* much information?!

Credit, I didn't exactly confess to Will that I've been investigating Lucy's case behind his back—with every intention of killing the bastard who took her life once we find him—but that wasn't personal. *This* was.

Or at least that's what the alcohol and pot are telling me.

"The real question is: *how* did they make that connection in the first place?" Luke asks.

"He told me they were comparing my DNA to the sample collected at the crime scene, and my father's DNA came up as a familiar match."

"*That's* what he told you?!"

I nod, and Luke immediately starts laughing.

"Um, no. You don't just '*run a sample*' and POOF! A match happens. They have to know where to look, and even then, they apply algorithms to narrow that shit down." Luke pauses to take another puff. "I hate to break it to ya, Cait, but your boyfriend's a liar."

"He is not my boyfriend, Lucas. But I'll give you 'liar.'"

I feel like such an idiot—not to mention humiliated—with a whopping batch of *furious*.

"Everything alright over there?" Cale asks me.

"Yeah, I think I'm just a bit too drunk."

"And a wee bit baked, too," Luke adds.

"Yep. That, too. I'm just gonna splash some water on my face."

I do my best to stand up and walk toward the restroom. I imagine Will stumbling onto every last torturous detail of my life, and the misfortune he must have felt afterward.

The idea is far too much for me to bear, and the more I think about it, the more pissed off I am getting.

I walk back into the room to find that both Cale and Lucas have passed out.

Grabbing my things, I type a quick text that Cale will wake up to in the morning, explaining how I'd decided to take a cab home.

I make my way out of the house and step into the yellow cab that is waiting for me near the curb.

Let's see what you have to say for yourself, Detective James.

38

The skies have opened up to release a downpour when I finally arrive. After instructing the cab driver to keep the meter running, I stumble my way up to the front door of Will's condo and start knocking.

Not even a minute later, I see his blurred physique appear through the rectangular window panes that are evenly-spaced along the entire length of the door.

When he finally opens it up, the sight of him takes my breath away. He is wearing a pair of gray sweat pants with a military logo printed on the lower left hip, and a navy-blue cotton tee.

He looks positively scrumptious—and confused.

"Hi." He takes note of the rain. "Come in."

Will steps to the side of the doorway, but I *refuse* to surrender my dignity.

So, I opt for a slurry interrogation instead.

"How long have you known what happened to me?"

"Are you drunk, Caitlin?"

"Why, yes I am, *William*."

"All right, come inside. After you've sobered up, we'll talk."

"No. Just answer the question. How long?"

"Caitlin, I will not have this conversation with you like this."

"Well, I'm not coming inside until you answer my damn question!"

"I swear to God, Caitlin. I'm not gonna ask you again." Will remains off to the side, demanding entrance.

I look into his eyes and immediately feel pained by the awareness of how pathetic my reflection must have been to him, after learning so many disturbing details about my life.

"You knew horrible things about me. Things I didn't even know about myself, and as if that wasn't bad enough, you kept it from me, and then had the nerve to sleep with me afterward."

Will holds his breath for a second, completely dumbfounded by what I've just said. He then takes a step toward me, rebuttal in tow, when a gust of wind carries my scent up to his nose.

"Wow. So, you're drunk, *and* you're high? That's fantastic, Caitlin. I hope you didn't bring that shit with you."

"Nope. I gave it back to Lucas."

"Oh, I see. Well before you say another word, let me remind you that I'm a cop, and neither you, nor your friends, have been granted immunity. Now get your ass in here so I can hose you down and make you some coffee."

"I don't need your *'immunity.'* What I needed then, and still need from you now, is your honesty! You even lied about that DNA match being 'random' when apparently, that's not even a thing!

"And meanwhile, I got to learn all the gory details of my life from Cale, after he performed a GODDAMN GOOGLE SEARCH! That's right, a Google Search! So, you know what? You keep your damn coffee because I've got a cab to catch."

I turn around and head down the porch steps when suddenly, I feel him grab my left elbow and spin me around to face him.

After his expression lets me know that I have *clearly* asked for it, he bends down to wrap his arms around my thighs and lops me up, and over his shoulder.

"HEY! Put me down, William!"

He ignores me, as he stomps his way through the front door, up the stairs, and into the master bathroom.

I do my very best to fight free when I suddenly find myself in the middle of a large walk in shower, surrounded by onyx tile.

Will sets me down, and within seconds, a spray of cold water induces an impromptu gasp of shock from my lungs.

"I'm going to pay the cab driver. Don't even think about coming out of there until you've sobered up."

Will leaves the bathroom, and I bitterly adjust the temperature.

Who in the hell does he think he is!

I stew in my anger as the water continues to beat down on my face; but the longer that it does, the more refreshing it becomes.

So, I slip off my clothing and attempt to wash away the fog of inebriation.

As it finally starts to fade, a heavy dose of shame for my behavior is left in its wake.

I shut off the water and peek out to find a white terrycloth robe on a hook near the stall. I slide my wet body into the robe and retrieve my once borrowed toothbrush from the holder next to Will's.

After scrubbing the alcohol and pot from my teeth, I head downstairs.

Will is sitting on the couch sorting through a pile of pictures and reports spread out in front of him.

He hears me enter but addresses me without turning around. "Would you like some coffee now?"

"That would be great, thank you."

He stands up and makes his way into the kitchen when I spot something familiar.

I approach the coffee table and carefully pick up one of the photographs from the pile.

Highly magnified, is the tattoo that Cale and I have been chasing. The enlargement of the image reveals details that were not visible to us before.

Colored in black-and-white, is an upside-down pentagram. The shape itself is constructed out of continuous chain-link that is joined together by a padlock positioned at the lowest point of the star.

Hidden beneath it, is the scarred tissue of what appears to be three cigarette burns.

I do my best to memorize every last detail of the image when my focus is abruptly-shaken by the sound of Will's footsteps leaving the kitchen.

I nervously return the photo to where I found it and hustle over to sit on the elevated hearth of a granite fireplace.

Will enters the room and hands me the coffee before then returning to his previous seat on the couch. He resumes sifting through reports when I realize he hasn't even bothered to look at me yet.

"Are you completely hating me right now?"

"I'm trying to, but you look entirely too cute in that robe."

Though he continues working, I am relieved to see a slight grin reach the corner of his mouth.

"How have you been?" I ask and take another sip.

"Miserable. You?"

"Yep."

Will stops working, then closes his eyes and sighs.

"Caitlin, I wanted to tell you. I just can't compromise this case, and I would expect you to be supportive of that."

"What makes you think what happened to me is even related to this case, Will?"

My eyes dart toward the tattoo as his do the same.

SHIT!

Cale and I had foolishly hoped that tattoo would remain random in the eyes of police, but Luke was right. They knew exactly where to look.

I set the mug down and rest my forehead in my hands while I attempt to massage a headache away.

"So, now that you're sober, can we talk about what you accused me of earlier?"

I lift my face up, trying to sort through all that I'd said in my drunken stupor.

"Something about my audacity to sleep with you? I'm still struggling with that one."

I hang my head and sigh, trying to find the words to explain my feelings of betrayal.

"Will, I have spent more than half my life trying to put puzzle pieces together. Most of which, mere fragments of the truth; and so much of who we are, is a direct reflection of how we came to be, and all that I have ever known about myself, is that I came from a background worthy of memory suppression for the sake of survival."

"Caitlin, what happened to you wasn't your fault. And while I understand how things like this take on a form of shame, it is completely uncalled for. The real shame belongs to the son of a bitch who put you through it. Quite frankly, I'm amazed by your resiliency."

"See! Right there! That's the problem. Before you knew all of this, I was just like any other girl, but now I've become some tragedy for you to solve, and I don't want to be that girl to you, Will! You should have given me an opportunity to choose for myself whether or not I wanted to be intimate with someone who viewed me in that way."

"Viewed you in what way?"

"Believe me, there is a vast difference between the girl you slept with and the one I wanted to be, and that makes your version of that night dramatically different than my own."

"Jesus. You've got that right."

Will tosses one of the reports onto the table in frustration. He stands up and walks around to sit on the edge of the coffee table in front of me.

"In my version? I didn't 'sleep' with you, Caitlin. I very much made love to you. And that girl I made love to is the same girl I interviewed the morning that her friend died. She is the same girl that gave me butterflies as we took a flirtatious stroll from the library to her dorm, and she is the exact-same beautiful and intelligent girl, that had me sweating in that kitchen for two hours so I could impress her with my mother's cooking.

"I fell in love with that girl, I made love to that girl, and while she broke my heart afterward, she is *still* the very same girl, that's been on my mind, every minute, of every day, since."

Will's words dredge up a very raw and uncut emotion from deep within me. I look down at my fidgeting hands, tears reducing them to nothing more than a blur. I search for the courage to say what it is that I *really* want to say.

"I am so sorry that I hurt you. And I know this is a lot to ask, but... do you think that maybe, you could forgive me for this one?"

Without hesitation, Will rises to his feet and pulls me into an ardent embrace. He then buries the side of his face into mine and releases an affectionate stream of air from his nose onto my skin.

Then, while caressing the left-side of my face, he moves in for a kiss, and I melt freely in his arms. Never have I longed for someone so deeply and I want nothing more than to feel him all over me.

Our kiss comes to a soft close.

Will leans his forehead against mine and peers into my eyes. "God, I missed you," he says.

"Me too."

"I'm sorry I couldn't tell you. I wanted to, I did."

"Well just out of curiosity, why *did* you tell me about my dad, if you couldn't tell me anything else? I mean, what was the point of that?"

"Well," he sighs. "When we discovered the connection between your past and this case, my captain started to question whether or not you might be involved too."

I pull back— "*What?!*"

"I told him that wasn't possible, but he doesn't know you as I do."

"Ok, so why didn't he just interrogate me then? Why tell me about my father at all?"

"He assumed that if you were involved, you might know more about your past than you were letting on. So—"

"He wanted to see how surprised I would be by those DNA findings."

"Exactly."

"And Gretchen? A patient advocate? Or just another means for analysis."

Will remains quiet.

"Wow."

"I know it was cruel, and I tried to prevent it, but he's my boss, Caitlin. My hands were tied. Just please believe that I tried to change their minds. I would not have agreed to put you through that."

"So, then why were you there for it? You didn't have to be."

"No, I didn't, but I wanted to be." He pulls me back into his arms. "I didn't want you to be alone when you found out." His eyes show remorse.

"I believe you."

Will leans his forehead into mine and sighs.

After a minute or so, he starts to dance us slowly. His embrace feels so safe and comfortable, and as we sway in place, I realize my usual need to run no longer exists.

Lifting his head, Will looks at me and grins.

"So, tell me beautiful. Do you know what comes after a big fight in a relationship?"

"The answer evades me."

"Well, allow me to show you then."

He tugs on my bottom lip and pulls me in for a sultry kiss that I hungrily accept.

After a euphoric night of forgiving each other—twice—I am rudely awakened by the persistent buzzing of my phone.

But my desire to remain in the comfort of Will's arms, has me ignoring it.

After the third attempt to reach me, however, I reluctantly break free from my comfortable place in his bed and reach for my cell when Will suddenly pulls me back down.

"Mmmm…where do you think you're going?"

"What? You mean you can't hear that incessant buzzing? It's enough to drive someone mad."

He laughs, "Yes, well, I'm no stranger to that doing what I do, but unless you're trying to solve a murder case, I'd say you have full permission to ignore it."

Oh William, if only you knew the irony of that statement.

He leans in and kisses the back of my neck, as my phone begins another round of buzzing.

Annoyed, I sit up and retrieve it off the nightstand to see that it's Cale.

Will sits up and kisses my shoulder, taking note of who's calling. "See, now I *know* you have permission to ignore it."

"You're hilarious. But it might be important. I'll just take it downstairs. I can make us some coffee while I'm down there."

Will looks slightly perplexed by my decision to answer Cale, and then my exit to do so.

While wearing one of Will's button-up collared shirts, I make my way down the stairs. Stopping two-thirds of the way down, I take a seat on one of the steps and dial Cale's number.

"Finally! Where have you been?" he shouts.

"Didn't you get my text this morning?"

"Yeah, I got it. So, imagine my surprise when Luke and I showed up at your dorm this morning with coffee, and you were nowhere to be found."

"Luke's with you?"

"Yeah, he's at the Java truck grabbing a crueler. So, where are you? We need to talk ASAP."

"What's going on?"

"I don't wanna say too much over the phone, but after Luke mentioned having access to those law enforcement databases last night, I decided it was too good an opportunity to waste."

"Dammit, Cale." I sigh.

"Don't worry. All I told him was that you were creeped out by the janitor and asked if he could look up his past charges. I didn't give him anything else."

"Okay, so did he find anything good?"

"Do you really think I would be calling you in a frenzy at seven in the morning if he hadn't?"

"Um, that's debatable, actually. Being, that you're a bit on the re-active side."

"Reactive? I'm not *reactive*." Cale cups the phone, and shouts, "Hey Luke! Am I reactive?"

I laugh, as he returns. "Yeah, no. Luke says no."

I suddenly become aware that Will has taken the seat directly be-hind me on the stairs, and is starting to rub my shoulders.

"So, where are you?" Cale asks.

"Um...well."

"I see."

"Listen, I'll be home in a bit, and we can meet up for lunch. K?"

"Yep." His tone is beyond annoyed, and I can already hear the lecture that is awaiting me.

"Great. I'll call you when I get back."

"Sounds good. Oh, and Cait, so that you know, I'm going to keep your current location between us. You think I have a problem with this? You have no idea how much it pisses Luke off."

"Actually, I do. Bye."

I hang up the phone and close my eyes, as I relish in the firm touch of Will's hands on my shoulders.

"Everything alright?" he asks.

"Yeah, he was just worried because we were drinking and I left without letting them know."

"So, I take it based on that conversation that my famous four-cheese omelet is out of the question this morning."

"I'm sorry, can I take a raincheck? I really do need to get back."

"For, Cale?"

"No, I have a paper to write."

"So, you didn't just make plans to meet up with Cale just now?"

"For lunch, yes. He's still behind in some of his classes and needs my help."

"Hm." He looks down.

"Is there something wrong with that?"

"Hey, listen, I'm not one of *those* guys, and I know you two are friends. I just can't help but notice how over the top his worrying can be. Particularly, where you're concerned."

"Well, can you blame him? I mean, the last time he had to go out searching for someone he cared about, he found his fiancée murdered, and she just happened to be my best friend."

"Yeah, see, that's just it, Cait. Your shared connection to her makes the odds of developing a stronger connection to each other, just a bit higher than I would like."

"Oh, my hell, not you too." I leave his grip and walk back up the stairs.

"Me, *too?*" he asks, falling in line behind me.

"Lucas accused us of that last night."

"Oh, so I'm not the only one who is seeing this? That's comforting."

"Yeah, well you're both dead wrong. Cale and I would *never* consider going there, and quite frankly, I'm offended that either of you would think that, to begin with."

I pick up my clothes, walk into the bathroom, and shut the door behind me to cut off this ridiculous conversation.

Will gives up, and I change my clothing.

I am so bothered by his insinuation, but I also recognize that he's right. Maybe not in the way that he and Lucas assumed to be, but Cale and I have definitely bonded over one particular pact, and the intense nature of it, calls for an equally intense relationship. But intense doesn't equal romantic.

Just then, I recall the recent course material from one of my psych classes suggesting that "intensity equals unhealthy" but then again, so does the need to kill someone.

39

Will drops me off at the dorms and I walk in my room feeling exhausted, and still a bit hungover from the night before. In fact, I question whether or not I have the energy to play P.I. with Luke and Cale today—but ultimately, my curiosity wins out, so I pick up my phone and shoot Cale a text:

I'm back. Where are you?

Just left the frat house. Be there in ten.

Oh, and by the way, I told Luke you went shopping this morning.

Me? SHOPPING?! Jesus, Cale.

I know, but I panicked.

And maybe you need to ask yourself if you should be doing something that requires me to LIE for you in the first place.

Hey, I did not ask you to lie for me.
You made that choice on your own.

**Well, I didn't want Luke to kill you.
I kind of like you ;)**

**Just tell him you went shopping
for some sheets or underwear. Even
you have to shop for those things.**

I couldn't tell ya where the sheet
aisle is or the underwear aisle, for that matter.

......
....

Yes?

**I'm giving you an opportunity
to recant your joke before my
imagination jumps to conclusions
that scare me for life.**

Jump away.

Would you do me a favor?

Of course.

**Could you not look at me for
the next couple of days?**

I erupt into laughter, as I hear a knock on my door. I open it up to find
that Cale is standing on the other side with his left hand covering his

eyes. He then smashes his right hand across mine and walks passed me.

I laugh and swat his hand away. "Grow up, Cale. Where's Lucas?"

"He ran to the store to pick up a few things. Should be here any minute though."

"Well good. That gives me an opportunity to tell you that I really don't like him involved in this, and I *especially* don't want him involved long-term if you know what I mean."

"Oh, I don't know, Cait. I mean, he broke into the FBI's database. Murder isn't *that* far behind, is it?"

"Oh, how I enjoy your sarcasm first thing in the morning after a night of heavy drinking." I collapse onto my bed.

"But I do think we need to consider bringing him in." Cale argues, "His place of internship is convenient, and we're gonna need connections like that to take these guys down."

"Wait—guys? *Plural?*"

Cale pulls out his phone and after playing with the screen hands it to me. "Just keep scrolling to the right."

I take in the first image and continue scrolling through. Each page is a different sex trafficking article in Virginia since the year two thousand.

I look up at Cale astonished.

"We can't just stop with one guy, Cait. I want the head of the snake, where it all began."

"But do you realize what you're saying? We could be talking hundreds here."

"So be it."

Cale's striking blue eyes are so sentimental, and yet so filled with loathing.

"Let's just take this one douchebag at a time. Then, we'll talk about the rest; assuming of course, that Will doesn't find out and throw us both in prison first," I say, handing his phone back.

"Yeah, and that's another thing, Cait. We need to talk about this fling, or whatever it is, that you've got goin' on with him. Is it serious?"

"Oh, come on, Cale. It's me! I don't do serious, remember?"

"You know, if he can read through your lies, half as well as I can, we're both screwed."

Lucas suddenly walks through the door, and I want to kiss him for interrupting us.

"This isn't over," Cale mouths at me, as I stand up to offer Luke a hug. He then hands me a bag of items, before taking a seat at my desk.

"All right, so? What the hell have you two been up to?" I ask.

"Well, Cale told me about your concerns with the janitor. So, I punched the guy into the system at work, and you were right. He has a rap sheet a mile long."

"Okay...but is that it, Luke? Because we already knew that."

"Um, no, Cait. That's not it."

Luke removes a folded-up piece of paper from his pocket and hands it over to me.

I open it up to find a crime scene photo of a young woman sitting in a chair. She is alive, but there is purple bruising around her neck—bruising that looks eerily familiar.

"Holy shit!"

"*Right?*" Lucas is clearly proud of his find.

"Okay, so then why hasn't he been arrested?" I ask, "Obviously, the cops have access to this information, too."

"Those were my thoughts exactly," Cale pipes in.

"So, do you think they might be watching him then?"

"Nope." Luke responds, "I checked into that, too."

"How?"

"Now, if I told you that, I'd have to kill you." Luke winks at me.

"Okay, well? If the cops aren't watching him, then I say we do some digging."

"Ah, but we are way ahead of you," Cale says.

I sit down on the bed, and Luke sits next to me.

"All right, so I did some digging. His name is Daniel Neil. He lives here on campus during the week, and with his mother on the weekends. Being that it's Friday, we should be good to search his digs here on campus."

"And where are his 'digs' exactly?" I ask.

"In the utility building."

Luke pulls out another piece of paper to reveal a hand drawn perimeter of the building marked with 'X's' and 'O's.' Each mark is showing the placement of doors and windows.

"This is the front door, back door, and cellar door. I took a walk over there, and the doors have your standard deadbolts, while the cellar has a combination lock. There are windows too, so we could potentially get in that way."

"*Only* if they're unlocked, though. We can't break a window and risk getting caught. And we're not getting into a deadbolt or combination lock, either, so we may be shit-out-of-luck," I say.

Cale pulls out his phone and starts typing things. He then hands it over to me, and I realize they are ahead of me on this point as well.

I push play on the video titled: "How to bust a master lock combination in 3 easy steps".

Of course, there is a video.

I watch the tutorial, as Luke reaches into his grocery sack to reveal a few practice locks and some walkie-talkies. Cale then looks over at me and mouths "Walkie-talkies"? I try hard not to laugh as Luke hands them out.

"We'll need someone to keep watch outside, and whoever that is can use these to alert the other two if someone shows up unexpectedly."

I raise an eyebrow to Cale, and he rolls his eyes.

Luke then hands us a lock, and after watching the video a few more times, we do our best to put its instruction to the test.

After three hours of practice, Luke and I have prevailed as the best candidates for taking a crack at the lock. Whereas, Cale just became more and more impatient with each fail, causing his attention span to go right out the window.

Of course, this made Cale the lookout by default, and he is far from happy about it, too.

We make our way across campus toward the janitor's campus dwelling, each holding a walkie-talkie and Cale is notably unnerved.

"Cait, no bullshit. If that guy is in there, *or* if you feel one hair on the back of your neck stand up, get your ass out of there. Got it? And call me if you get into trouble."

"What? You don't think that I could protect her in there, Cale?"

"Now is not the time to talk about this, Luke. Let's go." I pull his arm and force him to follow me toward the back of the building.

"Luke, he's just shell shocked after what happened to Lucy. Don't take it personally."

"Yeah, except that Lucy wasn't with someone when she got killed. If one of us would have been there, she would still be alive. This is clearly about him not trusting anybody but *him* to keep you safe, and that just pisses me off."

"Hey, all that matters, is that I trust you—and myself. So, let's get this lock picked. We can talk about this later."

Though, I am secretly hoping that he will forget about it by the time we finish up here. I can't handle any more discord between us. Losing Lucy was bad enough without the three of us losing each other, and we've been on some rocky ground lately.

Luke rolls his eyes and nods, as we finally reach the cellar. It has two large metal doors attached with hinges. The inseam holds the combination lock that aims to prevent us, and the rest of the world, from entering.

Thank God for nerds and YouTube.

After the two of us take turns doing our best to crack the lock's code, Luke finally finds the right sequence of numbers and removes the lock. I then take it from his hands and put it in my pocket.

Luke heads down the first few steps, shining a flashlight into the basement. After a few seconds of scanning the room, he walks back up and reaches for my hand to follow him down.

I grab the cellar door and close it behind me, as we head down the stairs. I then turn on my flashlight, making sure to illuminate every inch of the storage space until the light finally catches a door that leads out of the room.

We slowly creep through the darkened hallway, careful to check every nook and cranny along the way. Midway down, Luke shines his flashlight into an open doorway, and motion's me over.

I follow him into the room where the Janitor, or rather Daniel Neil, has been living. His dwelling has a generic appearance, furnished with a twin bed, a circle dinette table and chair, and one standup locker for his clothing. There are no pictures or defining characteristics of any kind to speak of around the room.

"Well, this should be a quick search," I say.

I lift the mattress to reveal a wire spring base, and through the springs, I see a foot locker. I kneel down and slide it out from underneath the bed.

"Damn, this guy is almost *too* boring," Luke says, sorting through his standup locker behind me.

"Maybe he prefers to keep his work and personal life separate, Luke."

"Or maybe he just wants to live under the radar. It's all so staged."

I unlatch the lid of the locker to find several personal items. Books on war, crossword puzzles, a handheld television, and a handheld game console with military style games.

I carefully set each item aside, until I reach what looks like an army rag folded into a perfect square. I turn the cotton package upside down, revealing tucked in corners. Gripping each one, I unwrap the bandana, and my heart instantly leaps into my throat.

Inside the cloth package are several journal pages folded in half—journal pages I recognize. I pull one of them out of the locker and start to unfold it when Luke pipes in behind me.

"You should see this weirdo's collection of origami in here."

I turn around, as he hands me an object made from newspaper.

A rose.

The look and feel of it in my hand triggers another whirlwind of hidden fragments to jar from my memory...

"Are you ready for my first question?"

Two knocks.

"Okay, is it a person?"

One.

"Is it an animal?"

One.

"A plant?"

Two.

"Okay! Is it really tall?"

One.

"Is it colorful?"

Two.

"Does it smell good?"

Two.

"Is it a flower?"

Two.

"Is it a rose?"

Two

"Yes!" I whisper my excitement, feeling proud of winning yet another game of twenty questions.

I feel so grateful for my friend, but he never talks to me, and sometimes I think he's not even real.

"I wish you would talk to me so we could play a real game. It's so lonely here."

I bring my knees up to my chest and start to cry, as the torment of isolation consumes me.

Lifting my face from my knees to wipe away the tears and snot, I see the bedroom door crack open and immediately freeze with fear. I hold my breath, as a hand slips into the crack and drops something onto the floor.

Still wary, I slowly crawl over to get a closer look at the object left for me. It looks as though it's just a crumpled-up piece of paper, but as I lift it from its resting place, I see that it's a rose. Carefully constructed out of newspaper, it is the prettiest thing I have ever seen in my whole life.

I cradle the gift in my hands and make my way back over to the air vent.

"Did you make this flower for me?"

Two.

"Oh, it is so beautiful!"

I clutch the flower in my hand and pretend to smell a fragrance that doesn't exist. Then, I reach my hand up and place it on the wall, imagining that my friend is doing the same. "Thank you for my pretty flower."

I lay down on the floor next to the air return and fall asleep with the flower tucked safely into my chest...

"Cait?!"

Luke is bent down in front of me, shaking my shoulder. My visual acuity continues to fluctuate, as Luke suddenly reaches for his walkie-talkie.

"Cale!"

"What is it, Luke?!"

I wipe away some tears and grip his wrist while shaking my head feverishly.

Luke pauses, unsure of whether or not he should respond to Cale, or listen to my pleas not to.

I mouth the word 'please' and he finally brings the radio back up to his mouth.

"Never mind, Cale. False alarm."

"*False alarm?* Remind me to kick your ass later."

Luke ignores Cale, as he assesses my current state and awaits an explanation.

"He'll just freak out, and come running in here, and we're not done searching yet."

"*That's it?* You're not gonna tell me what the hell just happened?"

I pause, debating on whether or not I should inform Luke about this *'friend'* of mine. Cale may want to invite Luke into this plan, but I'm still undecided.

Besides, I'm not entirely sure what I would tell him anyway. I haven't known for certain who wrote those journal entries up until now, and this is the first time I have recalled another child being in that house with me—*Oh, wait*—this *isn't* the first time!

I dreamt about him that night at Will's but the details were too fuzzy to make sense of it—*until* now.

There was a little boy who stayed in the room next to mine in that house; and actually, I think I may have even considered him to be a *friend*.

"*Hello?!*" Luke's patience has dissolved.

"I just got lightheaded, Luke."

"Are you sure?"

"Yes. Thank you, I'm good."

Luke continues scrutinizing me with his eye, as I then turn my attention to the journal pages stuffed inside the locker beneath the bed.

"What's that?" Luke asks.

"I don't know."—*Yes, I do.*

"Well, let's take a closer look."

Luke bends down to pick up one of the pages, and I really want to take it away from him. I want so much to protect him from whatever words might be looming inside of it.

I close my eyes when Luke begins to cite an excerpt from his page aloud. "She is so beautiful when she sleeps. I want to take care of her. She needs me to take care of her." Luke sets the page down and picks up another. "He is such a jerk! Sometimes I think about killing him. If I killed him, I would be protecting her. She would really love me then."

Luke suddenly stops reading and looks over at me with dumb-founded mockery. "Who in the hell is this whack-job talking about?"

I just shrug my shoulders. Considering all pieces of information that Cale and I have gathered up to this point, 'her' could be Lucy *or* me. Hell, we could be just two obsessions of *many* for all I know.

Luke picks up another page. "She wants me to talk to her, but if she hears how stupid I sound, she won't like me anymore. I want to kill that speech therapist for not helping me."

I instantly recall Daniel Neil's stutter while Luke continues to read excerpts from various pages.

"She tells me she is lonely. Today I made her a flower, and she loved it!"

Well, I guess that clears up who 'her' is.

Luke continues, "She made a new friend on the playground today, but she doesn't need *her*. She has ME!" He picks up another sheet. "Just when I had finally built up enough nerve to talk to her, they took her away from me! I have to find her."

I remain fixed in fear of every word that comes out of Luke's mouth. Words from a man that I once considered to be a 'friend.' A *savior*, even.

I sit with my eyes closed, wishing this wasn't my life. I start to feel nauseous, as all the words, nightmares, and flashbacks continue to swirl around in my head.

"That friend of hers is an enticing vixen. I want to hate her for taking my only friend, but she sucked me in too, and now I can't stop thinking about her. What a manipulative—"

"Stop, Luke. Just...stop."

"Are you okay?"

"Yeah. I just can't hear anymore."

"Okay well, this guy is clearly stalking someone. We need to take this stuff to the police. At the very least, they should know what he is up to. Don't you think?"

Shit.

"I don't know, Luke. I mean, stalking doesn't equal murder."

"Are you serious? He's a stalker, *and* he just happens to be the one who found Lucy? It's just too damn fishy, Cait."

"I think we need to take what we've found, and head back to the dorm before someone finds us. We can talk about it there."

We gather up the pages, and the rose I am so familiar with and make our way out of the building.

Cale is anxiously waiting for us near the cellar. I look him in the eyes, as I hand over the pages and flower that I know he will recognize as well.

We make our way back toward the dorm.

The anger festers, as I recall the earlier warning of danger that Daniel Neil had given to Cale and me.

'Love can make you do crazy things.'

He has been watching all of us for God knows how long, and what's worse, he is tormenting Rob and Cynthia with his sick fantasies.

But is it possible, for someone so capable of empathy and kindness during a time when I needed it the most, to be capable of *murder*?

Going back over the words from his last letter to Rob and Cynthia, I guess it could be possible that he was merely referencing the condition in which he had found Lucy in the garden that day.

And once more, he isn't the source of that tattoo we found on Lucy's phone, either—But one thing *is* certain. Daniel Neil was in that house with me, and he knows far more than he led Cale and me, to believe.

After returning to the solace of my dorm, Cale continues sifting through journal pages. The crease in his forehead and clenching of his jaw portrays a murderous rage.

I still haven't managed to stop shaking, and Luke is beyond calm at this point.

"I think we need to sit on this for a couple of days," I say, breaking the silence.

"Are you *crazy!?* We have to go to the police! NOW!" Luke shouts.

"Luke, all we have to go on right now are some journal pages. It's not enough to convict someone. And need I remind you that we just broke into the damn utility building? I'm not going to jail for evidence that won't get a conviction," I say.

"But they aren't even watching this guy, Cait! These letters could *at least* point them in a good direction!"

I have to deter Luke from his request. If Cale and I are going to go after this guy, we need him to back off—And if I wasn't sure about involving him in this plan before, I am sure as shit convinced of it now.

"Luke, we need more. Just give it until Monday. He'll be back on campus by then, and I say, we corner him with all of this stuff and see what he does. Maybe he'll hang himself with it, who knows."

"How about you, Cale? What's your take on all of this?" Luke asks.

But Cale ignores him. He is clearly too entrenched in Neil's memoir to comprehend what Luke has asked.

"I don't understand this. Don't you guys want the cops to catch this guy?"

"Yes"—*nope*—"Of course, we do, Luke. But I also want to make sure that we're able to show cause for the crime we've just committed, too."

Luke is critically eyeballing me, beyond disgusted by my response.

"Please, Luke?"

"Yeah, ok, fine. Whatever."

"Good."

I turn my attention toward Cale, who is still furiously analyzing what we've found.

"Cale?"

"Yep. Sounds good," he says.

"Great. Monday then."

I walk over and remove the pages from Cale's hands and walk them both out as the numbness starts to overwhelm my limbs.

Whether it was Neil who killed Lucy or the man who strangled my mother, I'm to blame for all of this. If it weren't for me, neither one of these men would have ever known who Lucy was in the first place.

I sink beneath my blanket of shame when a knock on the door startles me back into reality. I open it up to find that Cale is revved up and clearly ready to track this guy down. He brushes passed me, hands balled up into fists.

"Was Daniel Neil in that house with you, Cait?"

"Yes, but—"

"I'm gonna rip his fucking lungs right out! And we're *not* waiting until Monday to question this guy, Cait. I'll be DAMNED!" He is pacing the room.

"You're right. We're not. That was my way of giving us a couple of days without Luke breathing down our necks. We can't involve him, Cale. He won't be able to handle it."

"So, I noticed."

"We need to find out where this guy's mother lives and start there."

"All right. Then what? How are we gonna do this? I mean, do we take him somewhere? Do we do it in his mother's house? What?"

"Okay, you need to calm down. We don't have enough to accuse Neil directly—"

"Are you kidding me? Have you read this shit?"

"Yes, but if I'm gonna take someone's life, Cale, I want to be certain, okay? There is zero room for doubt here."

Cale sighs and sits down on the bed. He rests his elbows on his knees and places his face in his hands. He is unraveling. The anger is tearing him apart from the inside out.

I bend down in front of him and take his hands away from his face. "Hey, listen to me. We are going to get this guy, okay? We are. But you have got to keep your head straight. I mean, you are starting to worry me. The very last thing we wanna do is kill an innocent person."

Cale nods without looking up.

"And let's not forget about the tattoo, Cale. Neil is not the source of that, and without it, he could just be a creepy stalker that I once shared a prison with."

"Yeah, yeah, I know. It's just…" He exhales while shaking his head.

"I know. The resentment? That need for revenge? It's too much sometimes."

"Yeah. But say we do find that it was him. How do we, you know, take him out."

"I'm not entirely sure," I say.

The truth is, I haven't given that part much thought yet. I never entertained anything more than the desire to choke him senseless.

"But what I do know for certain is that before we can do that, we'll need a plan. Let's question him first, and if we find that it was him, we'll need to remain calm and design a foolproof plan that won't land us in prison—which also means, that you will need to reign in your anger."

"Fine, but I'll tell you one thing, Cait. We are not going anywhere until you've practiced shooting at the gun range. You saw Neil's rap sheet. Regardless of whether or not he's the one who killed Lucy, he's a violent son of a bitch."

"Do we have to—"

Cale places his finger over my lips. "It's happening, Cait." Then, while keeping his finger in place, he bends down to kiss my cheek.

"Tomorrow."

40

ITᴛ is barely six a.m. when Cale and I pull into the parking lot of an inconspicuous brick building.

Cale steps out of the car and retrieves a small, black duffle bag from the trunk. We head into the front entrance of the gun range to find a middle-aged man standing behind the counter.

Cale pulls out his wallet. "We'd like to reserve two hours, please."

Oh, joy.

"Will you be rentin' your firearms, too, son?"

"No, we'll be using our own, thank you."

The man hands a clipboard to Cale.

"I need each of you to write your names down, and next to your name, write down the type of firearm you'll be usin', along with its serial number. Then sign on the dotted-line, please."

I immediately feel on edge, as I recall Cale's first demonstration of the removed serial number from his illegal firearm—until I see that Cale is complying with the man's request without breaking a sweat.

It would also appear that he has obtained a second firearm for me because he is writing down a separate set of numbers next to my name.

Swell.

After Cale fills in the identifying information for both guns, we sign the ledger. The man then leads us into a room filled with sounds from a battlefield.

"Cale, what did you write down for serial numbers?" I whisper in his ear.

"My dad has two, nine-millimeter pistols that look similar to these, so I put those numbers down instead. That way, if we ever do get questioned by police, we can tell them we were shooting my dad's—neither of which would match a logistics test taken from the two we'll be shooting with today."

"Jesus, Cale. That's brilliant. But how did you know he wouldn't compare what you wrote down on the ledger to the guns we have now?"

"Let's just say the arms dealer I got them from told me to use this range for a reason." He looks back at me and winks.

After finding us a stall to settle into, the man leaves us and Cale begins to unzip his duffle bag. The sight of the guns inside it makes me uneasy.

"Cale, I don't know about this."

"Listen, I will not take you to Neil's place with me until I know that you can defend yourself."

"Um, *excuse me*, but if memory serves me right, it was me who brought you into this plan. So, know your role, Bradley."

Cale chuckles, as he removes the handguns.

"Do you remember how this works, or do you need me to show you again?"

"Well, let me see." I take one of the guns and accompanying clip sitting next to it. "Was it something like this?"

While bearing a presumptuous grin, I pop in the clip, cock the barrel back, remove the safety, and point it toward the center of the target.

"Short of the arrogance, I'd say that was damn near perfect." Cale grins as he places a large pair of protection muffs over my ears. Then, he grabs my shoulders and turns me around to face the target.

"All right, *Charlie's Angel*, let's see how good you are with the actual shooting part."

"And will you be the target, funny guy?"

He smiles, "See the circles on that sheet? Aim for the bull's-eye."

"That's it? Just aim for the bull's-eye?"

"Hm, yep. That's it."

I step inside the booth and remove the safety before aiming at the target. Closing one eye, I do my best to aim for the circle in the middle.

Then, once I feel I have perfected my aim, I place my finger on the trigger. With some hesitation—along with closing the other eye in anticipation of the scary sound that is sure to follow—I fire my weapon.

After the initial shock from the kick back wears off, I open my eyes and see that I am nowhere near the center. In fact, I have left the trace entirely.

I can just *feel* the smug look on Cale's face before turning around. After placing the safety back on, I decide that my only play here is to eat crow.

"Okay, so not *just like that*."

"Hm. Nope."

Failing to mask his grin, Cale shakes his head and removes the nine-millimeter from my hand.

"All right, so there were a few things wrong with that shot. First, you hesitated on the trigger, and hesitation can change the bullet's trajectory. So, next time, you'll want to apply a smooth and continuous pressure. Got it?"

I nod my head.

"Good. Moving on. Just before the shot, you closed your other eye, and you even turned your head. Now, I don't think I need to explain to you why that wasn't the smartest idea."—*And the smug grin is back*— "And finally, you'll need to work on your breathing."

After double-checking the safety, Cale positions my hands on the firearm while making corrections to my previous form.

Next, he steps behind me and corrects the position of my hips before then bending down and prompting a change in stance by tapping on my inner ankles.

Once Cale is satisfied with his corrections, he stands up and grips the back of my arms to correct my aim at the target in front of me. After placing his hands on either side of my waist, he aligns his face with mine so that he can see what I see.

"All right, Cait, I want you to visualize pulling back on the trigger and piercing the inner circle, but before you do, let's practice some breathing. I want you to close your eyes and arrange each breath into a slow and steady rhythm."

I slowly breathe in, and Cale joins my efforts as we then release a stream of air back out in unison. I can feel his chest rise and fall against my back with every breath we take.

In...out...in...out, and again.

We continue this pattern until the tickle of his whisper breaks my concentration.

"As you near the end of your next exhale, I want you to pull back on the trigger."

I nod slowly and focus on my breathing again. I close my right eye and try to visualize the target, as Cale suggested.

Once I feel my aim is accurate, I exhale slowly, and as the air leaves my lungs, I pull back on the trigger with a firm and steady motion.

I do my best to remain fixed, as I watch the bullet pierce through the outermost ring.

"Hey, not bad, Cait! Try it again."

I follow the same pattern and improve my previous mark.

"Much better. Keep it up."

Cale leaves the booth to prep the second nine-millimeter. His confidence is clear by the way he handles the firearm like it's another appendage.

Once his prep work is complete, Cale steps into the stall, and I decide to peek around the wall to observe his method. In just a small fraction of the time that it took for *my* shot, Cale then fires the nine and nails the bullseye.

"Pure luck." I snicker and go back to my booth.

"You better hope that luck has nothing to do with it or he might get the upper hand, smart ass."

I roll my eyes and prepare for another shot.

Time passes quickly, and my mark has improved with each shot taken. My latest mark has landed just one ring from the center—but my sense of accomplishment is dashed soon after, when I notice the gigantic hole in the center of Cale's sheet.

Ugh.

I remove my ear muffs and help Cale pack up our things. Once we have left the building, I decide to share my apprehension with him.

"You know, maybe guns just aren't my thing."

"Okay. So, enlighten me then."

"I don't know. I thought that maybe I could just collapse his airway with a rope or something. You know, 'an eye for an eye' and all."

"And exactly *how* do you plan to overpower this guy long enough to get a rope around his neck—and maintain enough force to finish him off? I mean, assuming that he won't cooperate with you."

"I was thinking maybe a Taser or a blow to the head first, smart ass."

"I think you watch too many movies."

"Look, when I think about what he did, it's not enough for me to just shoot him, Cale. I mean this bastard killed Lucy. I want to rip him apart with my bare hands."

"Oh, trust me. I would love to get up close and personal with the son of a bitch too, but I can't allow you to take that risk. The closer you get to him, the more likely you are of getting hurt."

We reach the Mustang, and Cale opens up the trunk to toss our bags inside.

"And I have to keep you safe because I gotta tell ya, Cait, I don't think I could handle failing yet another woman in my life."

"Cale, you didn't fail, Lucy."

"Goddammit, Cait. Yes—I did."

Cale slams the trunk down and turns to face me.

"I should have walked her up to your room. I mean, she was just one short accompanied walk away, from never having to die. Just five more minutes out of my fucking life to walk her inside, and she would still be here.

"So, yes, Cait. I did fail to protect her. I did. And I take full responsibility for that now." He lifts his finger up toward me. "But I'll be damned if I'm gonna lose you, too. So, we do this my way, or we don't do it at all. Got it?"

"Yeah. Okay."

"Good. Now, let's go pay a visit to Mr. Neil."

Cale unlocks the car doors, and we both step inside. His burden of guilt is palpable, if not excruciating, and *as always*, I find myself wanting to remove it from his shoulders.

But Lucas was right. I need to let him, and everyone else, sort through their own pain.

"Cale, I've been giving this plan of yours some thought. If you want to wipe out the 'head of the snake's' entire operation, we'll need a formal strategy to pull it off. It would be foolish to attempt it without one."

"So, this won't be a one-and-done deal for you then?"

"No, I think you're right. If we don't get them all, they will continue to exploit innocent children one-by-one. And besides that, once we finally *do* kill this bastard, we could become a target for *them*— which in turn, makes every single loved-one we know, a target, too."

"Okay, so we'll develop a strategy then."

"Great. I thought we could start by taking some combat courses. Like Jutsu, or something."

"Why?" Cale chuckles, "So, you can kick 'em to death?"

"Jackass."

After less than one hour, Cale pulls into the parking lot of Neil's apartment and turns off the engine.

"Should we just watch for a bit first?" he asks.

I mull over the options in my head, doing what I can to foresee every possible outcome for each one.

But as I reach the end of my internal assessment, however, my need for answers overrules caution.

"Nope. We're just gonna knock on his front door."

"Excuse me?"

"I think we need to catch him off guard. Remove any chance of him preparing a speech beforehand. If we decide that it was him, we'll come back later with a better plan. Besides, what could go wrong?" I smile.

"Yeah, I don't know, Cait. What *could* go wrong?"

"Just get your guns from the trunk, and while you're at it, see if you can locate your balls back there, too." I grin, as I open up the door.

"Dammit, Cait."

We meet at the trunk, and after carefully placing the guns into the waist-side holsters that Cale bought for us, we settle our jackets over them and make our way through the apartment complex.

Glancing at the address I jotted down before we left, I steer Cale toward building 'A.' We head up the staircase until we arrive at apartment two twenty-five. For the first time, I find myself grateful for the weight of the firearm next to my ribs.

I lift my hand to knock on Neil's door when suddenly, the shattering of glass jars explodes from the stairwell.

Cale and I instantly turn around, just as Daniel Neil abandons his bag of spilled groceries, and makes a run for it down the stairs.

I immediately bolt down the stairs after him while Cale bypasses them altogether and jumps over the railing instead. He catches Neil off guard, making it possible for him to grab the back of Neil's collar.

Cale yanks him back into the stairwell and pushes him up against the brick wall.

"Nice try asshole, but you've sorely underestimated what I'm capable of."

When I reach the ground level, I see that Cale has his forearm pressed underneath Neil's chin, and he is starting to cut off his airway.

"Cale, stop. We can't do this here."

But the rage in Cale's eyes has me worried that he is incapable of hearing me right now.

"Cale. Let. Him. Go."

"Fine."

Cale releases his arm but maintains his grip on Neil's shirt. "All right, Danny boy. We're just going to take a walk up to your place and have us a little chat. Got it?"

Neil nods as he continues to gasp for air.

Cale shoves him forward and I follow behind when my phone starts to ring. I pull it out of my back pocket to reject the call when I see that it's Will.

"Shit."

"What is it?" Cale asks.

"Nothing," I say.

But it continues to ring, so Cale finally turns around to look down at my phone and laughs.

"You know, I am trying to remember the last time that I was with you when he *didn't* call."

"Not the time."

I reject the call as we reach the top of the stairs.

Neil unlocks his door when my phone rings *again*.

Beyond annoyed, Cale turns around to face me.

"How about you take that, and we'll be inside when you're ready to join us."

But just then, Neil steps inside his apartment and slams the door shut.

"Shit!" Cale bangs his hands against the door and starts to pace the landing. "Dammit!" He then stops pacing and heads back down the stairs.

"Where are you going?"

Cale stops and looks up at me. "Are you kidding? He's probably calling the police, Cait!"

Cale continues his stomp toward the car, and I join him. As we reach the parking lot, however, a text from Will appears on my screen, and the message causes me to stop dead in my tracks.

**Please call me asap. I have some
news about your father.**

Cale notes my hesitation. "What are you doing? We have to go!"

I resume my speed behind him until we reach his car. Once inside, Cale pulls out his keys and fumbles to start the engine.

"Cale, I have to call him back. It's about my father."

Cale's anger suddenly changes to a look of concern. "Yeah, of course. I'm sorry. Call him back."

I swipe the missed call prompt, and after one ring, Will answers.

"Hey there, beautiful. I have some news."

"Oh?"

"We have officially cleared your father as a suspect in the case. It wasn't him."

No shit.

"Okay. So, what now?"

"Well, he wants to meet with you tomorrow. If you're open to it, that is."

My mind begins to race out of control. Not once has my father tried to contact me in the last nine years, so why now? What could have changed?

It then occurs to me that he might feel *obligated* to, now that police have tied us together.

Well, screw him!

I am so angry with him for not being there all this time, and that anger wants me to tell him to *piss off.*

But that little girl inside of me—the one who prayed so hard for him to find my mother and me? *She* wants something very different.

"Any chance I could get you to return to the here and now, beautiful?"

"Yes, I'm sorry. I just...I don't know. I guess I feel blindsided. I mean, why now?"

"I think that maybe you should ask him that yourself."

"I don't know, Will."

"I'll tell you what. Take the night to think it over. You might feel differently in the morning. But no pressure either way. Deal?"

"Sounds good."

"And hey, whatever you decide, I'm taking you to breakfast tomorrow. I miss you."

"Okay, sure. That sounds good, too."

"And you miss me too."

"Of course, I do." I try to hide my grin as I feel Cale's glare in my peripheral.

"All right, beautiful. I'll see you in the morning."

I hang up with Will and set my phone in my lap.

"What's up?" Cale asks.

"My father wants to meet with me tomorrow."

"Seriously? Wow. So, is that a good thing?"

"Honestly? I have no idea what to think, or how to feel about it. I mean, what would I even say to him?"

"You could start by telling him that you're relieved he's not a murderer."

"*Or* I could ask him where in the hell he has been for the past nine years."

"You could, but the guy has gone through a lot, Cait, and so have you. Maybe you should try to keep an open mind. At least until you've given him a chance to explain."

"Oh, believe me. I am trying to keep an open mind to *all* of this."

"Well listen, I'm happy for you. Even if your dad turns out to be a total asshole, at least you might be able to gain some closure out of this mess."

Closure?

No matter what my father has to say, I will never have closure until the man responsible for killing Lucy—and my mother—is dead.

41

I am antsier than I have ever been waiting on the leather sofa in Will's office.

After what seems like a decade of waiting, he finally returns. I immediately stand with anticipation, as he approaches me with a warm smile on his face.

"Well?" I ask.

"Well, he's a mess."

"What do you mean by 'a mess'?"

"I mean, he looks like a father who lost his daughter sixteen years ago and has finally found her."

"*Really?*"

"Really." Will sighs, as he adoringly reaches up and tugs on my bottom lip.

"So then....why wasn't he able to find me sooner? I mean, there had to be a record—"

"There was, but the county clerk's office had a fire in two thousand three, and your files were lost. So, he hired a PI, and he's been trying to find you ever since."

Hearing that my father hadn't *chosen* to forget my existence after his release from prison causes me to breathe a sigh of relief.

"He wants to meet you now."

I nod and start wringing my hands.

Will laughs and interrupts my wringing by cradling them both in his.

"Listen, beautiful, if you're not ready for this—"

"No, it's okay. I mean, yeah. I want to meet him."

"Okay."

Will kisses my hands again, before turning to leave his office. I immediately start to pace when the door opens not even a minute later.

I stop pacing as Will ushers my father into the room. The sight of him brings back another rush of memories.

"I'll be right outside if you need me," Will says and leaves the office.

My father and I stand in silence.

I study his face, recalling moments of happiness and laughter. Each memory as fond as the last and I feel my lip and chin start to quiver.

My father, too, wipes away intermittent tears, and the pain beneath them tells me that his search has been a very long and excruciating one. He finally clears his throat and breaks our silence.

"He must love you."

"Huh?"

"That detective."

"Oh. What makes you say that?"

"Well, his tone rang fondly anytime he would say your name; which mind you, was a direct contrast to the challenging tone he was using with every other word. I felt as if I had wronged him in some way." He smiles. "But then halfway through his questioning, I realized he was just sweeping the area on your behalf, and we only do that for the people we love."

I imagine Will interrogating my father and can't help but smile.

"Oh my, you have no idea how much you look like your mother." His expression turns weary. "Um, they told me that you'd forgotten most of what happened to you and everything before—"

"I *had* forgotten. But it's been coming back to me in waves since Lucy died." I start wringing my hands again.

"Right. I heard about that. I am so sorry for your loss. God knows you've suffered enough."

"We both have," I say to him.

My father nods, as a few more tears leave his eyes. He wipes them away and clears his throat again.

"You have a sister, you know."

"*I do?*" I try to scan my inner consciousness, "I'm sorry…I don't remember—"

"Oh, no. Not from before." He sighs with sad reflection. "I mean, your mom and I did try to have another baby, but it took us seven years to have you, so…it just wasn't meant to be."

"Wow, seven years?"

"Yeah." His chin trembles. "We fought hard to get you here."

My father's words cause my chest to hurt, and I want to cry for the childhood they fought so hard for—that never was.

"Her name is Ellie Marin, after—"

"Me. Yeah. I know that used to be my name."

"Well, I must say, Caitlin, is a beautiful name too."

"Thank you. So…did you remarry then?"

"Oh! I'm sorry. I guess I stepped out of order there, didn't I? Yes, I remarried, and her name is Patricia. She worked for the Private Investigator I hired to find you. She and I spent hours going over evidence together, and one thing led to another. It was unexpected."

"Yeah, well. Love has a funny way of showing up at the most inconvenient times."

Like with the Lead Investigator of your best friend's murder case, for example.

"*Or* when it's needed the most."

My father's optimism suddenly turns my pessimistic image back around to face me, and I'm surprised to find that I don't like what I see.

"Patti is anxious to meet you, and of course, we can't wait for you to meet Ellie. In fact, we're hosting a wedding for Patti's sister, Joyce at our home this Saturday. We'd love for you to come. No pressure, of course."

"Um...yeah. Okay, sure. I guess I could do that."

Just then, we hear a knock at the door and Will appears. "Mr. Jeffries, I am so sorry to interrupt, but I may have overlooked protocol a bit by letting the two of you meet before finishing up your statement this morning."

"Right, of course. Say, do you think I could trouble you for a pen first?"

"Sure thing."

Will opens the drawer to his desk and hands my father a pen and paper.

My father writes down his home address in Norfolk, Virginia, along with his telephone number.

"The wedding starts at eleven o'clock in the morning, and the reception is at one. No pressure to come to both–or either, for that matter."

"Okay. See you then."

I smile and accept the paper from his hands. He starts to walk out but then turns back around and whispers, "Oh and that's a plus one."

My father smiles as he leaves the office. I hear Will hand him off to another officer in the hall before walking back in and shutting the door behind him.

"Are you okay?"

I nod. "I have a sister."

"So, I heard."

"Right. I forgot that you knew my entire life story before I did."

"Hey," he sweeps the hair from my face. "I thought we were past that."

"We are, I'm sorry. It's just so *surreal,* ya know?"

Will kisses my forehead before pulling me into his chest and wrapping me up in his arms.

"Can I ask if you're free this Saturday?" I ask.

"For you? Absolutely."

"My father invited me to a wedding at his home in Norfolk. I'll get to meet my sister."

"Well if I may, Miss Beck—" He kisses my nose. "I would like to RSVP to that wedding—" A kiss to the lips. "And every other wedding, for the rest of your life." He then flashes the sweetest, not to mention the sexiest, smile at me.

"We'll see how it goes," I tease.

Will laughs and leans in to kiss me. My skin immediately heats up with anticipation when—

"Dispatch Fifty."

Will stops his attempt and reaches down to retrieve his radio, but keeps his adoring eyes on mine.

"James, fifty. Go ahead."

"Copy James. We've got a possible one-eight-seven and a ten fifty-six at the White Capel Apartment building in Baltimore. Over."

The mere mention of Daniel Neil's address over the speaker causes my heart to race.

"Copy dispatch, but that address is out of our jurisdiction. Over."

"Copy James, and affirmative on the jurisdiction, but we've got a suicide note that claims responsibility for that murder case you've been working on over there. Over."

Holy SHIT! Neil is dead??

"Copy. In route. E.T.A. twenty. James, out."

"I'm sorry, I've got—"

"Yes, of course! Go!"

Will kisses me before then rushing out of the office, and all I can do is stand here paralyzed.

Neil is dead, and he took responsibility for Lucy's death and—

Shit! Cale and I were just there!

My legs become weak with the possibility of Will discovering that we were just *at* Neil's apartment; harassing him, no less, and Cale's methods were far from inconspicuous, too. Anyone could have seen him assaulting Neil in the stairwell, which would only link us to whatever transpired there after we left.

And maybe we *are* to blame. What if our visit was the catalyst that finally pushed Neil over the edge?

But then again, there is another possibility here. Maybe the ass-hole who killed my mother did in fact, kill Lucy, and Neil is just one more scapegoat for yet another one of his murders.

Neil and I were both inside that house as kids, and that made us *both* loose ends. The 'snake' could have easily followed Cale and I to Neil's apartment and took advantage of an opportunity.

I leave Will's office and pull out my phone to text Cale, but as I reach the lobby, an image of Daniel Neil on the television screen, gives me pause.

A newscaster has begun her report on Neil's suspected 'murder/ suicide' after he and his mother were found dead in their apartment early this morning:

> *"Investigators say the cause of death was asphyxiation by carbon monoxide poisoning. The deaths were at first, considered to be an accident.*
>
> *That is until police found an apparent suicide note in the apartment taking full responsibility for the brutal murder of Luciana Capelli, last fall.*
>
> *The note, sources say, was signed by Daniel Neil, campus janitor of Mary Mackland University, who is said to have found the young woman's body."*

I don't know why, but my gut tells me this report is wrong. It's just... *too easy.*

I resume my walk down the hall and finish typing Cale's number when he suddenly calls me first. I answer, all the while anticipating a blow up from the latest news report.

"Cale—"

"So? How did it go with your dad?"

I pause, surprised by his question.

He doesn't know yet.

"Well? How was it? Is he a good guy or a total asshole?"

"Cale, have you seen the news this morning?"

"No, why?"

"Just turn it on. Channel seven."

I hear the television click on through the phone when— "*What the hell?!*"

Cale's reaction rings loudly in the background, intensifying my anxiety. He returns to the phone, and I try to ease his response.

"All right, just calm down—"

"*Calm down?* Did you really just tell me to calm down, because we were just—"

"*I know*, Cale. I know, and I'm coming over. Just wait for me. We can hash this out when I get there."

I hang up without waiting for a reply and make my way out of the police station.

After hailing a cab, I give the driver Cale's address. I can't help but feel incredibly angry—and ripped-off.

Neil was my only link to what happened inside that house. He was also the only one who showed me kindness while I was there. And what did I give him in return? Accusations and physical assault.

But again, I still don't know for certain that he wasn't the one who killed Lucy. And he *has* been tormenting Rob and Cynthia with those deranged notes, too. So, maybe I am allowing Neil's childhood empathy to cloud my judgment a bit.

Jesus. Could my life get any more complicated?

Just then, I pull up to the frat house and discover that Cale—*and Luke*—are standing on the porch in deep discussion.

Dammit. I spoke too soon.

Why did we have to involve Luke in all of this? No, correction; why did *Cale* have to include him in all of this? He is just too anxious to keep quiet but I cool my anger for now and get out of the cab.

Upon seeing me arrive, Cale motions me toward his car in the driveway. "Not here," he says.

We all get in the car and pull out of the driveway.

"I told you guys it was him! I knew it!" Luke shouts, "And *now* they'll probably search his room on campus and come up with evidence that we were there! They could try to blame us for this! We should have told them what we found like I wanted to."

"Worst case scenario, Luke, they find a hair or a fiber. Big deal. It doesn't exactly scream conspiracy. And besides, the guy left a suicide note. There aren't going to be any murder charges for his death; and therefore, nothing to blame us for."

I try to reassure him; all the while fighting my own queasiness over the possibility of Will finding out that Cale and I had just been to Neil's actual apartment not even twenty-four hours before his death. Our search of the utility building on campus is the very least of my concerns right now.

Cale pipes in, "Yeah, and even if they do find evidence that proves we were there, we could easily come up with a million excuses why. Like the fact that he was stalking us. And if that doesn't fly, we can pretend it was a prank or some stupid shit like that. No worries, Luke."

Luke nods, and finally, a little relief shows on his face. "But I knew it was him, though. I told you guys. I mean, you read his file and those freaky journal pages. The guy was a total nut-job!"

"It would appear so," I say, but again, not entirely convinced of Neil's "confession," either.

"I'm just relieved he is no longer out there, and we can finally put this bullshit behind us," Luke adds.

Cale and I subtly peek over at each other because this isn't over for us. Even if Daniel Neil *was* responsible for Lucy's death, he wasn't the one who started it all, and Cale and I have already decided to go after the head of the snake, along with his entire army.

My stomach suddenly growls, and I realize that my expectation to eat breakfast with Will this morning, has caused me to go without.

"What do you guys say we stop and get some breakfast? I'm starving, and I still haven't filled you in on my family reunion this morning." I motion toward a twenty-four-hour diner.

"Oh shit, that's right! Cale told me you were meeting your dad today. How did that go?"

"I'd prefer to fill you in over some coffee and bacon please."

Cale pulls into the parking lot, and we all jump out of his car. After walking into the restaurant, a hostess standing near the entrance leads us toward a booth in the corner.

"I've gotta hit the little boys room," Luke says, following an arrow toward the restrooms.

Cale and I take the menus from our waitress's hands, and as soon as she is out of earshot, Cale scoots in closer to me.

"You know, I can't help but feel incredibly pissed off for not being the one to take Neil out myself."

"Cale, have you stopped to consider that maybe this whole thing is just a bit too easy? I mean, what if the head of the snake just found someone else to blame for yet another horrendous crime. Neil was a loose-end, just as much as I am, Cale. The snake could have easily been watching him. Hell, he could be watching us right now."

"Cait, why do you keep defending Neil? He was an obsessed lunatic for Christ's sake! I mean, you read his journal!"

"Shh...lower your voice." I raise the menu up to cover my face. "I'm not defending him, Cale. I'm just saying that we need to consider all possibilities, and that is *all* I'm saying. And besides, he is not the man behind that tattoo on Lucy's phone."

"Whatever. All I'm saying is that you can't say for sure that it wasn't him."

"And that is precisely my point. I can't be sure of anything right now. Which is *why* we shouldn't be jumping to conclusions until we know more." I look down and mindlessly skim the menu.

"Well, either way, we're back at square one. He was our only solid lead, Cait."

"I know, and I have no idea where to take it from here, either." I set the menu down and begin to massage my temples.

"Well, actually...I do have an idea." Cale offers, "If you're up for it, that is."

"Let's hear it."

"What if we went back to that house where they found you. You know, the one in that crime scene photo from the article that I showed you. Maybe if we go there, you will remember something. I mean, everything you've remembered up 'til now has been triggered by something from your past, right?"

"Right."

The idea of stepping one foot inside of that house makes me want to hurl.

"Okay," he continues, "so, we'll head to Newport and check it out then. Shall we say, Saturday?"

Oh, no.

"Well, actually—" but I see Luke coming and have to change tack. "Actually, I think I will have the bacon and eggs."

"Figure out your orders?" Luke asks, sliding into the booth.

"Yep," I lie.

"Good, because I'm starving and I already know what I want." Luke motions the waitress over.

We give her our orders, and within thirty minutes, our food has arrived. Hunger overpowers my desire to share the details of meeting my father, and I choose to dive into my food instead.

After allowing me some time to eat, Luke finally pushes me for an update. "All right, so? Tell us everything," he says.

"Well as it turns out, my father has been looking for me all this time. He only failed to find me because the authorities never told him where I was, and my records were destroyed in a structure fire. So, he had no idea where to look. That's when he hired a private investigator. And of course, we already know that he wasn't able to find me either. Oh! And I have a sister, too, if you can believe it."

"Wow. So, you've inherited an entire family overnight." Luke says and takes a bite of his pancake.

"Basically."

"So, if we really wanted to find a silver lining in all of this, it would be that you were able to reconnect with your family. I think that's pretty great," Cale says while handing his credit card over to the waitress.

"So, when do you get to meet them?" Luke asks.

"This Saturday."

I nervously look over at Cale, but he just looks happy for me. "That's awesome, Cait. Really," he says.

"Yeah. Crazy cool," Luke adds.

"Thank you, both."

The waitress brings Cale the check, as Luke and I stand up to put our coats on.

We make our way out of the diner when Luke links onto my arm. "I am so happy for you, and I wish I had time to hear more, but my internship starts in one hour. I asked Angie if she could drop by here and pick me up."

Luke motions toward her car waiting in the parking lot. "I'll call you tonight," he says before kissing my cheek and slapping Cale's hand. "Thanks for breakfast, my man."

Cale and I wave Luke goodbye as he gets in Angie's car. We then head through the parking lot toward Cale's Mustang, and he opens the passenger door for me.

"Cait, I am so happy for you, really, and I know that Lucy would be, too."

I reach up and kiss his cheek. "Thank you. I just wish that she was here for this."

I get in Cale's car, and we head back to campus.

"So, you've got a wedding this Saturday, then?"

"Yes, I'm sorry—"

"Hey, don't apologize for that, it's a big deal! Besides, it shouldn't last more than a few hours, right? If you want, I could just pick you up from the wedding, and we could head to Newport from there."

Crap.

I sit in silence, suffocating between my rock and a hard place when I notice that Cale is analyzing me in my peripheral vision.

"Why do I get the feeling that you're about to tell me something that I don't wanna hear?" he asks.

I cringe, "Because I am."

"Okay. Let's hear it then."

"We can still go to Newport. I just won't be able to leave from the wedding, because Will is going with me. And Cale, before you say anything—"

"What are you doing, Cait? I mean, are you seriously getting involved with this guy?"

"I don't know...maybe."

Cale shakes his head. "Look, under normal circumstances, I wouldn't give a damn who you date, but this isn't just about you, Cait. If at any time he were to become suspicious about what we're doing, it would be the end for *both* of us."

I have no rebuttal.

"You know, maybe this relationship with Will, and having your family back, is giving you second thoughts."

"What? No. Cale that isn't—"

"Hey, listen to me." Cale throws his car into park and turns to face me. "I'd be grateful if it has. You are the only factor that has me second-guessing this entire plan on a daily basis. I hate the idea of you spending the rest of your life in prison, with all that you've got going for you. But Cait, I'm not backing out of this. I won't be able to sleep until it's done."

"I feel the same way. I just didn't expect any of this, you know? It's all just happened so fast."

"I know, and I mean it when I say that I'm happy for you, but you can't be involved with him and be in this plan with me. It's too risky."

I nod in agreement.

Cale gets out of the car and makes his way around to open the door for me. I step out and try to study his face for some insight into his thoughts.

He shuts the door and turns to face me. There is a look in his eyes that I haven't seen before; something soft in comparison to the usual anger.

"Cait, I'll tell you what. Take this weekend…with him, and your family, and see how you feel. You just might change your mind about all of this, and I hope to God that you do. But you *will* have to make a decision, either way."

Cale leans in and kisses my cheek before then stepping into his car.

I wave him goodbye, as he leaves me to simmer in the wake of his ultimatum.

42

I open my closet to sort through suitable options for the wedding when I spot the navy-blue cocktail dress I had refused to wear to the frat party last fall.

It's a dress I had never seen myself wearing in public, and of course, I did my very best to argue the purchase of it, too. But similar to her daughter, Cynthia has never been one to take 'no' for an answer.

I remember that day like it was yesterday.

Lucy and I had been looking through party dresses while drinking champagne and laughing at some of the hideous designs when out of the blue, she came across this dress and pulled it from the rack...

> *"Oh, Caitlin, you have to try this on! The color would make those blue eyes of yours pop!"*
>
> *"Yeah, I don't think so."*
>
> *"Cait, you are a five-nine, blue-eyed blonde, with high cheekbones, beautiful lips, flawless olive skin, and amazing legs! Why wouldn't you want to show that off?"*
>
> *"It's not me, Lucy."*
>
> *"No, it IS you. We just have to force it out of that little insecure box where you hide it, is all."*

Lucy coyly smiled, as she took the dress off its hanger and handed it over to me. "Here. At least go and try it on."

I started to argue, but she pushed it into my chest.

"Just do it, Cait!"

"You are a pain in my ass."

"I aim to please." Lucy smiled and held the dressing room door open for me.

I snatched the gown from her hands and stepped into the stall. After placing it on a hook, I began to undress.

"Cait, I'm going to find you some matching heels. Don't come out 'til I get back!"

"Oh, trust me. I won't."

I slipped into the dress, and it fit perfectly. The bodice had a sapphire encrusted trim that followed the contour of my breast, creating a heart shape at the top.

In between the breast was a subtle pleat made by two taut pieces of fabric that crossed over one another just below the sternum and continued toward the back.

The rest of the dress was navy chiffon that flowed into an A-line and ended just above my knee.

Within minutes, Lucy had pushed a pair of open-toed heels through the crack of the door. They had that same cross design stretched over the toes, and in the center of it, was a tear-shaped broach. It had two rows of diamond baguettes along the edge with a dark blue sapphire in the middle. The rest of the heel was covered in navy satin that left the top of my foot revealed.

I slipped on the shoes, and I was surprised to find that I liked them—surprised to find that I liked myself dressed in that way at all.

"Cait! Get your ass out here and show me them sexy legs, girl!"

I reluctantly opened the door, feeling rather exposed.

Lucy was sitting on a black-velvet couch shaped like an 'S.' She was holding a glass of champagne, and you would think it was Christmas the way she was postured with anticipation. I built up the courage to leave the stall, and she donned a huge smile on her face.

"Oh, Caitlin...come and see!"

Lucy motioned for me to step onto a round platform that was placed in the center of three tall mirrors. She then set her champagne glass down and walked up behind me.

"Damn girl! Look at you! And look at the back, it's beautiful!"

I turned around to see where those tight pieces of fabric had wrapped around to fasten in the center of my back.

Below the clasp, was nothing but skin—until just below my hip-line, where the navy chiffon continued to flow downward again.

I turned back around to face the mirror, and Lucy undid my loose braid to allow blonde, wavy locks to fall around my collarbone.

"Why, Miss Caitlin Beck. You are quite the knockout, you are."

"I feel so naked."

"That is the point." Lucy giggled and winked at me in the mirror.

Just then, Cynthia approached us from behind with her arms full of shopping bags. She set them down on the couch and joined us on the platform.

"Oh, Caitlin, honey. You look stunning in that. You really should wear dresses more often with those legs."

"See?" Lucy whispered.

I felt my cheeks become unbelievably hot as Cynthia and Lucy continued to "ooh and awe" over a dress that I felt so uncomfortable wearing.

"Well, my darling girls, we have a dinner reservation we cannot be late for." Cynthia motioned toward one of the saleswomen, *"Excuse me? We'll take everything she is wearing, wrapped up in boxes, please."*

"Oh, Cynthia, no. Really, it's okay."

Cynthia moved in beside me, and with her right hand on my back, placed her left on my arm.

"Just consider it a farewell gift for Mackland, sweetie."

Oh yes, I remember that day. How perfect it was. Sure, I hated the shopping, but I loved being with Cynthia and Lucy.

I pull the dress from my closet and hold it up to myself in the mirror. I feel the tears begin to flow as I remember the great-big smile on Lucy's face when she handed me the shopping bags.

Ah, what the hell. Lucy, this one's for you.

I put on the dress and move on to my hair. After filling it with loose curls, I lightly twist each side to meet in the back. I then pin it loosely, so that it softly rests just above the nape of my neck. The remaining hair in the back is tucked and pinned in the center.

For makeup, I have chosen a more neutral palette, consisting of bronzing lotion, light-pink lip gloss, a shimmery nude eye shadow to accent my brow line, and some mascara. It looks subtle but elegant.

As a final touch, I put on a pair of teardrop earrings that match the broach on my heels.

I stuff my phone and other desirables into the navy satin coin purse that came with the dress and look myself over in the mirror. I can't help but smile, as I imagine what Lucy's expression might have been if she were alive to see me dressed up like this.

Feeling rather antsy, I decide to leave my room and head toward the parking lot where Will has agreed to pick me up. After rounding the corner of the dorm, I see that he has arrived, and is stepping out of his car. He is wearing a crisp white button-up shirt, decorated with a pearly-gray tie that complements the gray slacks he is wearing.

I continue to admire Will in his formal attire as he dials a number on his cell. My coin purse starts to vibrate so I pull my phone out to answer his call.

"Hello, detective."

"I'm here, beautiful."

"So, I see."

I stop walking, as Will looks up to see me standing at the opposite end of the parking lot. He pauses to take in my appearance, and I quickly fill in his pause, "That suit is delish, by the way."

Will slides his left hand into his pocket and begins taking slow and deliberate steps toward me.

"I could say the same about that dress."

"Well, don't get too attached. I'm not exactly the dress type."

"Oh, trust me. The less attached you are to that dress, the better for me later."

"And what makes you think there will be a later?"

Will smiles and raises his finger up to deliver a silent 'shh.' He then arrives at where I'm standing and continues his casual walk around me with the most enticing look on his face. I feel his hand begin to lightly touch and tug at certain areas of fabric on my dress from behind—all the while provoking me with a desire to rip it off.

When he finally makes his way back around to face me, he keeps the phone held up to his ear.

"Oh, there will be a later," he says.

The combination of his smell, that smile, and his physique in that damn suit is unbelievably arousing.

I pull the phone away from my face and Will does the same. I throw my arms around his neck, as he grips my waist and pulls me in for a kiss.

After three hours of driving, we turn into a pleasant neighborhood, lined with large elm trees and modest homes. Will pulls up to the curb in front of my father's home and after removing his suit jacket from the backseat walks around the car and opens up the door for me. I step out, and Will takes my hand to walk us when my anxiety kicks in, causing me to hesitate.

"What's a matter, beautiful?"

"I don't know. I guess I'm nervous."

"Hey, if it becomes too much, we can go at any time. Okay?"

Will reaches up and tugs on my bottom lip with the most enamored look on his face, and it is all I can do not to attack him right here in the middle of the street.

"We better keep moving because you're about one tug of my lip away from me calling this whole thing off." I pull away, taking him by the hand to follow me.

"*Oh,* so you like that, do ya?"

I just smile and continue forward.

"You know, I can't say that I won't use that against you later," he says.

"And I can't say that I won't let you, either." I grin over at him as we reach the front porch of my father's brick bungalow.

We opted to forego the wedding, and the sign on the front door tells us the reception is in the backyard.

Making our way through a gate on the left side of the home, we step inside a large white tent. Scattered throughout the space are several tables covered with white linen and a vase of lilies.

I survey the wedding party when I notice my father nervously walking toward me.

"Caitlin, I am so glad you came." He leans in to kiss my cheek before then, shaking Will's hand.

"Nice to see you again, Detective James."

"Please, call me Will, Mr. Jefferies."

"All right, but only if you call me Joe."

"You got it."

Behind my father, is a woman with dark brown naturally curly hair, and warm brown eyes. She is beautiful, and much younger-looking than my father; I would guess around the age of forty. Whereas, my father will turn fifty this year.

"Caitlin, this is Patricia, my wife."

"Hello, Caitlin. It is so wonderful to finally meet you, and please, call me Patti." Her eyes fill with tears, and my father sends her a look of caution.

As if hearing about his sadness would be a burden for me? If anything, he is the one person who knows exactly what I went through, and have been going through, ever since.

Patti wipes the tears away when a younger woman resembling her walks up from behind. In the woman's arms is a precious baby wrapped in a white knit blanket.

"Oh, thank you, Jasmine. Cait, this is my sister Jasmine," Patti says.

Jasmine nods hello as Patti gently takes the baby from her hands. "And this is your sister, Ellie."

I look inside the blanket to see that Ellie is wearing a long white dress with a tiny collar around her neck. Covering her little head is a matching bonnet that ties into a pretty satin bow beneath her chin.

"May I?" I reach my arms out to hold her.

"Of course!"

Patti helps her into my arms, and I pull her in close enough to study her small features. I reach up to touch her hand when she suddenly grabs my finger. Immediate to follow is the faintest hint of a smile on her sleeping face.

I have never been so in love in all my life. I'm in complete awe of her perfection, and while my life is shrouded in darkness, I can't help but feel a grand sense of pride and promise for Ellie. She has a chance to live the life I never got to; celebrate birthdays the way I was meant to; and she will live that life surrounded by loving parents and a protective big sister to look after her, too. I will do everything in my power to keep her safe from the pain that I have known.

"Patricia thinks she has your nose and lips," my father says.

"Well, she does! I mean, she looks just like you in your baby pictures."

"I have baby pictures?"

"Of course, you do. I have everything." My father says, "Would you like to see them?"

I look back down at my little sister and try to imagine myself being at the center of a mother and father's attention long enough to have a photo album filled with baby pictures.

A few tears travel down my cheeks, as I look up at my father with defenseless longing.

"Yes, please."

43

The reception has started to die down, but I'm far too en-
thralled in family photos to notice.

My father pulls a pink album from the stack and hands it
over to me.

"Here's the one I wanted to show you."

I open up the cover to find that it's filled with pictures of myself
as a baby, gradually moving into my toddler years. Endless pictures of
birthdays, and holidays, and sunny days at the park.

I continue flipping through pages while my dad and Will sit nearby, and Patti sways Ellie in a chair next to my father. When I reach the
end of the album, I stumble onto a photograph of my mother's grave.

"Where is she buried?"

"Norfolk Cemetery. It's just a few blocks from here." My father
takes the photo and admires it with sadness in his eyes.

"Well, I guess I'd better get this food boxed up," Patti says while
reaching for a casserole dish on the table adjacent to us.

"Here, allow me." Will takes the dish from her hands. "Just tell me
where you want it."

"Oh, thank you, Will. The fridge in the kitchen would be great."
Patti then looks over at me and smiles. "Well, I'd say he's a keeper."

"He just wants to steal your recipes," I tell her.

"I heard that!" Will shouts, over his shoulder.

I grin, and watch him leave the tent.

"Caitlin, if it's alright, I have something I would like to give you," my father says.

"Of course."

I follow him into the house and down a narrow hallway until we step into an office lined with dark maple bookshelves. Each one is endlessly lined with books and decorative items, giving it a warm and traditional look.

Along the back wall is a desk centered between them, and two white wingback chairs facing the desk.

"Please, take a seat."

My father motions toward one of the chairs and then sits at the head of the desk. He opens one of the drawers to retrieve a small gift that is wrapped in white paper and a black satin bow.

"This is for you," he says.

I instantly note a touch of deep sadness hidden behind his smile when he hands it to me.

Removing the bow, I carefully undo the wrapping to see a small white box. I open the lid and tucked inside is a sterling-silver oblong-shaped locket attached to a silver chain.

I immediately gasp, "I know this locket!"

"Yes! That's right!" My father nods and smiles in relief of my memory, as tears start to leave his eyes.

Removing the locket from the box, I run my thumb over its shiny surface, trying to recall *how* I know it.

When I reach the tiny clasp on the side, I open it up to find a picture of my mother and I, carefully tucked inside. The sight of it triggers a new stream of memories...

My father is wrapping up the locket in a festive Christmas wrap, while I decorate a card made from construction paper....

A glimpse of me, proudly handing the card to my mother before jumping into my daddy's lap to watch her open her gift....

The memory of my father helping to fasten the locket around my mother's neck—when suddenly—my happy scene is replaced by an image of my mother wearing the same locket on the day we were thrown into that van...

The pain hits my chest like a sledgehammer, knocking the wind right out of me.

I look up at my father. "She was wearing this?"

My father nods, retracting inward with grief.

Oh, mom.

Anguish floods my chest as I gather up the locket into my fist. "I was there...when he killed her. I was blindfolded in the van, but..." I gasp, "I could hear her scream and plead with them not to hurt me."

I look up at my father, "And I prayed so hard for you to find us. I begged God to show you where we were!"

"Oh, my baby girl." My father stands and walks around the desk to kneel down in front of me.

"I looked everywhere for you. Everywhere! I tried so hard to find you." He winces. "And I can't even begin to describe the overwhelming sense of relief and mercy I felt on the day they found you alive in that house. Hearing that you had made it out of there is what kept me fighting.

"Even after they locked me up for the crime, I never gave up hope that I would find you."

His words are becoming inaudible. "And I swear to you that I never stopped searching after they released me from prison. Not one time did I ever!"

My father opens up his arms, and I am instantly filled with an upsurge of deep and repressed cries from that discarded and lonely little girl on a swing.

I fall into my father's arms, and all we can do is weep. Weep for the time we lost with her, weep for the time we lost with each other, and weep for the loss of a family torn apart by violence.

44

After leaving my father's home, we arrive at a beautiful cemetery, filled with trees and rolling hills.

"Do you want me to go with you?" Will asks.

"Thanks. But I think I need to do this on my own."

"I understand." He raises my hand up to kiss it.

I step out of the car and walk up a grassy knoll to where my mother is buried. Decorating her grave is a bouquet of fresh daffodils, and I immediately remember us picking them together as a child.

They were her favorite.

I bend down on my knees, and after years of separation, my mother now rests below me.

I reach out and touch the engraved words in stone, as more suppressed memories of her appear in my mind…her smile…her hair glistening in the sun as we walked to school that morning…the smell of her perfume.

I then imagine her being strangled to death as she wore the locket that my father and I had given her, and the weight of this causes me to shift off my knees and collapse to my side.

I reach up to touch the locket that is now resting around my neck, as the endless audio flashbacks of my mother's murder begin to surround me. Joining them, are the still frames of Lucy's brutally battered, and lifeless body.

Their loss is still as fresh and painful as ever, and like a dam breaking, the flood of it all overwhelms me. I grip onto a handful of earth and begin to cry.

I try to think of the life I could have with my father, Patti, and Ellie. I imagine introducing them to Rob and Cynthia and having holidays together with Cale and Luke. I even allow myself to imagine a life with Will.

But the instant that I picture their faces, I am reminded that my family isn't free. We haven't been free since the day that monster snatched my mother and me from that curb. And why? Because the man who caused all of this pain is still out there. It is he, who is free. Free to hurt children and free to kill.

A tremendous surge of animosity causes me to begin ripping clods of dirt and grass from the ground in a fit of bitter rage. With each tumultuous till of the earth, my anger, sadness, and grief, suddenly collapse into one perfectly centered mass that emits an insatiable thirst for blood.

That man is a living threat, and as long as he is out there, my family will never be free.

They will never be safe.

Just then, any sense of doubt I may have had before this moment is removed.

Pulling myself together, I sit up and wipe the tears from my eyes. After kissing the tips of my fingers, I softly rest them onto the polished granite and whisper, "I love you, mama."

I rise to my feet, tidy up my hair, and make my way back down the hill.

After retrieving my phone from my purse, I dial Cale's number and leave him a message.

"I'm all in, Cale. Let's end this."

45

Cale and I drive into Richmond and decide to stop and grab something to eat before continuing to, Newport News.

I am lost in thought over all that we have collected so far, and all that we have *yet* to. Snapping me from my daze is the fact that we've just passed the same string of stores for the second time.

I look over at Cale, and he is glancing back and forth between the windshield and his rearview mirror.

"What is it?"

"I think we're being followed."

"*What?* How do you know?"

"Because I've circled this block twice, and they're still back there."

"Shit. What type of car is it?"

"It looks like a silver sedan of some kind. I can't tell make and model though."

"Can you see what they look like?"

"I can't see any features, but I'm pretty sure it's a guy, and I think he's wearing a hat."

I sit and analyze the options in my head. Is it possible the police have found evidence to show that Cale and I were at Neil's apartment? Could they have figured out that I withheld Lucy's phone?

And if so, is it possible for Will to have known this without showing a hint of suspicion on his face while spending the entire day with me yesterday?

"Okay, I have an idea, Cale. Pull into that coffee shop over there."

Cale turns into the parking lot of a quaint looking cafe. I enter the diner, and after buying a latte, and a blueberry muffin, I scan the room in search of a quiet corner to sit in.

"Is there a point to all of this or does being stalked just give you an appetite?"

I ignore Cale and choose a spot to sit down at. After removing a notepad from my purse, I wrap my hair up into a bun and slide a pen above my ear.

Cale attempts to take the seat next to me, but I hold my hand out to stop him.

"Not there. I need you to sit on the other side of the table. Out of view."

"Out of view of what?"

"Of Will."

"Will? I thought we agreed—"

"Cale, do you trust me?"

"No. I'd make extermination plans with anyone."

"Not really the time, Cale."

He grins and takes the opposing chair.

I reach into my purse and pull out my phone to FaceTime Will. After a few rings, our connection is made.

"Wow, you really are full of surprises. I never pegged you for someone who would bother with FaceTime," he says.

"Well, I could always hang up and use voice call, if you prefer that."

"Oh, no you don't." He smiles. "So what are you up to, beautiful?"

"Oh, I was just studying for this test and needed a break. Been at it for hours."

I immediately take note of Will's surroundings. He is clearly at home, wearing casual attire, coffee in hand, and not an ounce of stress in his eyes.

It's not the police following us.

"Well, if you'd like, I could join you. Give you something else to focus on for a while," he says.

Cale rolls his eyes and scoots his chair back to leave the table.

Great.

"Well, as much as that offer appeals to me, I'll have to take a raincheck. These past few months have really distracted me from my schoolwork, and I think it's high time that I move on with my life."

"I couldn't agree with you more, but just out of curiosity, do you plan on moving on with or without me?"

"Hmm...I think I might take you with me. Although, it could prove to be a rather bumpy ride, Detective."

"With you, I'd expect nothing less. You look incredible by the way."

"Liar."

He laughs. "I miss you. Are you sure you don't need someone to read off note cards or something?"

"I'm sure. But how about I take you to dinner Monday night? After my test is done. I can't afford your distractions beforehand."

"So, you're gonna make me wait"—he looks down at his watch—"thirty-two hours before I can see you again?"

"Anticipation, Will. Remember?"

"Mmm-yeah. Except that I don't need long periods of time to anticipate being with you. It starts the second you walk away from me."

"Wow, you really are quick with those mushy one-liners, aren't ya?"

"Is that your way of calling me cheesy?"

"You said it."

He laughs. "I can't help it. I'm a hopeless romantic...and you bring out the Shakespeare in me. It's almost as if I have finally found my Juliet."

"Oh, dear, God."

Will smiles. "Now *that* was cheesy."

"And thank God you were joking. I would have ended this relationship right here and now."

"Well listen, Caitlin, all jokes aside? Nothing I say to you is scripted, okay? You just make me happy, and when I'm happy, I want you to know it. I can't help how that side of me chooses to come out. So, take it, or leave it."

"Hmm..." I look off into space.

"You know, I was only trying to be polite by giving you an out. What I *really* meant to say was deal with it."

I roll my eyes. "And there's that authoritative persistence I adore."

"I fight for what I want."

"Well, in that case, I promise to meet you for dinner on Monday," I lean in and lower my voice to a whisper, "and after we're done eating, I'll let you fight for dessert."

Will slowly releases a stream of air with pierced frustration and wipes his face down with both hands.

"You are quite possibly the cruelest woman I have ever dated."

"I'll make it up to you, I promise."

"Yes, you will." He smiles.

"All right. Well, I better get back to it. I'll see you Monday."

"You've got yourself a date, beautiful."

"Bye," I say, with a wink and end our call.

After gathering up my things, I toss the untouched-muffin and latte in the trash. I then exit the café and see that Cale is sitting on the hood of his car. His look is stressed, making it painfully clear that we won't be moving on until I address this with him.

"Cale, I had to make sure it wasn't him, and the only way for me to do that was to actually *see* where he was."

"I don't know whether to laugh or be extremely pissed off by you insulting my intelligence, Cait. You really have no intention of ending things with him, do you?"

"Listen, I did consider it, but the idea of not having access to what he knows, made me question whether or not it's the right play for either of us in the long run."

"Ohhh, I see. So, this is just you, taking one for the team, then."

"Cale, if I end things with Will, I won't be able to do what I just did. We won't have any way of knowing what's going on inside of his head, or what the authorities may or may *not* know."

The lie induces immediate shame, and it's a two-headed snake. Not only am I withholding the truth about my feelings for Will from Cale, but I'm also belittling my relationship with Will by minimizing it.

The truth is, while the idea of having an inside connection with authorities does appeal to our plot, that's not what stops me from letting go of Will, and I would never intentionally use him for information.

Somewhere along the way, I have actually managed to develop feelings for him, and I'm just not ready to call it quits yet.

Cale suddenly removes his keys from his pocket and hops off the hood.

"All right, Cait. If you really want me to believe that being involved with him, is what's best for *both* of us, then fine. I'll humor you. And hell, I'll even back off. But just so you don't have to lie to me again in the future, I would just like to state for the record that you clearly love this guy."

"Excuse me?"

"Don't, Cait. I've never seen you like this before, so I know it's serious. Just..." he pauses, playing with his keys. "Be careful, okay? For your sake, and for *ours*." He unlocks the doors, and we get in the car.

"In the meantime, though," he continues, "what in the hell are we gonna do about that tail?"

"Well, I think the wrong play is to let them know, that we know, we're being followed."

"Okay, so what do you have in mind?"

"Get back on the Interstate. We're gonna check into the first hotel we see."

"That's your plan? To let them know *exactly* where we are staying?"

"No, my plan is to give whoever it is something *else* to watch, Cale. We'll check in, call a cab, and sneak out the back door."

"Hmm, not bad, Beck. But who do you think it is?"

"Well, I don't think it's the authorities, so we have to consider the alternative. That snake is still on the chopping block for killing my mother, regardless of whether or not he killed Lucy, and now that Neil is dead, I'm the only one left who can point the finger.

So, it could be him or his entire operation for all we know. I mean, you saw how skittish Paula was. We may have attracted some unwanted attention with all of our digging around."

"Hey, if that's the case, let 'em come."

"I think I'd prefer the cops," I smirk.

We pull out of the cafe parking lot, and within a few short blocks, I direct Cale toward a Howard Johnson Hotel. We decide to park near the entrance—but request a room close to the back—as to not tip off our unwelcomed visitor to the vicinity of our room.

After making our reservation, the host tells us to take the center hallway. But unsure as to whether or not our tail is watching us through the lobby windows, we decide to take the hall to the right, instead. We then exit through the side door and re-enter the hotel from the back.

We locate suite one twenty-four, and once inside, Cale calls for a cab while I begin to stage the scene.

I start by turning on the television and setting the volume high enough to create some buzz, but low enough, to avoid complaints from the neighbors.

Then, I draw the drapes closed and request an early morning wakeup call from the concierge.

"All right, let's go," I say.

I then apply the 'Do Not Disturb' sign on our way out the door.

"You know, it really is scary how calculated your mind works sometimes," Cale says.

"Hey, I started watching C.S.I."

I wink at him, as we leave the hotel to meet our awaiting cab.

After making it to Newport, we settle into a hotel that is located a few short blocks away from the old house.

"We should probably get there before sunrise. To avoid being seen," Cale says.

"Sounds good. Although, after getting a look at the neighborhood, I highly doubt anyone walking these streets would be sober enough to notice us." I sit on the edge of the bed and remove my locket.

"May I?"

Cale reaches his hand out, and I hand it over to him. After carefully unfastening the latch, he opens it up to reveal a picture of my mother, and what is now a picture of Lucy on the other side of it.

Cale brushes his finger across the photo when his expression fades from adoring to sadness.

"I never wanted to be a Lawyer. It's not what I wanted at all. Hell, if I'm being honest, I never wanted to go to Mackland, either. That was my dad's plan, and I hated it—but Lucy made it okay for me. She gave me hope that I could live that life, as long as she was there to live it with me.

"But do you know what eats at me every day? And I mean, every-single-day? That I never told her that. Never one time did I tell my future wife the damn truth about who I was, or what I really wanted to be. She loved a lie." Cale's forehead is creased with regret, as he closes the locket and hands it back over to me.

"Cale, she knew."

He looks at me in complete surprise, "What?"

"She already knew that you felt that way. You're not as covert as you think you are."

"She really knew?" Cale blinks his eyes a few times to fight back the tears.

"Yes, and she planned on telling you that before the wedding, too. She was worried you were under the impression that *she* was set on that life and wouldn't love you otherwise.

"But she didn't care about any of that, Cale. She told me she would have married you whether or not you were an unemployed drifter or a Fireman."

"Wait—she actually said a Fireman?"

"Yep. She talked in high school about how much your face would light up anytime you saw a fire truck pass by." I laugh. "She said your eyes would glaze over like you were a ten-year-old boy, daydreaming about climbing ladders and rescuing some damsel in distress."

Cale's smile in response to this piece of information is so endearing, and it is now, more than ever, that I am indebted to Lucy for confiding in me all those years. What a privilege it is, to possess a prized secret, so beloved, that it would cause that look on his face.

I hope you can see this, Lucy.

"She loved you, Cale. It wouldn't have mattered to her what you did, as long as you did it together."

Cale nods and wipes his eyes with the back of his hand. "Thanks, Cait."

"You're welcome. And hey, you can still make it up to her."

"How?"

"By following your dream. It's not too late, ya know. Make it so that the next woman you fall in love with, knows exactly who you are, and what you want to be."

"Well, actually," he chuckles. "I won't be sharing my 'true self' with the next one either. All plans considered, that is."

And with those words, I feel a colossal pit in my stomach. Cale may have believed that he could not rest until this job was done, but the relief I just watched come over him, tells me there might be some hope left in him yet. He can still be the man he always wanted to be.

He can fall in love, get married, and have children—but if he stays on this path with me, his life could end before it ever began.

And besides, if Daniel Neil did kill Lucy, then her killer is already dead, and what happened to my mother isn't Cale's fight.

"Well, I'm gonna crash," Cale says, drawing back the covers. "We've got an early morning, and I'm wiped out."

I nod in return, as I decide to slip away from this room and explore that house—without him.

46

After retrieving the 9mm pistol from the safe in our room, I was able to sneak away from the hotel without waking Cale.

Using the map on my phone, I reach a back alleyway that appears to run directly behind the house I was held hostage in for so many months. I walk with caution until the arrow on my phone shows that I have reached my destination.

To my right, is a back gate that enters the yard. I carefully release the latch and step through it. After closing it behind me, I turn and face the house.

Even with minimal moonlight, I can see that it has been abandoned for some time now.

I make my way through tall weeds until I've reached the back door. With little hope that it's unlocked, I try the knob anyway and confirm my suspicions.

Just to the left of the porch, however, is a basement window and only one side is boarded up. I quietly hop down into the well and give the window a try, but as expected, it is locked, too.

After turning on my flashlight, I shine a light in the window to look for signs of life, but all I can see is an empty room.

I remove my jacket and place it up against the window. With the butt of my flashlight, I then deliver a muffled—but effective, blow to the glass. While using my sleeve to protect my fingers, I reach around and unlock the window. Once open, I step down into what looks to be more like a crawl space and shine my flashlight around the room.

I listen for any signs of people, or God knows what else, but the house is silent. So, I make my way toward some stairs and slowly hike my way up until I've entered the kitchen.

The room is old and stale, but in the center of it stands a clean table with one chair. In the middle of the table are a plastic bowl, plate, cup, one set of silverware, and an oil lamp.

Someone has been living here?

This possibility calls for every hair on the back of my neck to rise as if some lowly drifter will pop out of hiding at any minute.

While gripping the flashlight in my left hand, I reach down and remove the 9mm with my right. Allowing the firearm to lead the way, I sneak through the kitchen and into the adjoining living room.

As I turn the corner, my ears immediately recall the sound of heavy footsteps dispersing all around the house. A methodical-rhythm of soles created by the S.W.A.T. team that rescued me from my hiding place underneath that bed.

Reaching the staircase, I grip the railing to begin my ascent. My skin suddenly tickles upon recalling the blanket that a S.W.A.T. member had wrapped around me just before we had fled the scene. My eyes follow a ghostly image of us, as it rushes past me down the steps, and out the front door.

I resume my ascent until I finally reach the room I called home for almost six months, and allow the luminescence of my flashlight to lead the way in.

To the right of me, is a metal frame twin bed, just as I had left it— short of the pink ruffled bedspread. The mattress has been tossed aside, exposing its metal springs.

Taking a few more steps inside the room, I recall the sounds of shouting from downstairs, causing me to turn toward the hallway. An imaginary plate of peanut butter sandwiches then slides across the floor toward my feet. A show of kindness and mercy from a beaten and neglected little boy, who longed for the same love and nurturing I longed for as a child—until that kindness turned into resentment after his only friend in captivity had been ripped away from him.

But did Neil's bitterness remain contained to nothing more than a decade of anonymous stalking and obsession? Or was he actually capable of murdering Lucy?

The memory of him, causes me to shift my gaze toward the air return that served as our only pathway to human connection, consoling us for weeks.

I slide down the wall next to the vent and feel oddly comfortable. Leaning my ear against the wall, I lightly give it two taps in remembrance of our endless games of twenty questions.

Turning my attention back toward the bed, I suddenly recall the memory of hiding objects of affection inside a tiny hole in the mattress, which now lies between the metal frame and the wall.

I immediately stand and place my 9mm in its holster, before making my way over to lower the mattress down onto the box spring. While illuminating every inch of fabric, I slowly make my way around the mattress, feeling for an opening.

Halfway into my search, I find what I am looking for, and shine my light inside. Crumpled and stuffed tightly together, are several origami objects.

Bittersweet emotions fill my chest, as I recall how much I had loved receiving them.

Removing each gift, one-by-one, I sit on my bottom to sort through what I have found: More flowers, an elephant, and a heart. Each one filled with messages I would have been too young to read at the time...

> *You are so beautiful...*
> *Things are better with you here...*
> *I'm sorry they took you, but I'm happy that you're*
> *here...*
> *I hope we can always be together...*

Curiosity now demands that I move to the room where Neil once resided. I carefully illuminate each corner of the hall and staircase, before entering his room, and I am immediately floored by what I find.

In all, this is a very well-kept room. Located in the center is a bed, with actual bedding on it. There is a desk in the corner with a chair and on top of that desk is another oil lamp.

I open up the middle drawer to find a journal tucked away inside. A journal with writing I have become all too familiar with, making it clear that Daniel Neil must have been keeping this room, this entire house, like a shrine.

The binding on the journal has a handwritten time stamp of *March 2017*. The inside shows a blank slate, and of course, it will remain that way. Daniel Neil died just after the start of March, so he never got the chance to write in it.

I return it to its rightful place and search through the rest of the drawers when—*Jackpot!*

Located in the bottom right drawer of the desk, are several journals banded together in chronological order. The first one, dated: *December 1999 - June 2000*, the year I was kidnapped, catches my eye. I remove it from the bunch and start flipping through pages:

> *She like's peanut butter...*
> *Her smile is so pretty...*
> *He yelled at her, and I wanted to kill him...*
> *They said she has a buyer coming soon, but I*
> *won't let them take her!*
> *Police came and took us away. My father*
> *escaped and won't come back for me. She is all I have left*
> *now...*

"Oh my God."

Neil wasn't a fellow prisoner at all, but the son of my captor? The man who killed my mother, and deprived me of my childhood—*was a father?* My anger intensifies at the mere thought of it.

I trade the journal for another dated: *December 2006 - June 2007.*

Today was supposed to be the day I would take the swing next to her, and tell her who I am. Remind her of our time together, but she wasn't there…

It's been over a week, and she hasn't been back to the Rec Club. I am worried she will never come back. I have to find out where she is…

Today, I built up the courage to knock on her door, and her foster mom told me she was adopted by that conniving bitch, LUCY'S family! She took her away from me, but I WILL find her!

I continue trading journals in and out, making my way through their various years and entries.

They thought they could keep her away from me, but I'm smarter than ALL of them. I found her in no time at all…

That Lucy seduced me, too. I want to rip out her throat, but her smile is rather exquisite from afar. Maybe she can save me, too. Deliver me from my hell. But I can't talk to her like this. I will have to find a way to clean myself up a bit…

She is blinded by this 'Lucas.' He is nothing more than a weasel! Their love is a farce. He can't offer her what I can…if only she knew…

A JOCK?! He couldn't possibly hold more brain cellsthan players on his team! Their love is continuously flaunted in my face, but I know who she REALLY wants. I will become the man she desires. One of professional stature, and when I do, I will find the words to tell her the truth, and she will be MINE. Someday. ALL mine.

At last, I have found the means to become the man she desires. A fabrication of some records, made possible by my superior ability to manipulate one's emotions. We are quite the pair, but she will never measure up to mi fiori.

Her father was released from prison today. I can't let him find her and ruin what we have...

It was almost too easy. Just a little gasoline, a match, and Marin Jeffries no longer exists. Nobody will ever come between the love I have for mi fiori...

I feel a chill as I set the journal down.

Neil had been cataloging my every move from the time we left this house, until the time he took his own life—or was killed—but either way, he lived a life plagued with obsession and fantasy.

That center mass of vengeance for the man who caused it all, for his father, continues to multiply with each passing minute. Along for the ride, is my rather perverse excitement for the day when I will finally take *his* life into my own hands.

I return the latest journal to the bunch and spot the *'Holy Grail'* dated: *October 2016 - February 2017.* This will outline all events between both Lucy and Neil's death, so I decide to take it with me and slip it into my knapsack.

Scanning the room with my flashlight, I land on the air return, and a faded memory of something hidden inside of it enters my mind.

I walk over and pry the vent from the wall. After carefully placing it to the side, I use the edge of the floor to scoot myself into the opening.

Breaching the darkness with my light, I bend my head down into the shaft to find a gap beneath the floor. The light then catches a glimmer of metal, hidden between the floorboards.

Finding the object with my hand, I pull it out to reveal a lunch box decorated with dinosaurs and an undisturbed layer of dust. I replace the vent and start to lift the latch of the box when I am harshly awakened by the sound of intrusive footsteps coming from downstairs.

I immediately turn off the flashlight and slip the lunchbox into my knapsack with the journal. I then decide to tip-toe toward the hallway for a closer look, all the while praying that what I heard was nothing more than a figment of my imagination.

But my hope is painfully cut short by a glow being cast over the railing from that oil lamp in the kitchen.

Unsure of who might have entered the house, I turn back around to scan the room for an out, but the only window in this room is boarded up like the rest.

The front door is my only remaining option.

I sneak into the hall and feel for the railing with only the faint glow of that lamp to guide me. I grip it tight and close my eyes to heighten my hearing. The sounds that follow suggest that someone is unloading a grocery sack in the kitchen, but who?

Daniel Neil is dead, and I doubt a homeless person would bother with keeping his belongings in such pristine conditions—*Oh shit! His father!*

The snake is still in hiding, and where better to hide, than your own, run down, and forgotten home?

And once more, if the snake was our tail in Richmond, this dwelling puts him close enough to leave his post for some shut-eye before resuming his pursuit tomorrow.

I frantically debate on whether or not I should fight or flee when a pit in my stomach tells me that it's time to stop running and do what I came here to do. *It is time for you to kill him, Cait.*

But how? I could attempt to sneak down the stairs and shoot him with my nine-millimeter—but what if he hears me coming, and has one aimed at me when I get down there, instead?

Yeah, going downstairs was a bad idea.

As this internal debate continues, my focus becomes less concerned with holding still and my foot shifts positions inadvertently. The slip causes a creak in the floor, which then prompts an immediate release of cortisol into my bloodstream.

I wish for my presence to go unnoticed, at least long enough to come up with a plan for attack, when it occurs to me the activity from the kitchen has stopped. I open my eyes to see a shadow enter the living room and do my best to quietly slip into the nearest room—also known as my childhood prison.

After carefully removing the gun from my hip, I adjust my vision in the dark and search for a place to hide, but there is just one option before me.

No, please. I can't.

The sight of the twin bed fills me with vertigo when the faded memory of Lucy's efforts to 'beat my nightmares' suddenly appears in its place. The faint echoes of her voice…the pocket knife…our initials...

"You don't have to be afraid anymore, Cait..."

Tears stream down my cheeks as I force myself to lay face-down on the floor, and slide underneath the bed while maintaining my view of the door.

After a lifetime of nauseating anticipation, I hear the footsteps finally reach the top landing of the stairs and begin to travel down the hallway toward me.

A rapid trauma response induces a playback of past nightmares and silent prayers for God's protection and guidance. I close my eyes and pray for him to see me through this one, too. For my mother and Lucy, to help see me through.

Just then, the stranger's feet announce their arrival near my door, causing my eyes to fly open. I squint through the crack under the bed, just in time to see the dark shadow creeping its way past my door and into Neil's bedroom, instead.

Once I am certain the footsteps are well-inside, I carefully scoot out from my hiding place and creep into the hallway. While holding the nine-millimeter pistol in my left hand, I carefully grip the top and cock it backward. I then slink up against the wall and attempt to peek into Neil's bedroom, but as my vision adapts, the figure standing in front of the desk becomes more visible, and it's *not* one of familiarity. This outline is far from the burly man I remember in my nightmares.

Must be a drifter.

The oil lamp on the desk suddenly turns on, prompting me to flee. I reach the stairs and tip-toe my way down. The drifter may not be the man who killed my mother, but for all I know, he is far worse.

Upon reaching the bottom of the stairs, I slide against the living room wall to avoid from being seen over the upstairs railing, but the instant I enter the kitchen, my survival instincts become less concerned with being seen, and far more desperate for freedom.

So, after what could only be described as an Olympic-worthy leap, I reach the back door, and quickly unlock the deadbolt.

Upon turning the knob, however, the door fails to open and my nerves become frayed. I double check the deadbolt and knob again, to verify they are indeed, unlocked, but the door will not open.

A blanket of dread overwhelms my circuits when I realize that I am trapped in this house—*AGAIN!*

Just then, I hear some movement in the room above me, which throws my panic into overdrive.

Scanning the door, I look up to see another cross latch positioned at the top of it. Too far up to reach, I pick up the kitchen chair and place it next to the door. The second I step onto the seat, I hear the footsteps from above start to make their way down the stairs.

I urgently reach up and unlock the latch.

Stepping off the chair, I turn the doorknob and feel instant relief by the cold night air that greets me.

Breaking free, I duck and run through the weeds toward the back gate. With each panicked step replacing the other, I run for my life, all the while expecting that whoever was in that house will reach out at any moment, and yank me back inside.

I'm nothing short of relieved when I finally reach the back gate without incident. I slip into the alleyway and pick up my speed.

Without looking back, I flee the scene with my heart in my stomach, and a knapsack of evidence on my back.

47

I walk back into the hotel, praying that Cale is still asleep, but the cussing I hear on the other side of the door when I get there makes it painfully clear that he is not.

I reluctantly insert my key card and walk in the room. Cale is swearing on my voicemail, which will be sent to a powered-down phone in my purse. He suddenly hears me walk in and tosses his phone on the bed.

"Where in the hell have you been? Do you have any idea how worried I've been? DO YOU? I mean, dammit Cait! We've got God knows who, out there following us, and only God knows for how long!"

Cale turns to walk over to a chair in the corner of the room and sits down. Resting his right elbow onto the sidearm of the chair, he begins to rub the stress from his forehead.

"You have NO idea how scared I was, Cait."

"I'm sorry...but I just couldn't take you with me."

"What?"

Cale looks up, and his expression prevents me from saying another word. Then, with a wind of exasperation, he leans forward, drops his forearms onto his thighs, and clasps his hands together.

"Please don't tell me you went to that house without me. Just please, don't tell me that's where you've been."

Cale closes his eyes, hoping to hear some other excuse, but I remain silent. So, he opens his eyes and looks up at me.

"Did you?"

I clear my throat, which suddenly feels like it hasn't seen a drop of water in days.

"Yes, but—"

"Ah, JESUS, Cait!"

Cale stands up and rubs the front of his face down with both hands. His dirty-blonde hair is tossed, and his blue eyes are full of fear and frustration. He walks over to sit on the bed and puts on a pair of white Nike's.

Then, after grabbing a navy-blue hoodie from his overnight bag, Cale slides each one of his arms into the sleeves and pulls it up and over his head. His aggravation is immeasurable, and I can tell that he is fighting hard to bite his tongue.

"Cale, where are you going?"

Avoiding my gaze, he reaches behind me to fetch his keys and heads for the door. He cracks it open and pauses. He doesn't turn around, just stands there holding the doorknob.

"You know what, Cait? Sometimes you can be so selfish."

Cale walks out of the room and slams the door behind him, as his words punch me right in the gut.

Sure, I know I can be selfish sometimes, but hearing someone say it out loud, carries an incredible sting.

I sink onto the bed and attach my phone to the charger. It turns back on and Cale's slew of texts and voicemails start to roll in...one after another...like tiny sirens exhibiting his panic.

I close my eyes and feel my heart break with each ping. I try to call him, but the buzzing on the bed nearby makes it clear that he left his phone behind.

Serves you right.

I feel the tears starting to flow, as I sit in my shame. I finally walk over to the window to see if I can see him anywhere, but it's just an empty parking lot. I close the curtains and debate on what to do next, when I hear the key card and turn to face his return.

Donning nothing short of exhaustion, Cale walks back in the room and stops halfway between me and the door, fiddling with his keys.

"I was going to make you sit here and worry about me for a few hours, but I just couldn't do it."

Cale tosses his keys aside and looks me in the eye.

"You can't do that to me again, Cait."

"I know."

"Do you? Do you really know? Because sometimes I don't think you have a fucking clue. I think you've gotten used to doing things on your own and you prefer it that way now. You don't think twice about rushing in to help someone you care about, and yet none of us are allowed to do the same for you. And it's such bullshit, too, because you're not alone anymore, Cait. And you are not the only one who is affected by the choices you make, either."

"Cale, you just seemed so full of hope after our talk earlier. I was worried you felt obligated—"

"Oh, no. Don't do that. Not with me, because I'm here. We're in this together, you and I, and I haven't given you one goddamn reason to leave me out of this race. I'm all in, Cait. All in."

I wipe the tears that are involuntarily leaving my eyes with my sleeve. I take a step toward Cale, but he immediately puts his hand up to stop me.

"No." He keeps his hand up and locks his eyes with mine. "I need you to promise me something, Cait—no, you know what? Fuck that."

He takes a step closer and points his finger in my direction. "You *will* promise me, that you will never put me through that again. And if you give a shit about me at all, Cait, you will keep that promise to me. Because if you don't, I will walk away. I will walk away from you, and do this on my own."

The wind is instantly knocked out of me, as I imagine Cale leaving my world. The truth is, I'm afraid. Afraid of loving, afraid of loss, and I've never questioned my methods to avoid any of it—*until now.*

I will forfeit every defense that I have, if keeping them, means losing Cale in the process.

I open my mouth to admit how willing I am to wave the white flag. To finally let my guard down and say—out loud—that losing his friendship would devastate me. At the very *least*, Cale deserves to hear that from me right now.

But that innate fear of rejection continues to choke my words when I suddenly notice through the blur of my eyes that Cale's posture has softened.

"Cait, I know you're afraid, and I understand why, but don't you get it? I'm the one at risk here, not you. This resistance you're giving me right now? I stand to lose far more in this relationship, because of it."

"I know." I nod. "And I promise, I will never do that to you again. Whatever you need from me, I'll do it. Just…" I wipe away more tears. "Please, don't go."

Cale moves in and wraps his arms around my neck to pull me into the most comforting embrace. I immediately grab onto his sweatshirt and rest my head against his chest.

"Thank you for coming back," I say.

"Yeah, well, who am I kidding? I couldn't get rid of you if I tried."

I step back and shove him, which causes him to fall onto the bed laughing.

My knapsack, which was teetering on the edge of the bed, suddenly falls to the floor, and the lunchbox I collected slips out.

"Hey, what's that?" Cale asks.

"I found it inside the air vent that separated my room from Neil's." I pick it up. "I haven't had a chance to look inside of it yet because I got interrupted."

Cale's jaw tightens, causing me to regret my words and redirect, "I also brought back his most recent journal."

I remove the memoir from my bag and hand it over to Cale, before then, taking a seat in front of him to explore the lunchbox.

I open the latch and lift the lid to find a treasure trove of pictures. The first photo I see reveals a young woman in her twenties cradling a baby in a rocking chair. Behind the picture is a newspaper article, but before I can explore it further, Cale looks up from Neil's journal.

"Hey, listen to this, August sixth, two thousand sixteen: 'He ran away like a coward, and all I have to remember him by are the burn scars he inflicted after I'd failed to keep a close eye on his victims. I was weak then, and he was right to punish me, but I am far from weak now. I have become stronger and more masterful than he ever was. These scars are no longer deserved.

"So, first thing tomorrow morning, I will honor my father by covering them up with his signature tattoo. I will wear it proudly until the day we finally reunite as father and son.'" Cale crumples up the page and tosses it across the room.

"Well, Cait? There's the confirmation you were looking for. He had the motive, the obsession, and *now* we know, he had that same fucked-up tattoo."

"So, it was him."

"Yep. That son of a bitch killed Lucy and *then* took the easy way out before I could get my hands on him. Fucking coward!"

Cale brings his hands up to the back of his head with his eyes closed and exhales. I know this confirmation has him feeling immensely ripped-off for not being the one to take Neil's life, and I admit that I feel the same.

But Neil isn't the only one on the chopping block for us. He didn't kill my mother.

So, while I can't help BUT feel the same irritation that Cale does—especially when I consider that we did just have him in our bare fucking hands—and RIGHT before he killed his mother, too!

Oh, boy, Cait. Breathe.

I close my eyes and try to reign in my anger.

After all, there is still someone out there who deserves the fate that Cale and I had intended for Neil, so we have got to keep our eye on the prize, and aim our rage forward.

"Remember, Cale. The head of the snake."

He nods, and releases another stream of air, before finally opening his eyes to continue his search through journal pages.

I return my attention to the photo I am holding and spot a label on the back that reads: "Carol and Isaac". The newspaper article I found with it outlines the details behind the death of *'Carol Stalin, mother to four-year-old Isaac Stalin.'*

"Oh my God, Cale. I think I just found our best lead yet."

"And what's that?"

"Well, first of all, it looks like Neil's real name was Isaac Stalin."

"Makes sense. You were given a new name, too."

"Yes, but now we have a *real* name to search, and according to this article, his mother's name was Carol Stalin."

"Does it say anything about his scum-sucking father in that article?"

I scan through each sentence. "No. Just that his mother died of an 'accidental' overdose."

"So that woman he gassed himself with, wasn't his real mother, then."

"I would guess that he was eventually adopted like I was."

Cale raises an eyebrow, and whistles while shaking his head. "Man, you two really did lead parallel lives, Cait."

"Yeah, until they crossed paths, and he murdered my best friend!"

"Well, what do you say we stop by the cemetery after we're done here, and dance on his grave a little bit."

I chuckle. "Yeah, sure. We'll just stop by and do a little jig."

"Oh, what I wouldn't give to see you jig, Caitlin Beck."

Cale laughs, and the joyful sarcasm in his voice takes me back to a time when the sole focus of our friendship was centered around who could nail the other one, with the wittiest comeback.

"What-da-ya say we put the celebration on hold until we've killed every last one of them first," I say.

"Fair enough. And hey, once we finally *do* kill them all, we can sprinkle their ashes across Neil's grave before I piss on it."

Cale's attempts to lighten the mood finally pay off, and my veiled laugh bursts through pierced lips.

"There she is." He smiles.

"You know, we truly are disturbed individuals, Cale."

"Undeniably so."

Cale winks at me and unfolds a faded piece of paper when—"Holy shit! I just found his birth certificate! '*Isaac Stalin*, born October thirty-first, nineteen ninety-one—'"

"He was born on Halloween? You're joking, right?"

"Nope. You couldn't make this shit up."

"Wait a minute, that would mean he was twenty-five when he died."

"Right. So?"

"So, Daniel Neil was twenty-eight, Cale. Or at least that is what the news report said."

"Well, his dad was still out there when the two of you were removed from that house. Maybe the Feds had to change his age to ensure his safety."

"Yeah, you're probably right."

"So, do you think we can move on from discussing his age now? I mean, I know how groundbreaking that was."

"You may proceed, smart ass."

"Thanks, I appreciate that. Especially since you cut me off before I had a chance to read the best part. It *also* says here that he was born in Harrisburg, Virginia to Carol and *Edgar* Stalin."

"Edgar," I state back.

"Yeah. Edgar." Cale smiles.

"Well, I gotta say, I'm encouraged. Now that we have their names, we can run them all through one of your nifty Google searches, and come up with something useful," I say.

"Or maybe someone else could run that search for us. Someone who has access to the Feds records."

"Cale, no."

"I'm just sayin—"

"Well, don't."

"Look, all I'm asking is that you *at least* consider bringing in Luke. We could use the help. And remember, according to him, the Feds access to information far exceeds my Google searches."

"Fine. I'll think about it."—*No, I won't.*

Just then, I come across a photo with several men crowded together in a half circle. Each one is holding their right sleeve back to flaunt the very tattoo that Neil aka *Isaac Stalin,* was referring to so proudly. I scan each face in the photo, one-by-one, and count a total of fifteen. Fifteen men involved in the abduction of God knows how many children, and there could easily be more.

Too many to find without help.

My attention is suddenly pulled in the direction of a little boy standing off to the side. The date stamp tells me he was just eight years old at the time of the photo. He is admiring the men with a deep sadness and longing in his eyes.

A chill runs through my body, as I absorb the image in front of me. The face of a boy, surrounded by a sadistic gang of men, who devoted their lives to exploiting the innocent. A little boy raised by the very man who inflicted so much pain and suffering onto me, and everyone around me.

My stare burns a hole in the last face that Lucy saw when she died, and once again, my inner psyche finds itself the target of an excruciating case of sensory overload. Within my grasp, lies the solution to a puzzle I have been fighting so hard to find, but now, so desperately long to forget.

A confusing whirlwind of images from our time together invokes an immediate urge to vomit.

Then, as if a switch has abruptly turned off, I am filled with a harsh sense of nothingness. Void of all emotion, my sights become callously directed toward the promise of complete resolution before me.

At last, I have found what I am looking for, but it's complicated now, and there are just too many of them to find. Unfortunately, we *will* need some help to pull this off.

"All right, Cale. As much as I hated the idea before, you were right." I hand over my find. "We are going to have to involve Luke."

48

I carry my overnight bags to the parking lot and pass them off to Cale.

"How are you feeling?" he asks me.

I take in a nice deep breath, as a welcomed thought of impending peace washes over me.

"Eager," I reply

"Hold the train!"

I turn to see that Lucas is hustling down the walkway, overnight bags in tow.

"Did you get it?" Cale asks him.

"Yep. We're golden." Luke flashes a sly grin.

I step into the car, wishing that Luke didn't have to be involved in this way, but unfortunately, it couldn't be avoided. There wasn't a single piece of information in Isaac's memoirs that would help us find Edgar and the other fourteen men in that photograph. So, it became clear to both Cale and me, that to pull this off, we would need the type of information that only Luke could provide us—and it would be impossible for us to request what we needed from Luke, without taking him with us. The inevitable anxiety that would ensue by not knowing what we were up to would deem him too unpredictable, and we just can't take that risk.

So, that left Cale and me with only one option: Allow Luke to be involved enough to prevent an explosive response—but not enough—to know of our entire plan. For Luke, this would just be a recognizance mission.

We hit the highway toward Singer's Glen, Virginia, where according to Luke, was Edgar Stalin's last known place of residence.

Conveniently located just five miles outside of Singer's Glen, is a cabin belonging to Cale's family, where we plan to set up post.

I sink back into the headrest when my phone starts to buzz. I attempt to ignore it, but it's persistent. I reach into my bag and see that it's Will. I give the side of the phone two clicks, sending it straight to voicemail, before then shutting it off completely.

"So, what else did you come up with, Luke?" Cale asks.

"A lot. Although, I didn't find much on Isaac. His records must have burned up in that fire with yours, Cait, but I found a lot on his parents. Edgar Stalin was raised by the system, spending most of his life in and out of prison. He was being investigated for sex trafficking but disappeared from the FBI's radar about a year before your abduction. And as you already know, Carol Stalin, tragically died from a heroin overdose."

Luke hands me a manila folder, and I remove its contents to find mug shots of the man who killed my mother. His familiar eyes express nothing short of evil.

"I did find some child abuse charges involving Isaac though," Luke continues. "Burns that were inflicted by his father. He's a sick son of a bitch, I gotta say."

"Yeah, well. The apple didn't fall far from the tree, did it?" I look back at him.

"Well, at least Neil had the common decency to take himself out."

"Not Neil." Cale corrects him, "Isaac."

"Same difference," Luke says.

"Right," I say.

I continue sifting through the valuable information compiled in my lap.

"So? What do you think?" Cale asks me.

"I guess we should start with Singers Glen as planned, and see what we come up with. Maybe he's been back there since he lived there last."

"And no doubt some of the locals will know who the Stalin's are. I mean, that town only has like, a thousand people living in it," Luke adds.

Just then, we reach the entrance to a driveway that is heavily guarded by a rod iron gate. Cale types in some numbers on the keypad, and it opens.

The road before us is paved with black gravel, and lined with endless trees and shrubbery. Once we reach the end of it, Cale turns off the engine.

After exiting the car, Luke takes both of our bags from the trunk and heads up the white wooden steps connected to a white wrapped porch.

"It's open," Cale says, and Luke heads inside.

I am now aware of the beautiful gardens surrounding the property and look over at Cale.

"Cabin?"

"Yeah, well. I find that 'cabin' is just another word for vacation home these days." Cale smiles, and motions toward the white cottage before us. "Shall we?"

"Ladies first," I say, with a smile.

Cale takes the lead, and I follow him up the stairs and into the house.

Once we have entered the foyer, our attention is pulled toward the large living room on the left.

While the house appears to be fully furnished elsewhere, this room is empty—except for Luke, who has fallen onto his knees with his back turned toward us. Directly in front of him is the metal lunchbox I discovered inside Isaac's room, with a single photograph on top of it.

"See something familiar?" I ask him.

Luke's eyes remain locked on the image below, as he stretches his left hand out from his lap, slowly curls each finger into a fist, and knocks on the wooden floor beneath us—*twice*.

49

With Luke's knock, I instantly recall the moment when I first laid eyes on the photograph he is holding. An image of fifteen sadistic men, and a sad little boy with three freshly made cigarette burns on his upper arm. A little boy with a familiar face.

The face of a friend.

The face of Lucas.

The moment I'd laid eyes on him, a devastating surge of confusion overwhelmed me, but once it had finally settled, I knew everything...

Lucas *is* Isaac.

Lucas was in that house with me.

Lucas found me and befriended all of us.

Lucas framed Daniel Neil.

And Lucas killed Lucy.

At that moment, Lucas died. He was no longer the close and trusted friend that Cale and I had thought he was. He was no longer the friend I once shared toffee peanuts with, and laughed with, and cried with. He was *Isaac Stalin*—a sociopathic monster, who gained our love and trust by using ruthless manipulation. He then *used* that trust to murder someone who loved him dearly.

That very fact morphed the rage that Cale and I had previously felt, into something far greater than when he was previously believed to be a stranger.

It became *personal.*

Cale and I remain silent, as Isaac rips up the photograph and sprinkles the pieces into his lunch box. He slowly rises to his feet, prompting Cale's casual posture to shift into a defensive one.

Isaac turns around to face us, and the curvature of his right eyebrow bears the signature of a serial killer. The pupils of his eyes have widened, and his grin has turned baneful.

Like a predator observing his prey, Isaac exudes a darkness that mocks the face I once believed to be a friend—*but that never existed.*

"So..." Isaac casually removes his glasses, and blows hot air onto the lenses, before rubbing them clean with the bottom of his shirt. "What is this, an IN-TER-VENTION?" he hisses.

"Something like that," Cale responds.

"All right, so tell me then—" Isaac puts his glasses back on before unexpectedly banging his hands together. "WHAT'S it gonna be? An FBI raid? A straight jacket?" He chuckles. "I mean, all you've got is a stupid photo."

"Oh, I'd say we have more than that," Cale says.

I bend down to retrieve the journal entries from my bag. Then, without removing my glare from his eyes, I slowly begin to circle the room.

While swiftly sliding my right hand across the stack of pages, I bitterly make it rain by ejecting each page into the air around him.

I feel nothing but anger toward this person, who abused the love we had for him—who abused the love that *Lucy* had for him. He is nothing short of a liar, and my rage has created a disconnect between the man I thought he was, and the man he actually *is.*

"My *beloved* Lucy..." I slowly begin to mimic his words with intense malice as I continue to circle him.

"How I once longed for your love and affection. The taste of your lips...I remember them like it was yesterday. But you left me. I did everything to become what you desired. A big college man with a bright and prosperous future. And even though you still chose him over me, I FORGAVE you anyway! I was still GRACIOUS enough, to give you another chance! But you refused my advances, Lucy. Refused to let me take his place."

Upon my return to the doorway, I stop and look Isaac dead in the eye. "And for THAT, I *had* to kill you." I grit my teeth, as I toss the remaining pages onto the floor.

Isaac's face is blank, as he starts to clap his hands slowly. "Bravo, il mio fiore. But sadly, it is true. I *did* have to kill her. I mean, she just wouldn't listen to reason, and I can't for the life of me figure out why! I mean, I made my way into Brunick Solutions, for Christ's sake! Even you've gotta give me some credit for that one, Cait."

"You know I would if the credit actually belonged to you."

"Oh, that's right!" Cale pokes, "I was going to thank you for the information you gathered for us on your loser of a father, but I guess I should save those props for Angie."

Isaac chuckles and waves his finger. "I do have to admit, that was mighty clever of you. Ya know, getting me involved in your plan just long enough to get me here. Impressive strategy. Even for you, Cale."

"Well, we needed the information, and you made it abundantly clear in your journal that you no longer trusted us after we'd chosen to question Neil *without* your help. You know—after you went out of your way to frame him," I respond while folding my arms.

"Hey, it was *you*, who gave me someone to blame. I just followed your lead. So, technically, that one is your fault."

I painfully recall Isaac's strategy to frame Neil laid out in his journal, after Cale and I had so blindly announced our suspicions of him.

And like any sociopath would, Isaac *then* seized the opportunity to plant journal pages and origami work throughout Neil's dwelling on campus during his "recon" mission, before we searched it.

"You didn't have to kill him!" I shout.

"Hey, I only planned to frame him, but the two of you insisted that we keep what we found a secret from the police—which I found to be rather odd coming from the two people who *supposedly* loved her most. It was then that I began to follow the two of you around. And hey, for what it's worth, I hadn't exactly planned on killing the guy when I first got to his apartment, either. I mean, I only wanted to know what you two had talked to him about, but he *saw* me kill her."

Cale and I glance at each other in a show of confusion and Isaac raises an eyebrow.

"Oh, I'm sorry, did you not know that?"

We both remain silent, and Isaac laughs.

"OOPS! Guess I forgot to mention that one in my journal. Sorry about that. Any-who, I showed up after the two of you had suddenly vanished, and there was instant fear in his eyes when he opened the door. I knew right then and there that he knew what I had done, and well? I just couldn't let him live after that."

I shudder, as I recall the earlier warning of danger that Neil had given us about the crazy things that love can make someone do. A warning I misread *entirely*.

"And hey," Isaac continues, "if you would have just included me in your plan to visit Neil's apartment, I wouldn't have needed to do that. It's not my fault you're disloyal friends."

"*Disloyal?!* Did you really just use that fucking word with us?! You don't know the first thing about what it means to be *loyal*!"

"Now, that is just not true, Cait." Isaac says calmly, "Angie is a prime example of loyalty. When I needed to present flawless transcripts to get into Mackland, she made it happen. When I needed to get into Brunick Solutions, she made it happen. *She* is the epitome of loyalty."

"Oh—PLEASE! Does Angie even know who you *really* are?!" I shout.

Isaac places his hand over his heart. "Oh, she knows that I too am just a lowly outcast." He then drops his hand, rolls his eyes, and laughs. "Or maybe that's just her. She was a sad and needy misfit who needed someone to love her, and I unselfishly gave her my affection. So, giving me something in return, was the very least she could do."

"Shit, you are *far* more certifiable that I thought you were," Cale says.

"Certifiable? Really, Cale? Because I would say that Lucy was the certifiable one. I mean, what beautiful, intelligent girl, wants to marry *you*? What could you possibly offer a woman like that? A life of you, sitting on the couch watching sports, while she tended to your many spawn—who no doubt, would have been just as dumb as you are!"

"Dumb is needing someone to hack into a computer so they can get into college," Cale's says.

"Well, if they wouldn't have taken Cait from me, I wouldn't have needed to run away from my foster parents home, and drop out of school! I wouldn't have needed to steal clothing—*just* to fit in—and I wouldn't have needed to bounce around from one hostel to the next, completely void of roots!"

"Not to mention a soul!"

"Oh, BOO-hoo, Cait. So, you lost a friend. BIG DEAL! I lost my parents!" Isaac suddenly puts his hand up to his mouth and giggles. "Oh, wait—I completely forgot about your mom."

"I swear to GOD I am going to make you pay for all of this!" I shout.

Just then, Cale reaches over and touches my arm. I am always lecturing him on keeping our emotions in check, and yet here I am allowing mine to take over.

"And exactly how do you plan on '*making me pay*,' Cait? Once again, all you have are some journal pages and a few photos. I could easily destroy them, just as I destroyed your records in that fire. So, you see, I still have the upper hand in all of this."

"Oh, but I beg to differ," Cale says.

"Oh, BUT I DO, Cale!"

Isaac begins to walk in circles and talk with his hands, "See, no matter what happens today, I will ALWAYS be at the center of your torment. I will always be the one who made your worthless lives forever shrouded in her blood"—Isaac pounds his fist against his chest— "ME! I DID THAT! I *sqeeeeeezed* the life right out of her!"

Just then, Isaac's expression dramatically changes to one of *sincere* pleading. He stops walking and directs an eerie, almost *child-like*, gaze in my direction.

"Don't you see, Cait? She came between us. We had a special bond, and then *she* came along, and took it all away from me!"—He laughs— "And THEN! Then, she tricked me into believing that she cared about me. That she loved me even!"

Isaac's expression abruptly changes back to anger. "But she was A LIAR! She made a fool out of me! Out of *us*!"

"She did love you! We all did!" I shout in return.

"NO! She screwed me!" Isaac tsks, as he starts to circle the room again. "And I just never guessed her to be someone who would spend the rest of her life with someone so mindless." He stops and tips his head down, to peer at Cale over the tops of his glasses. "But hey, buddy, for what it's worth? I did try to talk some sense into her. I tried telling her that she was misguided, and needed to remember what it was like being at the center of my affections. Hell, I even kissed her." He chuckles, as he throws his hands up in the air. "But she pushed me away. SHE—pushed ME—AWAY! HA!" Isaac shakes his head and chuckles again, "Ungrateful bitch."

Cale takes a step forward, and I immediately raise my arm out to stop *him* now.

"Oooh...something I said, Cale?" Isaac places his hand over his mouth, before lowering it back down. "You'll have to excuse me for not giving a fuck."

Cale allows his posture to relax again.

"Nah, you know what? Keep running your mouth, asshole. You're just making it easier."

"Oh, and what are you gonna do, frat boy? Hire a hitman with daddy's money?"

"At least I have a daddy."

Cale's comeback has triggered a look of rage to form across Isaac's face.

"*Oooh, something I said, Isaac?*" Cale hisses.

"You know, I *reallllyyyy* wish you could have been there, Cale—seen her face. I mean, what a sight it was to see her *beg* and *plead* for her life as I STRANGLED THE SHIT RIGHT OUT OF HER!"

Cale bursts forward, just as Isaac takes a momentous leap, and launches the lunch box from the center of the floor toward Cale's face. He then takes advantage of the distraction, by shoving Cale against the wall.

Cale is abruptly knocked off his feet, causing his firearm to break loose from his grip.

I immediately reach around to find mine, when Isaac then slams me against the wall. Within seconds, he has wrapped his hands around my neck, and with a blinding rage, begins to methodically apply pressure. The look in his eyes is so tyrannical and cruel. I feel a stream of tears trail down my cheeks, as I find myself wanting to call out to my former friend. A 'friend' I once thought would never hurt me. I frantically search his eyes, but that person is nowhere to be found—*Because he never existed, Cait!*

I slide my forearms up between Isaac's and urgently push against them, desperately trying to break free from his grip, but his pressure only amplifies, causing my vision to become skewed.

Just then, Isaac's head is suddenly jerked backward by Cale's generous grip of his hair.

Cale flings him against the opposing wall like a rag doll and makes a beeline for his sternum, but just as he is about to make contact, Isaac reaches into his back pocket and removes a pocketknife.

"LOOK OUT!"

I shout to warn Cale but it's too late. I watch in horror and astonishment as the knife viciously pierces his side and he falls to the floor.

Oh my God, NO!

Once again, I grip my firearm and cock it backward, when Isaac grips onto my wrist and tries to take the gun away from me. We stumble around the living room, when he suddenly backhands me across the face, violently sending me to the floor.

After landing on my side, the impact causes the gun to fly from my hand. I quickly roll onto my stomach and attempt to reach for the handle, when I'm blinded by a crushing blow to my right wrist by Isaac's boot. I scream in pain, as he kneels down and gets close to my ear. "Uh-uh-uh, Cait. I don't think so."

Isaac grabs the pistol from my hand and inadvertently releases the cartridge from its handle. He then chuckles in response, and tosses the cartridge out of the room, before dropping the pistol back onto the floor next to me.

I roll onto my back to face him when I catch some movement coming from Cale.

Isaac instantly follows my gaze, and upon seeing Cale, rolls his eyes and turns back around to face me.

"WOW! He is a stubborn son of a bitch, isn't he?" Isaac raises his pointer finger up. "Would you excuse me for a moment?"

Then, while raising his knife, Isaac turns back around to face Cale, when he is abruptly knocked off his feet by the sweeping of Cale's leg against his ankles. The knife flies from Isaac's hand and lands next to Cale, who then snatches it up, and skims the blade across Isaac's thigh.

Their tussle continues, as I slowly inch my battered body across the floor toward the gun behind me, all the while careful not to take my eyes off Isaac.

I continue to watch as he manages to get away from Cale's clutches and stagger to his feet.

Cale does his best to stand in succession, but Isaac dropkicks him in the face, sending him back to the floor. Then, while applying pressure to a bleeding thigh, Isaac spots Cale's nine-millimeter on the floor and stumbles his way over to pick it up.

"You know, Cale, this really is a somber day. I mean, it didn't have to come to this. It wasn't *your* fault she was such a manipulative bitch." Isaac is short of breath, as he picks up the gun.

While keeping an eye on his every move, I slowly reach my left hand back until I feel the cold steel of the pistol beneath my fingertips. I then rise to my feet, just as Isaac begins to taunt Cale by teetering the gun back and forth with his words.

"You—were just too—damn stupid—to know what she was capable of." Isaac stops and points the firearm at Cale.

"Uh-uh-uh. I don't think so," I mock, gripping the gun with my uninjured left-hand—*my dominant hand.*

Isaac turns around and instantly laughs at the sight of the gun. "MAN! It is a good thing you're pretty, Cait!" He chuckles some more, then finally points toward the removed cartridge resting in the foyer. "I emptied it, remember?"

"Yeah, I remember." I take aim. "But you missed one."

As the last bit of air leaves my lungs, I thoroughly pull back on the trigger and the bullet lands right between Isaac's eyes. The blow to his forehead induces a look of shock on his face when he is abruptly-knocked off his feet.

Stunned by the blast, I just stand in place.

Once the ringing in my ears subsides, I maintain my aim and slowly walk toward him; in search of final confirmation.

My heartbeat thuds loudly in my ears, when Isaac's face suddenly comes into view. His eyes are open, but there is no life. No more anger between his brow. No more taunting. No more Isaac.

No more Lucas.

My breathing becomes deep and rapid, as the shock of what I have just done starts to register.

That "peace" I'd expected to follow this moment, has yet to show itself, as my rational mind struggles to reconcile with the lifeless result of rage in front of me. Instead, grief overtakes my limbs, and I collapse down onto my knees.

That hole left from my childhood has widened, and I am more than willing to surrender myself to it when Cale is suddenly next to me. He takes the gun from my hands, which startles me from my stupor.

"Oh my God, Cale. What have I done?"

With his right hand applying pressure to a bleeding wound on his side, Cale uses his left hand to sweep the hair away from my forehead.

My eyes connect with all the love and compassion inside of his, and I immediately start to cry.

"Hey, it's okay. Shh…" Cale moves his hand from my hair to gently grip the back of my neck, urging me forward.

Feeling lifeless and weak, I accept Cale's invitation and slink toward him. He pulls me into his arms, and we fall back against the wall.

Hyperventilation meets a barrage of sobs when a heavy dose of old and suppressed pain *finally* breaches the surface.

I bury my face in Cale's chest and begin to cry uncontrollably. He gathers my body up into his lap and tightens his grip around me. The warmth of his breath on my head provides solace, as he begins to lightly stroke my hair.

"Shhh, it's all right, Cait. It's all right. This time, it's me, who's got you."

EPILOGUE

After falsely reporting to authorities, that our weekend getaway with friends became an unexpected plan for Isaac to kill us, we now find ourselves sitting on the tailgate of an ambulance in front of Cale's vacation home.

Paramedic's diagnosed Cale's stab wound as a "mild laceration in need of stitches," and I was diagnosed with "soft tissue damage." Neither of which requires an emergent trip to the E.R.

I only wish the damage to my psyche was that benign. The inner peace I'd expected to follow the killer's death continues to be a farce. It's a peace I believe to have overly-romanticized like any highly emotional person would do, and as a Psych major, I should have seen this coming.

Allowing such volatile emotions to pave the way, is sure to produce devastating results. I have taken someone's life, and while his inner monster led to justification at the time, my rational mind is now condemning that behavior by reminding myself of his inner *good*.

Endless late-night conversations, and adorned inside jokes that can only be formed by a close friend's observance of your blunders. The many hugs and healing laughter when I needed it.

A peanut butter sandwich when I needed it.

Isaac was an abused child, deprived of love, who somehow found it within himself to lend me some compassion when all hope was lost.

So, peace was never meant to make an appearance on this day. Not by killing someone I had loved so dearly and *believed* to love me, in return.

I was never meant to experience anything more than grief and despair. For no matter, how insidious Isaac turned out to be, I still lost *Lucas*, and my love for *him* was very real.

And so, here it is, I have lost yet another loved one. The body count is devastating, not to mention infuriating, and while I'm left to drown in this pool of exponential loss, the very source of it all roams free. Free of remorse. Free from persecution. Free to live.

But not for long.

Edgar and I share no ties. No laughs. No late-night conversations. Just a bitter hatred.

And so, it will be *Edgar's* death that is sure to grant me that inner peace that I long for.

As for right now, however, I would settle for a week's worth of sleep.

Wrapped in a blanket, Cale and I sit together in silence. Riddled with overwhelming exhaustion, I rest my head on his right shoulder. He wraps his arm around my waist in return and kisses the top of my head.

"How ya doin', slugger?"

"Not great."

"Yeah." He rests his chin on my head. "Me neither. Although, technically, you did save my life."

"Just let me know where to send the bill."

Cale laughs and kisses my forehead again.

I maintain my forward gaze until I hear a familiar voice to my right. I lift my head to see that another officer is chauffeuring Will toward us.

"Oh boy." I sigh. "Looks like my acting skills are about to be tested."

"Nah, you'll do fine. I'm not worried about it."

"But you said it yourself, Cale. If he can read me, half as well as you can, we're screwed."

"Yeah." Cale limps off the tailgate. "But I don't think he can." His eyes become soft, amidst an esteemed grin. He then pats my knee, before turning his attention toward Will. With a show of truce, Cale extends his hand, "Detective James."

"Please, Cale. Call me Will."

"Right." Cale looks back at me and grins, before turning back around to grip Will's shoulder with his left hand. "Say, Will. May I offer you a word of caution? You know, man to man."

"O-kay?"

"Good, because I think it only fair that I warn you."

"Warn me of what?"

"Simply this," Cale leans in. "If you hurt Cait, I'll kill you."

Will is stunned, as Cale lifts his hand from Will's shoulder, and slaps him on the arm before then walking away.

Will watches him go, before turning back around to face me. "Does he know that threatening a cop is a federal offense?"

"I doubt if he would care." I grin while stepping off the tailgate to meet him.

Will's face is contrite, as he takes one look at the bruises on my neck and immediately pulls me into his arms. I rest my head against his chest, grateful for the comfort of his embrace.

"You have no idea how worried sick I've been. I've tried calling all day to warn you."

I pull back, surprised. "Warn me?"

"Yeah, we discovered that Stalin killed Lucy this morning. We've had some glitches in our computer system, so we called our IT guy, and he found a hacker's signature. After a few hours of triangulating signals, he was able to unravel the hacker's steps, and we put two-and-two together. That son of a bitch managed to interfere with his DNA results—which were an exact match to the sample we'd collected under Lucy's fingernails, by the way."

"Yeah, well, he didn't act alone, Will."

"I know. We arrested his girlfriend this morning. Anyway, when that call came in as a fatal shooting, I thought I'd lost you." Will sighs, and rests his face in my hair. "God, I would have never forgiven myself. I am so sorry that I wasn't here."

317

"Me, too."

"*Really*," he boasts.

"Yeah, really." I pull back and flash a playful grin. "Maybe then I wouldn't be covered in all these bruises."

He laughs. "And here I thought you were about to confess that you actually needed me."

"Oh, so it's a confession you're after?"

"If it involves your feelings for me, hell yes."

"All right, William." I wrap my arms around his neck and connect my eyes with his. "I think I'm falling in love with you."

Will smiles with instant witticism. "I'm flattered."

"Not exactly the response I was looking for, but I'm so happy for you."

Will lets out a subtle laugh, as he tugs on my bottom lip and pulls me in for a wistful kiss—which is rudely cut short by one of the local police officers.

"Detective James?"

"Yes, what is it?"

"May I have a word with you, sir?"

"Certainly." Will smiles at me. "I'll be right back, beautiful."

I smile and nod, as he follows the policeman—who just gave me a look of scrutiny.

What the hell was that?

Confused, I watch them reach the patrol car. Upon opening the trunk, the officer hands something over to Will and *there's that look again.*

I direct my attention toward the item that Will is holding and see that it's Luke's—*Isaac's*—cell phone.

Within seconds, I feel as though I am about to be unmasked. Neither Cale, nor I, had thought to ditch Isaac's cell phone during all the chaos, and between his involvement with some of our searches, and his recent activity of following us around, there could be anything on it—*Oh, please, God, don't let there be anything on that phone!*

I immediately scan the area, in search of Cale, when I spot him sitting on the porch. His eyes connect with mine, and I urgently dart them toward the item that Will is holding.

Cale follows my gaze and immediately falters upon recognition.

I stumble my view back over to Will, who is now, looking back at me. His facial commentary speaks nothing short of bewilderment, as he then shifts his eyes toward Cale.

Will's expression causes my body to flush, as fight-or-flight withdraws the blood from my limbs.

Returning my sights over to Cale, he reverts his back onto me, and while we have yet to speak a single word, our message to each other is clear.

He knows.

ACKNOWLEDGEMENTS

This book would not have been possible without the love and support of my husband, Barry, and our two wonderful children. You are the most important people in my life, and I could not have finished this project without your love and support. I love you all so much!

Thank you to my parents, Russ and Bambie, for your love and support with everything I do. Thank you so much for always being there when I need you. Thank you, mom, for reading my rough draft. I always knew you would be the first one to read it, and I am so grateful for all your insight! Love you so much, Mom and Dad!

A big thank you to my second parents, Kathy and Brent, for showing me so much love and support for half my life now. I love you guys so much, and I am grateful to call you my family!

Also, a big thank you to my siblings: Zack, Whitney, Tori, Lia, Rick, Mike, McKenna, Matt, and my adorable nieces and nephews. Every single one of you means more to me than you could ever know. I love you all so much!

Thank you to my best friends, Kresha and Sarah, for their unbreakable friendship that helped to inspire the special bond between *Lucy* and *Cait*. I love you both "more than my luggage."

Thank you to my "truth-tellers" Jamie, Jess, and Melissa, for reading my rough draft and offering your much-needed insight. I love you all, and I am so grateful to call you my *Friends*.

And finally, a BIG thank you to my Editor, Katrina Diaz, for your superb editing skills. I am not here without you. I would also like to thank NY Book Editors in general, for their services.

www.ingramcontent.com/pod-product-compliance
Lightning Source LLC
Chambersburg PA
CBHW020230180626
46810CB00006B/2116